Lake Chelan Revisited

Twenty-seven short stories.
Eighteen pages of visitor information.
Thirty-one photos and a Lake Chelan map.

Photo: *Jim Tarbert on a ridge above Hart Lake, Lyman Lake, and Lyman Glacier in the Glacier Peak Wilderness between Holden Village and Glacier Peak in 1970.* Photo by Jim Clouse.

Jim Tarbert

9/15

Jim Tarbert lived on an apple orchard near Manson, Washington in the 1940s and early 1950s. He has since explored Lake Chelan and the surrounding lakes, hiked the high mountain trails, and enjoyed a variety of activities in the local communities.

Jim shares his experiences and knowledge of the area and its history with this collection of fictional short stories and visitor information.

Visitors relax in the sun and catch their dinner from the dock at Stehekin in front of the North Cascade Lodge. They can hike to Rainbow Falls—or take the bus.

Dedicated to the memory
of Joe and Edna Tarbert,
and Dick and Don.

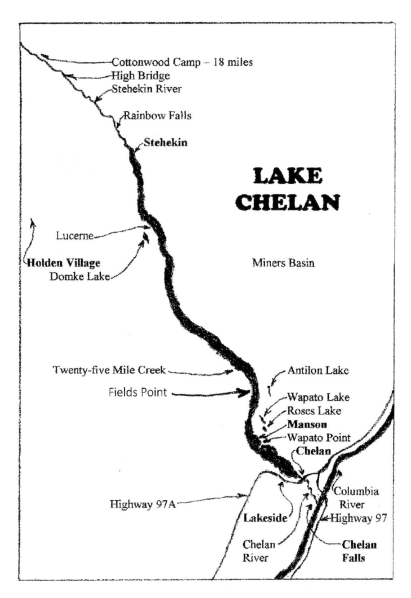

*Lake Chelan and locations mentioned in
short stories and visitor information.*

Lake Chelan Revisited

Short Stories and Visitor Information

Lake Chelan - Long, Deep, and Narrow

Lake Chelan is the largest, longest, and deepest natural lake in Washington State. The Chelan River, at the lake's southern end, connects it to the Columbia River. It is the state's shortest river.

The lake is over fifty miles long and two miles wide at its widest point, but averages only a mile in width. The lake is 1,500 feet deep, the third deepest in the nation.

A glacier extended from the top of the Cascade Mountains to the Columbia River over 10,000 years ago, forming the valley and Lake Chelan. Water pours into Lake Chelan from the Stehekin River at its northern end and from streams all along its shoreline.

Steep terrain surrounds most of the lake, making all but the southern end of the lake inaccessible by road. Residents and tourists access the northern part of the lake by boat or seaplane. Dedicated hikers can reach the head of the lake following trails over difficult terrain.

Agriculture and the residential population are mostly restricted to the fertile, rolling hills at the south end of the lake. Recreational opportunities exist all around the lake.

<u>Photo</u>: View from the public dock in Chelan in front of Campbell's Resort. The view is typical of the south end of the lake—calm water, a fishing boat, a paraglide, orchards, and vineyards on the hillsides with mountains in the background.

Pie for Breakfast

Katie Benson locked her cabin door before she hid the cash she received for thinning apples. *Now I have four hundred dollars stashed away,* she thought. *I need to earn another hundred dollars. Then I can divorce Ken and purchase a bus ticket to go home.*

She opened the door to catch any hint of an evening breeze before she dumped water from a bucket into a wash pan to scrub her hands and face.

Mother would have a fit if she could see me now, washing with cold water from an irrigation ditch. Would she believe I'm too tired to walk to the cistern to pump clean water, and it's too hot here to start a fire to heat water or cook supper?

After she dried her hands and face, she sat on a wobbly chair to rest her head on the cabin's small table for a moment. She was sleeping soundly an hour later when the sun disappeared behind Slide Ridge on the south side of Lake Chelan.

Aldorf Gourmand knocked on the cabin's doorframe a few minutes later.

"Good evening, Mrs. Benson. Is Ken on his way home?" he asked, as he stood on the step outside the open door.

Katie jerked awake and jumped up, biting her lower lip as she took a step back, staring at the huge, homely man. She noticed his sweat-stained shirt, dirty face, and his ten-year-old, 1938, Ford pickup parked behind him.

"I don't know," she stammered, hoping he would leave. She recognized Aldorf as an orchard worker and knew he lived in one of the cabins at the far end of the migrant camp.

Ken must owe him money from a poker game. That's

the reason men usually came to the cabin looking for him.

"He'll be here soon, won't he?"

"Does he owe you money for a poker game?" she asked, disgusted that her husband spent all his time playing poker and chasing skirts.

"You know gambling isn't legal in Washington State," he admonished. "I'd rather call this a loan payment. Ken said he'd be here after work today."

"Ken didn't come home last night, and I don't know when he'll return." *And he didn't work today, and he'll never work again if I continue supporting him.*

"He isn't likely to miss supper. I'll sit on the bench in front of your cabin to wait for him."

Katie watched Aldorf slump onto the bench, looking as tired as she felt.

He's right. Ken won't work, but he'll show up for supper. This is payday. He'll want to use the money I earned this week to pay his gambling debt.

She shuddered, visualizing what would happen when Ken demanded money. She didn't want to endure another beating now that she'd paid an attorney to start the divorce process. She turned her back to Aldorf and sat down at the table to hide her quivering chin.

After a gentle breeze cooled the cabin interior, Katie shoved paper scraps and kindling into the firebox to start a fire. When the wood flamed brightly, she adjusted the damper and sliced potatoes and onions into a frying pan.

While the potatoes simmered, she mixed ingredients to make biscuits. She placed the biscuits in the oven and stirred the potatoes, adding salt and pepper.

Ken hadn't returned when she pulled the biscuit pan out of the oven.

He knows Mr. Cooper pays his orchard workers after work on Friday. He should've been here two hours ago.

She placed potatoes and a biscuit on a plate and

turned to go outside to take advantage of an evening breeze. Then, before she reached the door, she realized Aldorf was still sitting on the bench in front of the cabin.

She couldn't eat in front of him, and it was too hot to stay in the cabin. She quickly filled a plate with potatoes and added two biscuits.

"Ken would already be here if he planned to eat the supper I prepared for him," she said as she handed Aldorf the filled plate and a fork.

"You don't need to feed me," he said, as he hesitantly accepted the plate, "but I do thank you."

Katie sat on the doorstep to eat and watched Aldorf out of the corner of her eye. She noticed he had washed his hands and face while she cooked supper.

He must've walked to the irrigation ditch behind the cabins to wash.

Aldorf ate the potatoes and a biscuit like a man who had worked hard all day, filling a need rather than savoring a satisfying meal. Then he slowed down and seemed to taste the second biscuit.

He smiled when he looked up from his plate. "This is very good, Mrs. Benson. I've never tasted a better biscuit."

"The biscuits would be better if I had an icebox to keep butter and jam."

"This biscuit's so light and fluffy, it melts in my mouth. It doesn't need butter or preserves."

Katie blushed. She couldn't recall Ken ever complimenting her on the biscuits even though he knew she won blue ribbons for her baked goods at the Conway County Fair back home in Arkansas.

"I have cherry pie for dessert," she blurted out, forgetting for the moment she needed to get rid of Aldorf to avoid taking a beating when Ken returned.

Embarrassed by her impulsiveness, she jumped up to rush into the cabin to get a slice of the pie she baked before daylight that morning.

Aldorf ate the pie so slowly she feared he didn't like it. Baking in a wood-burning stove was a new experience for her, but the pie turned out better than she could've hoped. She wasn't sure how to react, other than blushing foolishly, when he finished and smiled at her again.

"You're in the wrong occupation, Mrs. Benson," he said. "You should be baking goods in a restaurant or a pastry shop instead of thinning apples in an orchard."

Now she was completely flustered. "Thanks," she mumbled.

"How old are you, Mrs. Benson?" he asked.

She gasped. "Old enough," she snapped, startled by the personal question.

"Old enough to survive in a camp full of grown men?"

"I'm married."

"I don't see a husband. Neither do the other men."

"They wouldn't dare bother me."

"Even if Ken doesn't come home tonight?"

"I'm a lot older than I look. I'll be eighteen tomorrow."

"And you'll get older fast. Do you realize what migrant life and working in orchards will do to you? You're an attractive young lady now, but you're going to look like an old woman in ten years."

"I'm not staying. I'm going home," she said before she could stop herself. She didn't know why she told him what she was going to do. Her plans were none of his business.

"Ken didn't say anything about leaving."

"He doesn't know I'm leaving. I've saved four hundred dollars. As soon as I save another hundred dollars, I'll have the money I need to divorce him and take a bus back to Springfield, Arkansas to live with my parents," she said, hastily, compelled to defend her action.

Aldorf didn't respond immediately, giving no hint of approval or disapproval.

Katie stood up, biting her lower lip again, reacting silently to his silence. She had no reason to have confided in this man, and she certainly didn't need his approval. Flustered, she reached for his plate and rushed into the cabin to dish up another piece of the cherry pie for him.

Aldorf ate the second piece of pie with an appreciative smile on his face.

Children stopped playing and returned to their cabins for the night. Adults turned on ceiling lights, casting bright light out open doors.

Katie sat on her cabin's doorstep, watching Aldorf eat the pie. *He should leave now. It's obvious Ken isn't going to return, and I need to go to bed. Tomorrow will be another long day, climbing a twelve-foot orchard ladder. I still need a hundred dollars.*

"I came here from Oklahoma," Aldorf said. He spoke so softly he could've been talking to himself.

"I stayed to work in my family's business for five years after high school. Then I decided I wanted to make something of myself on my own. I've been here for two years, and I'm going to stay. Manson and Chelan are wonderful communities."

Katie placed her hand over her mouth to hide a yawn as she listened. Exhaustion, heat, and a full stomach conspired to make her drowsy.

"Why did you leave home?" Aldorf asked.

Startled by the personal question, she responded with a silent, disapproving glare. She realized she had asked herself the same question more than once since she ran away from home with Ken nearly a year ago, thinking she would never find another man as handsome or debonair.

Marrying the thirty-year-old man she loved was her ticket to a better future, she had believed. Now she realized she had lacked the experience needed to know the difference between infatuation and love.

She hadn't known about Ken's temper, refusal to work, or persistent philandering. Now the dream had evaporated, so she was going home to her parents, defeated.

"Have you read the Chelan newspaper lately?" Aldorf asked, breaking into her thoughts when she didn't answer.

She shook her head to indicate she had not.

"A small restaurant is for sale in Chelan. The owner needs to retire to take care of his sick wife, so he's offering reasonable terms for a quick sale. A friend wants to buy the business. He knows how to manage a restaurant and cook, but he needs help.

"He's not a baker, and he can't wait on customers. I know he'd hire you to bake and wait tables. He'd take you on as a partner if you have five hundred dollars to invest to help him get started."

Katie was suddenly wide-awake, considering what he was proposing. She remembered how much she enjoyed working in her parent's restaurant in Springfield. Her elation lasted for only a few moments, however. Then reality crushed her.

Ken will never allow me to take a job in a restaurant. He needs to keep me stranded in migrant camps where no one will notice my bruises.

Aldorf watched her flicker of excitement fade before he spoke.

"We are part of a never ending tide of people migrating here seeking opportunity, Mrs. Benson. Most of the men who own the orchards where you've worked this past year moved here just like us. They worked hard, saved, and bought an orchard."

When she didn't respond, Aldorf said, "Daylight will be here before we know it, and we both need to work tomorrow. You best go to bed. I'm going to sit right here and wait for Ken."

Katie went into her cabin, closed the door, and stripped. She washed her body with the tepid water she heated when she cooked supper. Then she crawled into bed.

Despite her exhaustion, she had difficulty falling asleep. She couldn't stop thinking about the man sitting in front of her cabin. His intimidating appearance, inappropriate questions, and abrupt manner frightened her. She sensed, however, there was something she didn't understand about him.

He must realize Ken isn't going to come home tonight. Why is he still sitting in front of my cabin? She had one last thought as exhaustion forced her into a deep sleep.

Should I have locked my door?

Ken hadn't returned when Katie woke up the next morning. She breathed a sigh of relief. Then she smiled.

It's my birthday. I'm eighteen, an adult.

She jumped out of bed to open the door a few inches to peek out. A hint of approaching daylight revealed Aldorf, sitting on the bench in front of her cabin with his head resting against rough siding. He snored softly.

Frying potatoes and warming leftover biscuits took but a few minutes after she dressed and started a fire. She had just finished placing the food on two plates when she heard a knock on her door.

Katie held Aldorf's breakfast plate in one hand when she pulled the door open. There was enough light now for her to see water dripping from his hair as he stood on her doorstep.

He walked to the irrigation ditch to wash.

"I want to wish you a happy birthday before I go to work."

"Thank you. Eat this before you go," she said as she pushed the plate toward him. "You can't work on an empty stomach."

"I don't know how to thank you for your kindness," he said, as he accepted the plate and sat on the bench to eat.

"I'm just sorry you had to wait all night for Ken," she said, as she sat on the doorstep with her plate.

"You're not responsible for your husband's behavior. I can't wait much longer, though. Thinning apples every day gets me closer to reaching my goal. There are unlimited opportunities here for anyone willing to work, Mrs. Benson."

Katie felt a ripple of excitement as his previous comments flashed through her mind. *I can bake and wait tables.* She wanted to know more about the restaurant he had mentioned, but she didn't ask.

Ken will never allow me to wait tables. People will see my bruises and ask questions.

"Don't leave yet," she said, impulsively. "I baked the cherry pie for my birthday. You can help me celebrate by eating another slice."

Before she returned with the pie for Aldorf and a slice for herself, she retrieved her hidden savings and stuffed the money in her back pocket.

Ken's still my husband, so I'm morally responsible for his debts. The decision made her feel better although it meant she would have to start saving again for the divorce and a bus ticket.

After they finished eating the pie, Aldorf set his plate to one side and stood up. "I thank you for breakfast and the pie, but we need to get to work as soon as I take care of the payment I mentioned last night."

As he spoke, Katie stood up to take the money out of her back pocket.

"I'll pay the money Ken owes you if I have enough to cover his debt," she said.

"Hold on a minute, Mrs. Benson. I said I was here to take care of a loan payment. I never said Ken owes me money." Aldorf reached in a back pocket to get his billfold as he spoke.

"I don't gamble, but a friend thinks he's the world's best poker player. He tried to fill a straight flush on credit. All Ken had to do to win was show his hand. My friend drives a truck and had to leave town on a long haul. He asked me to deliver the money. Since Ken hasn't returned, I'll give the money to you."

Katie gasped as if she had received an electrical shock. *Ken has never won before. This isn't possible.*

Confused, she accepted the folded bills he handed her. She shoved the money in a front pocket, too surprised to clarify her thoughts.

"Uh-oh, we're in trouble," Aldorf said, softly, before she had time to realized what he had done.

She turned in the direction Aldorf was looking, just in time to see Mr. Cooper park his car next to Aldorf's pickup.

The orchardist had a concerned expression on his face. The look mirrored that of a recent employer when he fired Katie because Ken wouldn't work. They had to vacate the cabin the orchardist provided and live in her car for a week until they found another job.

"This doesn't look good," Aldorf whispered, as Mr. Cooper walked toward them. "He can't tolerate anyone being late for work, even on Saturday."

"I'm sorry," she said. "I shouldn't have offered you the pie. I've made you late for work."

"Good morning, folks," Mr. Cooper said. "I fear I have some bad news."

"If it's about being late for work, it's my fault," Aldorf said, quickly, before Katie could react.

"No, Aldorf. This concerns Ken. If you're a family friend, you might want to hear what I have to say."

"Has something happened to Ken? Has he had an accident?" Katie anxiously asked, alarmed by the orchardist's words and demeanor.

"He hasn't been in an accident. Apparently, you hired an attorney in Chelan. He called this morning to say police arrested Ken. He spent the night in the Chelan County jail in Wenatchee."

Katie bit her lip and hung her head to hide tears. Twice before, she had used her hidden savings to bail

Ken out of jail for drunk and disorderly.

"How much is his bail this time?" she asked.

"No bail this time."

She snapped her head up to look at him.

"Oh no! What'd he do?"

"Nothing here. Your attorney discovered Ken was already married when he married you. In fact, he was married to at least two women in Arkansas and one in Missouri when he married you.

"Your attorney obtained a warrant to have Ken arrested, and an officer is escorting him back to Arkansas. They left Wenatchee at three this morning on the east-bound, Great Northern passenger train."

Katie started crying, loud, wet sobs.

The red-faced orchardist babbled sympathy.

Aldorf gently grasped Katie by the shoulders to set her on the bench. He pulled his handkerchief out of a back pocket and handed it to her.

"The attorney said your marriage to Ken is null and void. You're not married. He said your initial payment covers expenses for correcting the records in Arkansas. Your car is parked behind a tavern in Chelan."

Katie wiped away tears as Mr. Cooper talked. She assumed the men believed she was shedding tears of resentment over Ken's betrayal. That was only partly true. Although a dozen emotions overwhelmed her, she realized she was mostly brushing away tears of relief.

Mr. Cooper mumbled, "Let me know what you plan to do," as he turned to walk toward his car.

Aldorf watched the orchardist leave. Then he turned to watch Katie as mixed emotions confused her, reflected in facial features as she rubbed away tears.

"Calling you Mrs. Benson no longer seems appropriate," he said. "May I call you Katie?"

"Yes, of course," she sobbed as she looked up at him. The concerned expression on Aldorf's face startled her.

"Katie, do you have any of your cherry pie left?"

She nodded her head. "Two pieces," she said.

"I suggest we finish your pie, Katie. Whether you realize it or not, you've just been liberated," he said, expressing the feeling she had been trying to hide behind tears. "I believe a celebration is in order, and I can't think of a better way to begin than with a piece of the best pie in Chelan County."

Katie suddenly giggled, despite her tears, as she jumped up to give him a quick, impulsive hug. She turned and ran into the cabin to get the pie, leaving the startled man standing with his mouth open.

They ate the pie slowly, without talking. Katie savored the overpowering sense of relief that washed over her.

I'm free. Free from my terrible marriage.

Yesterday, she realized, she would've immediately purchased a bus ticket to flee back to the security of her parent's home in Arkansas. Aldorf's comments had given her a new perspective, however.

I can still have a better life here if I stay and work hard enough. I'm an adult. I can do this.

"Orchardists don't allow single women to live in their cabins," she said. "I need to find a job. Can you tell me more about the restaurant your friend wants to buy?"

"You can learn all about the restaurant after I shave and change into clean clothes. I'll take you to Chelan to find your car. Then we can stop to look at the restaurant.

"I can guarantee you a job working for the new owner. The restaurant has two small apartments overhead. The new owner is going to live in one apartment, and you can live in the other one. You will own the apartment if you invest five hundred dollars to become a partner in the business."

Katie knew a partnership was out of the question because she only had four hundred dollars saved. She would jump at the chance to take the job, however.

"How do you know so much about this restaurant and know the buyer will hire me?" she asked.

"I didn't tell you everything, Katie. First, tell me what you see when you look at me."

Katie gasped involuntarily, shocked by the startling request. She realized she would've told him he looked like a dangerous, homely brute if he had asked yesterday. Now, she realized, there was much more to this man. For one thing, she still couldn't believe Ken had actually won a poker game.

Where did Aldorf get the money he gave me? Why did he spend the night in front of my cabin?

She took a deep breath and looked Aldorf squarely in the eye as she searched for the proper words to tell him the truth.

"I see a very kind, compassionate man I'd be proud to call a friend," she said.

"Would you be proud to call me your business partner?"

"I don't understand."

"I told you a friend wants to buy the restaurant. Actually, I'm the one who wants to buy the business, but I realize my appearance upsets people until they get to know me. I was afraid you would immediately reject the idea of working at the restaurant if you knew I'm the one who wants to buy it.

"My father taught me to cook and manage a business in his restaurant in Oklahoma. But I can't bake or wait on customers, Katie. I need your help to make this restaurant a success.

"You can be an employee or a partner. The owner wants a thousand dollar down payment on a contract for the building, business, and inventory. I have nine hundred dollars in my billfold. I can thin apples for another ten days to earn enough to make the down payment. I'd rather purchase the restaurant today with you as a partner, if you'll invest five hundred dollars."

"I only have four hundred dollars saved."

"You have a hundred dollars in your front pocket that

Ken won playing poker. He's gone now, so the money is yours."

Katie clamped a hand to her mouth to stifle an impulsive reaction. Now, finally, she realized what Aldorf had done.

I told him I saved four hundred dollars to divorce Ken and buy a bus ticket. He gave me a hundred dollars of the money he saved for a down payment, so I can become a partner.

She wanted to hit him, hug him, or both, but realized a physical reaction wasn't appropriate. She suspected he still hadn't told her everything.

When did he learn the police arrested Ken? He had to have known last night. Did he stay at my cabin all night to protect me? I want to know—someday.

When she could trust her voice, she said, "You've found a business partner if you'll allow me to use my tips to pay the hundred dollars I owe you."

Aldorf grinned and nodded his head before he said, "The owner has the paperwork ready to sign. We can move into the apartments after we meet with him this morning. We'll have time to open the restaurant for supper tonight if we hurry. We need to pack our belongings in my pickup and let Mr. Cooper know we're leaving."

"Does our restaurant have a name?" she asked.

"How does *Katie and Al's Cafe* sound to you?"

"I think *Al and Katie's Cafe* sounds better. It will be the first restaurant listed in the phone book."

"Good thinking, Katie."

"If we hurry, I'll have time to bake a cake for supper tonight. Customers can help us celebrate our first day in business."

"And an eighteenth birthday, Katie. Your day of liberation and the beginning of a bright future in a land of opportunity."

Chelan - A Tourist Mecca

Chelan is a popular vacation resort with a wide variety of options available for accommodations, ranging from deluxe hotels to tent sites. Visitors can easily identify and reserve lodging on the internet. See pages 172 and 287 for details. Heavy demand for facilities during the summer months dictates making reservation well in advance for hotels or campgrounds. Dining options include drive-ins, pizza parlors, cafes, and deluxe dining.

Camping and R. V. sites surround the southern portion of Lake Chelan from Twenty-Five Mile Creek on the south shore to Manson on the north shore. Some tent sites are available for boaters at docks along the northern end of the lake. Tent sites are available at most high mountain lakes surrounding Lake Chelan.

You can bring your own boat and bike or rent them. You can learn to water ski, snorkel, or scuba dive. Turn to page 169 for information about attractions you can enjoy during a Lake Chelan vacation.

Photo: Fishermen of all ages fish from the docks surrounding Lake Chelan. This photo, taken from the public dock in front of Campbell's Resort in Chelan, shows a happy fisherman displaying the five pound, twenty-one and a half inch Rainbow trout he caught as I arrived with my camera.

Blood on His Hands

I will never forget the shocking discovery I made at our neighbor's pig farm on my fourteenth birthday, or the lesson it taught me about human nature.

After breakfast, Mom baked a cake for my birthday party while I helped Dad clean the barn. As we forked clean hay into the last stall, the siren sounded at our rural fire station.

"Let's get going," Dad shouted.

We ran to our pickup with shovels, tossed them in the back, and raced to catch up with the fire truck. We spotted the truck a few minutes later and followed it to Mr. Pardee's farmhouse. Dad parked in the driveway beside several neighbors' vehicles.

I could see Mr. Pardee standing on his front porch talking to neighbors. No smoke drifted from his house or outbuildings, so this wasn't a fire call. An accident seemed more likely.

Neighbors called our volunteer fire department for any emergency because our farming community didn't have a police officer, ambulance, or hospital. Neighbors responded to help any time the fire siren sounded.

"What's wrong?" Dad asked a neighbor as we hurried toward the farmhouse.

"Joe Pardee's daughter's missing," the man said.

He might've heard me gasp. I had gone to school with Linda Pardee for years. She had just graduated from Manson High School, a few weeks after her eighteenth birthday.

When we reached the porch, an agonizing howl arose from the back of the house. Everyone ran around to the backyard where Mrs. Pardee stood just inside an open window in what I assumed was Linda's bedroom.

I could see blood on the sill under the raised window.

"Someone has taken her," Mrs. Pardee shrieked through the open window.

Our neighbor, Mr. Farwell, kneeled to look at the ground under the window. "The tracks in the dirt are too large to have been made by Linda," he said.

"There's blood on the window latch," Mr. Pardee said. "He must've cut his hand on the latch when he forced the window open."

"Who could have taken her?" asked Mr. Halstead, another neighbor.

"The pig farmer," shouted Mrs. Pardee.

"Why the pig farmer?" Mr. Halstead asked.

"I forgot about him," Mr. Pardee said. "Eric Talmer arrived at daylight to buy grain for his pigs. I helped him load grain sacks on his truck until milking time. He drove away while I milked cows in the barn."

"He stole my baby," Mrs. Pardee shrieked hysterically. Then she started crying uncontrollably, just as I believed my mother would if someone stole my little sister.

The men around me exchanged silent glances for a moment. Then they ran to their vehicles. I followed Dad to our pickup, and we joined the caravan racing toward the pig farm.

"This could get ugly," Dad said.

"Do you think he has hurt Linda?" I asked.

"The window sill had a lot of blood on it, and Eric Talmer's a strange acting man. I don't know what he might do."

Dad followed our neighbors several miles up a canyon behind Roses Lake to the pig farm, giving me time to think about Mr. Talmer. I remembered our teacher saying an explosion severely injured him a few years earlier during the 1944 invasion of Saipan.

"Now he wears an eye patch, and he can't hear," she said. "He avoids people because he doesn't understand what they're saying. He bought the abandoned farm after his injuries healed, and he doesn't welcome visitors."

Dad parked our pickup in Mr. Talmer's driveway alongside our neighbors' vehicles. A truck, loaded with grain sacks, sat beside an old barn. I could hear pigs squealing and grunting in a dozen pigpens surrounding the barn.

As we joined our neighbors to approach the farmhouse, Mr. Talmer stepped out from behind the barn.

"He has a knife," someone yelled.

I could see blood dripping from the blade on the knife Mr. Talmer held in his hand as he walked toward us. He had blood on his hands and the front of his coveralls.

"Where's my girl?" Mr. Pardee shouted.

Mr. Talmer stopped, but he didn't respond.

"Looks like he might've already killed her," said Mr. Baker, another one of our neighbors.

Mr. Farwell shouted, "She needs help if she's still alive."

As if given a silent signal, men spread out in all directions to search for Linda.

Mr. Talmer still held the knife in his hand, looking confused, as I followed Dad to one side of the barn.

We ended up beside a pigpen. The pen held three, huge boar hogs behind high walls. I made the mistake of looking in the boars' pen.

Mr. Pardee said the pig farmer bought grain to feed his pigs, but these boars weren't eating grain. They were eating meat. I looked at what I assumed were Linda Pardee's remains and lost the special birthday breakfast Mom cooked for me.

We raised a few pigs, so I knew they will eat anything. Mom's favorite rooster made the mistake of landing in our pigpen one morning before feeding time. Nothing remained but feathers, and not many of them, when I arrived with the slop bucket.

Neighbors quickly gathered around the boars' pen. They talked quietly for a minute. Then everyone turned to walk toward Mr. Talmer.

The pig farmer stood in the same spot, looking frightened now. As the men started to surround him, he thrust the bloody butcher knife out to protect himself.

Dad must have realized things were about to get out of control because he grabbed my arm and whispered, "Get my rifle." Then he turned to our neighbors. "We need to wait for a deputy," he shouted.

"A deputy will take all day to get here if one comes at all," someone said.

"And my daughter will still be dead," Mr. Pardee said, choking the words out between sobs.

I jumped in the pickup while they were arguing and pulled Dad's rifle out of the gun rack. Then I heard a shot.

"You missed him," someone shouted.

I turned back toward the men just in time to see Mr. Talmer running toward the boars' pen. He dropped his knife as he climbed to the top of the wall surrounding the boars. Then he started to jump over the wall, but he lost his balance and fell in the pen on his back.

"Are you crazy?" Dad yelled.

"He killed my girl," Mr. Pardee said as tears wet his cheeks. He held a small pistol in his hand, staring at it as if he couldn't believe he had it.

Dad walked over to Mr. Pardee, jerked the pistol out of his hand, and shoved it in his back pocket.

Then squealing and chomping sounds drew everyone's attention back to the pen where the three hogs were going berserk.

I shoved Dad's rifle back on the gun rack, and watched as the men hesitantly walked toward the pen. Before they reached it, a speeding car approached with someone frantically honking the horn.

Everyone stopped and turned to watch the car.

I didn't recognize the driver until the car jerked to a stop and Mrs. Pardee jumped out.

"Linda's safe," she shouted as she rushed toward her

husband.

"What do you mean, she's safe?" Mr. Pardee asked.

"She just called from Coeur d' Alene, Idaho. She and Andy Milner ran off during the night to elope. They were married at ten o'clock this morning. Andy cut his hand opening the window. It was his blood on the windowsill."

A stunned silence followed Mrs. Pardee's words. Then someone mumbled, "Oh no! What've we done?"

The men turned suddenly to rush toward the boars' pen.

I didn't follow them. I remembered Mom's rooster and knew what they would find. I walked behind the barn and stepped inside to avoid the scene in the pen.

The inside of the barn was dark, so I flipped the light switch next to the door. Then I stood there, stunned, staring at a hanging carcass.

I realized then what Mr. Talmer was doing when we arrived. The blood on his knife, hands, and coveralls came from butchering a hog. The bloody wheelbarrow he used to haul the waste viscera to feed the three boars still sat under the hanging carcass.

As the men pulled Mr. Talmer's body from the pen, the siren sounded at the fire station. Our traumatized neighbors seemed relieved to have an excuse to leave. They avoided eye contact as they moved silently to their vehicles to respond to another emergency.

"I'll wait for a deputy sheriff," Dad said.

I didn't know what Dad would tell a deputy. I did know Mom had baked a cake for my birthday party, but I was in no mood to celebrate after learning our rush to judgment left every one of us with blood on our hands.

Manson - A Village by the Lake

If you seek a small town atmosphere, Manson is the place for you. The quiet town of the writer's youth has transformed itself into a destination resort while retaining the small town appeal. Yes, you may detect some favoritism here.

You can stay at a lodge or resort at Manson and still be close to the water slide, miniature golf course, go-carts, bowling, arcade games, and horseback rides in Chelan and swim at the dock in Manson or pick blueberries at Blueberry Hills.

Adults may enjoy wine tasting at local wineries surrounding Manson, gambling at the Mill Bay Casino, or leisurely dining in a western atmosphere at Blueberry Hills.

In addition to Lake Chelan, several small lakes near Manson provide recreational opportunities. You can swim, fish, hike the foothills, pick berries during the summer, and hunt in the fall.

Take a drive to view the apple orchards and the mountains. Bring your binoculars to view birds and mule deer. The black stump on the hillside may turn into a bear if you watch it long enough.

Photo: Apple orchards and foothills near Manson.

A Guardian Angel for Christmas

Tears wet my cheeks as I watched her on my security monitor. I was watching Cristina, Cristina Sortino whom I had loved with all my heart for the nineteen years since I first held her in my arms. She couldn't possibly do something so stupid, could she?

I hoped I was mistaken when I witnessed their first transaction, but there was no question the second time. The young man was a drug dealer, and his customer was my beautiful Cristina.

The transactions took place at Gino's Grocery, my son's business in Chelan, where Cristina worked as a checker during the busy Christmas season.

I accepted a position at the store after my business failed in 1972, nineteen years earlier. The sign on my office door said *Diego Sortino - Security Officer.*

The young man—I had learned his name was Seta—was not alone the third time he entered Gino's Grocery. My good friend, Leo Berone, entered behind him.

No one knew Leo Berone worked for me, and no one in Chelan would recognize him. He was my confidential employee before I lost my business in the big city. We grew up together on the mean streets in the old country. I immigrated legally. Leo did not.

I watched the drama unfold on the monitor in my office. The drug dealer tried to act like a customer as he inspected the fruit baskets and Christmas cards on his way to the back of the store.

Cristina closed her checkout station after Seta entered. She walked past the vegetable and fruit display in the produce aisle to meet him near the restrooms. She held two twenty dollar bills in her hand, clearly visible on my monitor, as she approached him.

Seta concealed a small bag in his hand.

As they started to make the exchange, Leo Berone stepped between them with his back to the young man. His broad shoulders blocked Seta's view for a moment.

Leo flashed a badge in front of Cristina as he handed her a note. "Go in the restroom and read this," he ordered in a low command voice that demanded compliance. Then he quickly walked away.

I knew Cristina would be too startled to question the badge or Leo's authority. Who knows what an undercover officer looks like?

Tears flooded Cristina's eyes, matching my own, as she rushed into the restroom, avoiding Seta's futile attempt to grab her arm to stop her.

I assumed Cristina would read the note in the privacy of a booth. I knew what the note said. I wrote it. What I wrote was very explicit.

Cristina, you have only one chance to give up drugs. Tell Seta to leave the store and never return. If you ever purchase drugs again, I have to tell your father. You need to think about what will happen if he finds out you have used drugs.

Cristina stayed in the restroom for several minutes as I sat in my office, watched the monitor, and wiped away tears.

Seta waited outside the restroom, pacing like a caged animal.

Would she tell him to leave the store, or defy the instructions in the note and buy the drugs? I didn't know. I wanted to go rescue her as I had done in the past, but I forced myself to stay at my desk and watch the monitor.

Cristina's eyes were red rimmed from crying when she finally stepped out of the restroom to face the drug dealer.

"What're you trying to pull here?" he shouted.

I held my breath as I waited to hear her answer.

"I'm done buying from you. Leave the store and never come back," she said as she tried to push past him.

Seta grabbed her shoulders and slammed her up against the wall. "No one is going to cut in on my business," he snarled through bared teeth, spraying spittle in her face.

Leo reappeared, as I knew he would, before the confrontation could escalate. He grasped the young man firmly by the throat, picked him up, and packed him out the back door.

I knew Seta would never sell drugs again. He would disappear just as my first wife and her drug dealer disappeared after she refused to give up drugs.

Attorney fees bankrupted my business in the big city before prosecutors dropped murder charges against me for lack of evidence. They couldn't disprove my attorney's contention that my wife and the drug dealer fled the country.

The big city prosecutors didn't know Leo Berone existed. His name wasn't on any official records, and we never met in public or talked on the phone. We still met at safe locations where I could pay him in cash and give him instructions.

After the confrontation, I erased the tapes from the security cameras. No evidence remained to show Seta and Leo Berone visited Gino's Grocery or met Cristina.

I watched the monitor as Cristina finished her shift at the checkout station and walked back to the employee's locker room to get her purse and jacket. I heard the expected knock on my office door a few minutes later.

Cristina stood outside my office when I opened the door. Her eyes were still red rimmed from crying as she rushed into my arms and started bawling.

"Grandpa," she cried, "I've done something really stupid this time."

I held her in my arms and let her cry. She had acted foolishly, but granddaughters are too precious to allow any fault to diminish their grandfather's love.

"Yes, Honey. You made a serious mistake this time," I said. I spoke quietly and hoped she wouldn't notice my tears.

"What if he comes back?"

"He won't come back, Cristina. You'll never see him again," I said. I could feel her tremble, suggesting she understood what I was implying.

No one in our family ever discussed my big city problems to my knowledge, but she surely heard rumors about her grandmother's disappearance and the months I spent in lockup while prosecutors pressed charges—and my business plunged into bankruptcy.

"I'm afraid, Grandpa. What'll happen if Daddy discovers what I've done?" she asked, as her tears wet the front of my shirt.

I knew she had good reason to be afraid if my son, Gino Sortino, realized she used drugs. Gino learned by watching me that there is a severe price to pay for bringing dishonor on the family. My behavior became his behavior, Old World behavior—unacceptable in the New World, in rural America.

"Your father won't find out if this never happens again."

"What should I do, Grandpa?"

"You should go home, Cristina. Hug your mother and father. Help your mother decorate the Christmas tree and bake cookies. Go back to school after Christmas vacation and finish your studies."

"Bad things happen at the university, Grandpa. I'm afraid to go back there."

"The university will be a safe place for you next semester. I'm giving you a guardian angel for Christmas to watch over you while you're at the university," I said, thinking of my good friend Leo Berone. Now, I was the one who was trembling.

"A guardian angel for Christmas?" she said as she wiped away tears to look up at me.

"Yes, Honey. Your guardian angel will make sure you don't do anything that will bring dishonor on your family," I said, sadly. I loved this girl. She was the one bright spot in my life after all the trouble I had in the big city. I didn't want to lose her, but...

"Thank you, Grandpa. I need a guardian angel."

This view of Woodin Ave., Chelan's main street, is from in front of the museum. Campbell's Resort, on Lake Chelan's shoreline, is visible at the end of the street with snow-capped mountains in the background. The historic Ruby Theatre is on the right side and the Chamber of Commerce Visitor's Center is on the left side of the street.

The New Boy in Town

You can think of a hundred reasons
    Not to go to that new school,
When you're the new boy in town,
And your name is Meadowlark Brown,
    And you will feel like a fool.

You know some well-meaning teacher
    Will stand you at her side,
To introduce you to the class
By your first name and last,
    For a reaction, you cannot abide.

You always tell each new teacher
    That your real name is Joe,
But they just pat you on the head and smile,
And study the official record awhile,
    And say "Meadowlark Brown" very slow.

You would think a teacher wiser,
    The kid's reaction is always the same.
They start by just laughing at you,
And then it turns to ridicule,
    And who is a boy to blame?

You cannot explain to your classmates
    About your hippy parents and their drugs,
And how they thought it was a funny game
To give you a ridiculous name,
    That marks you for each new class thug.

So you try to get the kids to laugh with you
    By telling them your time tested story,
About how your dad watched sports at the bar,
And named you after the globetrotter star,
    Hoping his son might aspire to like glory.

But you know the new school will be a disaster,
    And you really don't want to go.
It is no fun being the new boy in town
When they will treat you like a clown,
    And you just want to be a regular Joe.

The New Boy in Camp

Roy Cascade believed Mr. Short's migrant camp near Manson would be the same as other camps he had stayed at in '48 and '49. He could hear someone playing a mouth harp at one of the cabins. A woman hung wet garments on a clothesline strung between two posts. He could see children sneaking around the cabins. They had a white flag on a short pole stuck in the ground at each end of the dirt road that ran between the two rows of cabins. He remembered playing capture-the-flag when he was a youngster.

Then he noticed the petite girl. She sat on a bench in front of one of the cabins across the road. A grimace distorted her facial features as she stared intently toward the south end of the camp.

Despite her nervous demeanor, Roy knew he would find a way to meet the girl. But he needed to wash first. He was still hot and sweaty from hitchhiking.

He found a water bucket on a shelf beside the wood-burning stove in his cabin. A couple of minutes later, he used a hand pump to fill the bucket at a cistern near the north end of the camp. When he finished pumping water, he straightened up and turned around.

The girl stood behind him, holding a bucket in a stained hand. She used her free hand to push long, tangled hair from over sad, blue eyes. Streaks on her dusty cheeks could have come from wiping away sweat or tears.

"Hello. I'm Roy Cascade. I can fill your bucket for you," he said, assuming she needed water to wash after picking apples all day.

"Thanks. I'm Colleen Sherman," she replied, as she handed him the bucket.

Up close, he could see she was younger than he had first believed. An oversized, bulky sweater concealed any hint of her physical development while a brief, longing glance suggested maturity beyond her years. Her dark eyes never stopped moving, scanning the area south of them.

"How long has your family been here?" he asked, as he pumped water into her bucket.

"Since yesterday. You alone?"

"Two cousins will be here tomorrow evening. They're picking the last trees in an orchard near Yakima. I hitch-hiked ahead to reserve a cabin."

"Our last stop was in Union Gap, a few miles from Yakima."

"Was that your mother at your cabin?"

"Yes. My stepdad's gone. He always goes on a drunk when we get a new job."

"My cousins aren't old enough to drink, so I don't have that problem. We're all twenty."

"I'm going to be seventeen in another month," she said, making direct eye contact with him for the first time. Her defiant glare told him he better believe her.

He looked down at her bucket when water spilled over the sides. *She might be seventeen in another month, but she looks more like fifteen up close.*

"Mom asked me to get water so she can make strawberry Kool-Aid. You want some?" she asked, after a brief pause seemed to convince her he wasn't going to question her age.

"I'd be a fool to say no," he said. "Let me pack the bucket back to your cabin. I need to heat some water and wash while your mother makes the Kool-Aid."

Several minutes later, Colleen's mother handed Roy a glass of the bright red liquid. He noticed the woman, who looked to be fifty but was more likely thirty-five, moved as if every muscle in her body ached.

"I'm Charlene Ryman, Colleen's mother," she said as she placed an arm around her daughter's shoulders.

Roy read Mrs. Ryman's protective posture as a warning that his intentions toward her daughter better be honorable. "Thanks for the drink," he said. "I'm Roy Cascade. This is a real treat." He took a sip of the drink, resisting the temptation to ask about Colleen's age.

"It'd be better if we had ice," Colleen said.

Roy noticed her cheeks were pink from a fresh scrubbing, and she appeared to have brushed her hair. She was wearing a different, cleaner, oversized sweater now. *She's still looking toward the south end of the camp. Afraid of something.* He glanced in that direction. Nothing.

"You'll have ice again when we finish picking apples and go home," Mrs. Ryman said.

"And a refrigerator, running water, and an indoor bathroom," Colleen added.

"You two can sit on the bench to drink your Kool-Aid while I fix supper. Roy, you're invited. I didn't see you packing groceries when you arrived."

"Thanks. I'll chop some firewood for your stove and bring some candy bars for dessert," he said, as he sat down on the bench in front of the cabin.

Colleen sat beside him to sip her drink. The bench was short. Their hips touched and her shoulder rested against his arm. The temperature had dropped noticeably after sunset, making her body heat very noticeable.

"Where's home?" he asked.

"We stay in Salinas, California with my grandparents when we aren't following the harvest."

"We're almost neighbors. My folks have a small farm south of Salinas. My cousins and I are going to buy farms. We'll follow the harvest for three more years to earn enough money for down payments."

"I'll probably follow the harvest forever," she said, sounding hopeless. "My stepfather wants to get rid of me.

He wants me to marry Ed Lander, a forty year old drunk."

"You're too young to marry."

"Mom was sixteen, the first time."

Roy wished he knew what to say to Colleen. He knew many migrant women married, aged, and died young from overwork, neglect, and abuse. Marrying someone other than a migrant like Ed Lander was unlikely as long she lived in orchard cabins.

"Have you thought about getting a job in a store or an office so you don't have to travel?"

"Of course, but they want someone with a high school diploma. I'll never graduate while I'm moving every week or two for most of the year. Did you graduate?"

"I graduated before I started following the harvest," he said, uncomfortable with the direction the conversation was going.

"You were lucky."

"I always keep a couple of paperback books with me. I'll give you one if you'd like to have something to read," he said, to try to change the subject.

"That would be nice."

"I'll get a book for you after I chop firewood for your mother.

After they finished eating fried potatoes and onions smothered in heavily peppered, flour gravy, Roy and Colleen sat on the bench, looking at the pictures in a paperback book. He had just handed her a Baby Ruth candy bar when an incredibly gaunt man stumbled around the corner of the cabin.

"That's my stepfather, Max," she whispered.

If she hadn't previously commented about her stepfather's drinking, Roy might've believed the man was an amputee teetering precariously on two, poorly crafted, artificial legs as he wobbled past them to enter the cabin.

Max slammed the door shut. "I need twenty dollars

right now," he bellowed. He slurred his words so badly they were barely discernable through the door.

"We don't have twenty dollars. We're broke until I get paid on Saturday."

A loud smack, which sounded like a hard slap, brought Roy to his feet to reach for the doorknob.

Colleen grabbed his arm to stop him. "Don't go in there," she pleaded. "Mother knows what to do."

As Colleen spoke, Roy heard a loud grunt that sounded like someone had taken a hard blow to the gut. Then the bedsprings creaked when a weight fell on the mattress. Roy was still standing on the front step a moment later when Mrs. Ryman opened the door. He could see Max crumpled on the bed, lying face down.

Mrs. Ryman stepped out of the cabin and closed the door. She rubbed a red spot on her cheek as she said, "I'm sorry you had to witness that."

Roy didn't know what to say. He felt foolish standing there with a candy bar in his hand.

Suddenly, a man roared, "What in the hell are you doing here?"

Roy whirled around to face a two-ton blimp. The man exhaled whiskey fumes strong enough to wilt a charging grizzly bear.

Colleen squealed and jumped up from the bench to cower behind Roy.

Mrs. Ryman took a step back. "Ed Lander, you don't have any business here," she shouted.

"Like hell I don't. Your worthless husband came here to get the twenty dollars he owes me. I don't see him or my twenty dollars."

"Max is sleeping. We won't have any money until payday on Saturday. You'll have to wait until then."

"I ain't going to wait. If Max can't pay the twenty dollars he owes me, Colleen leaves with me right now. That was our deal when Max bet the money. He'd pay the twenty dollars tonight if he lost the bet, or he'd let me take Colleen now instead of waiting until we're married."

"I'm not ever going to marry you," Colleen howled from behind Roy. "I'd rather be dead!"

Ed's flushed face turned even redder. He doubled his fists as he turned his attention toward Roy. "I ain't gonna leave her here where the new *boy* in camp can court her with candy bars," he bellowed. As he spoke, he tried to step around Roy to grab Colleen.

She screamed and jumped back.

Roy grabbed the axe he used to split firewood for Mrs. Ryman. He raised it to a threating position as he moved to stay between the enraged man and the girl.

Ed stopped abruptly when he noticed the axe. "A deal is a deal," he shouted defiantly as he took a step back.

"You know a man can't use his step-daughter as collateral for a bet. Get out of here, or I'm going to chop you down to size," Roy said as he swung the axe in a half circle, forcing Ed to take another step back.

"You better do what he says," Mrs. Ryman shouted. "That axe is sharp, and he's about to take a chunk out of your hide. You're not welcome here, Ed Lander. Colleen isn't *ever* going to marry you."

Roy noticed people watching from the cabins across the road as Mrs. Ryman spoke. He could hear them talking among themselves, too softly to make out words.

Ed looked around, startled, apparently, to discover witnesses. "I'll be back to get Colleen later. You better be gone when I get here," he shouted, thrusting a finger toward Roy. "Max promised Colleen to me, and you better not interfere," he added. Then he turned to stagger away, grabbing a clothesline post for support for a moment as he wobbled past it.

As Ed released his grip on the post, Roy threw the axe overhand, sinking the blade right where Ed's hand had been. Roy heard a loud, "Ugh" sound from bystanders.

Ed disappeared around the corner of a cabin without realizing, apparently, that he would've lost his fingers if Roy had thrown the axe a second sooner.

"You almost took his hand off," Mrs. Ryman said.

"I use an axe all winter to chop firewood to sell when there are no crops to pick," Roy said. "He would've lost his hand if that had been my intention."

Roy wasn't surprised he had difficulty sleeping. The first night in a migrant camp was always the most difficult.

New neighbors always produced different sounds, smells, and problems although he had never run into a situation as serious as the one he had just encountered. He expected a baby would cry, someone would snore louder than a braying donkey, and noisy kids would play late into the night. He didn't expect to have a huge drunk try to run him out of camp or need to defend a girl he had just met.

The three glasses of strawberry Kool-Aid he drank also interrupted his sleep along about midnight. He had to step outside for a minute.

Unfortunately, a full moon illuminated the camp. He could see two teenagers sitting cheek-to-cheek on a bench in front of a cabin across the road from him. They could see him, so he had to walk all the way to an outhouse behind the cabins.

He sighed audibly in relief before he stepped out of the outhouse to return to his cabin. He had taken only a couple of steps when he heard movement behind him. Before he could react, something struck him alongside the head. Fireworks exploded in his skull as his legs buckled under him.

Several men held Roy down when he tried to get up. One of them tried to twist his arm behind his back. Roy swung his free arm, hitting the man in the face.

"Ouch! Dammit. He's awake now," the man shouted. "Get a rope. Tie him until the deputy gets here to hand-cuff him."

Awareness hit Roy all at once when he forced his eyes open. It was daylight. Mr. Short, the orchard owner, was the one calling for a rope.

Three men sat on him, pinning him to the ground. Several spectators stood around him in a circle, watching. They looked angry enough to lynch him.

Before he could spit dirt out of his mouth to ask why they were holding him, someone tossed a rope to one of the men. They quickly tied his hands and feet. Then they picked him up, packed him to a storage shed, and dumped him on a yellow-stained floor next to open, sul-fur-concentrate containers that smelled like rotten eggs.

Mr. Short gave him a disgusted look as the men rushed out of the shed to breathe fresh air. Someone slammed the door shut.

Roy heard a key turn in the lock. He tried to figure out why they were mad at him, but his head felt like someone had used it for a punching bag, clouding his thinking, making him drowsy. He fell asleep.

Someone shook him, gently. "Wake up, Roy."

Roy recognized Colleen's voice. He opened his eyes just in time to see her pull a knife out of her pocket.

"Not much time. Already afternoon," she whispered, as she cut the ropes. "They found you and Max behind the cabins this morning. Max is dead. They think you killed him."

Roy gasped, shocked. "Why?"

"His billfold was in your pocket."

"Didn't kill Max," he mumbled, as he shook the ropes loose. Glancing around, he noticed she had pried the back window open.

"I know. Max went to Ed Lander's cabin after Mom kicked him out last night. His watch is missing. You didn't have the watch, just his billfold."

"Watch?"

"Antique pocket watch from his grandfather. Only thing he owned besides his old car. Could've paid his gambling debt to Ed with the watch. Traded me instead."

"Ed killed him?"

"Of course. He's stupid and greedy. He put the empty billfold in your pocket to frame you, but kept the watch. The watch's gold chain broke. Max replaced it with a cheap silver-colored chain. Easy to see. You need to prove Ed has *that* watch before the deputy gets here.

"Ed told Mom he was going to Manson for the day, and gonna move me to his cabin tonight. He'll get drunk before he comes to get me. If a deputy takes you to jail, you'll never prove you're innocent, and Ed will kidnap me."

"Can't the deputy arrest Ed for forcing himself on you?"

"You know police treat us like trash. Don't care what we do to each other. We're gonna work today to get gas money. We need to leave before Ed comes for me."

Roy walked to Manson to locate a pickup with the homemade canopy Coleen described. As expected, Ed had parked the vehicle near the tavern in the middle of the block-long, business district.

Finding Ed was the easy part, Roy realized. He had no idea how he could prove Ed had the watch. Ask him? No. Poking a grizzly bear with a stick would get him killed. He looked around, trying to decide what he should do.

The tavern had a vacant lot on each side, separating it from other buildings as if they wanted no part of the business. Roy suspected they didn't, judging by the clientele loitering in front of the building.

He decided an overgrown vacant lot on the opposite side of the street would be a good place to sit while he considered his options. He could lie down in the tall weeds to hide if he spotted a patrol car.

Despite his expectation that the police were out in force looking for him, he had yet to see a deputy at five in the afternoon when a pickup stopped in front of the tavern.

An elderly man eased himself off the front seat of the pickup. He stood in place for several moments to get his balance before he hobbled toward the tavern entrance. After he stepped up onto the boardwalk, he stopped to speak to the men loafing in front of the tavern.

Voices carried to Roy in the cool breeze blowing inland off Lake Chelan. The loiterers addressed the man as Mr. Mansfield.

"Need pickers," he said.

The vagrants shrank away from him as if he were a vampire.

Mr. Mansfield turned his back on them, in apparent disgust, and entered the tavern.

A half hour passed before he exited the tavern. He stopped to talk to the loafers again, with no better results. Then he started toward his pickup, admiring the gold pocket watch he held in one hand.

Roy jumped up to run across the road when he noticed the watch had a silver-colored chain attached to it.

"Mr. Mansfield," he said as he approached him. "Heard you're hiring pickers."

The man studied Roy for a moment. "Experience?"

"Two cousins and I have followed the harvest from California to here for two years."

"When can you start?"

"My cousins will arrive at Mr. Short's orchard before six tonight, ready to start picking. Told them I'd meet them there."

"I'll stop. It's on the way to my orchard."

Roy realized he was taking a chance by going back to Mr. Short's migrant camp. He was betting his freedom the watch Mr. Mansfield had in his pocket was the one taken from Max, and he had just gotten it from Ed Lander or someone who had purchased it from Ed. If he was wrong, he would likely end up in jail for a long time.

The seriousness of his gamble became apparent as they approached the camp. A deputy sheriff and Mr. Short had parked their vehicles in front of Mrs. Ryman's cabin. They were talking to her and Colleen.

When Mr. Mansfield parked beside the patrol car, Roy could hear Mrs. Ryman and the deputy arguing.

"The boy didn't kill Max," she said, angrily. "Ed Lander killed him, and he's going to kidnap Colleen if you don't arrest him."

"All I have against Mr. Lander is your wild accusations. I have solid evidence against the boy," the deputy replied. "He had your husband's billfold in his pocket. Solid proof. What more do you need?"

Roy didn't have a chance to find out how the argument would've ended because Mr. Short spotted him and Mr. Mansfield getting out of the pickup.

"There's your killer right there," Mr. Short said, pointing his finger at Roy.

The deputy's eyes widened, in apparent alarm. He jerked his revolver out of a holster and aimed it at Roy.

"What's going on here?" Mr. Mansfield asked, looking at Roy for an answer.

"What time is it?" Roy said.

Mr. Mansfield frowned, seemingly puzzled, but reacted instinctively. He pulled the watch out of his pocket to look at it.

"That's Max's watch," Mrs. Ryman yelled.

The deputy shifted his revolver to point it at Mr. Mansfield.

"Don't point that gun at me," Mr. Mansfield bellowed.

"Mr. Mansfield, please tell the deputy where you got the watch," Roy said, knowing the answer would mean freedom or jail.

"Paid a bartender twenty dollars for this watch not more than a half-hour ago. Ed Lander used it to pay his bar bill," he replied, angrily. "What in the hell is going on here?"

"That watch belonged to my husband," Mrs. Ryman said. "Had it with him last night when he went to Ed Lander's cabin."

Mr. Mansfield turned to Roy, his face turning red in anger. "Told me you wanted a picking job *just* to get me to stop here with this watch," he accused.

"I want the job, if the offer is still open."

As Roy spoke, he heard a vehicle coast to a stop behind him. He assumed it was his cousins until he turned around.

Ed Lander had a smug smile on his face as he stepped out of his pickup. "Ya caught your killer," he said. Then he seemed to notice Mr. Mansfield for the first time. "What're you doing here?"

Mr. Mansfield opened his fist to show Ed the pocket watch.

"That's Ed Lander," Mrs. Ryman shouted. "He killed my husband."

The deputy started to swing the revolver to point it at Ed, but reacted too slowly.

Ed's beefy, backhand blow to the side of the deputy's head knocked him off his feet. Then Ed lunged toward Colleen, grabbing her before she could run. He clutched the screaming girl to his chest as he backed toward his pickup.

"Don't try to stop me. I'll snap her neck," he bellowed, as Colleen kicked her heels at him and continued screaming.

The deputy, lying on his back in the dirt, pointed his revolver at Ed.

"Don't shoot. You'll hit Colleen," Roy yelled, when he realized the deputy didn't have a clear shot.

Ed glanced at Roy and chuckled. "You're just a wimpy *boy,* like I thought." Then he turned his back to them to reach for the handle to open his pickup door.

As soon as Ed turned his back to them, Mrs. Ryman handed Roy the axe she had picked up when Ed grabbed Colleen.

When Ed gripped the handle to open the pickup door, Roy threw the axe overhand, just as he had practiced hundreds of times to relieve boredom when he chopped firewood all day during winter months.

Minutes later, the deputy raced from the scene with his siren screeching to transport Ed and his severed fingers to the hospital in Chelan.

Mr. Short paid Mrs. Ryman the wages she and Colleen had coming, and agreed to let authorities know no one would claim Max's remains. Mrs. Ryman had already packed Max's old car so she and Colleen could leave.

Roy and Colleen stood to one side, talking quietly.

"It'll take me three more years to save enough for a down payment on a farm," he said. "That'll give you time to graduate from high school and turn eighteen. I'll look you up then to see if you'd like to go to a movie."

"Don't want to wait three years," she whined, wiping away tears.

Roy's cousins parked beside Mr. Mansfield's pickup as Roy and Colleen talked.

Lonnie Cascade stepped out of the pickup and started laughing. "Roy, didn't take you long to find a pretty girl," he said.

Lorrie jumped out of the passenger side of the pickup. She ran to Roy, threw her arms around his neck, and hugged him.

"Missed you Roy," she said. "Had to chop my own firewood last night and wash the dishes all by myself."

Colleen turned loose of Roy's arm and stepped back to look at Lorrie. "Didn't tell me you had a girlfriend," she accused, as tears started running down her cheeks again.

"We're both going to meet people we like in the next three years, Colleen. It's part of growing up."

Colleen hesitated for a moment. Then she turned her back to him, ran to Max's old car, and crawled in beside her mother.

Mrs. Ryman backed the car up to turn it around to leave.

"Are you finally ready to go?" Mr. Mansfield asked, impatiently.

"Yes sir, we're ready to go pick apples," Roy said.

"Not yet, Roy," Lorrie said. "Don't you think you should stop that girl, and tell her I'm your cousin?"

"I'll tell her in three years, if she hasn't found *Mr. Wonderful* before I buy my farm."

The Old Man in the Outhouse

The old man was sleeping on the floor when I opened the door to the outhouse at Rainbow Falls.

"Sorry, I didn't hear the bus," the old man mumbled as he opened his eyes. The outhouse was an oven in the middle of August. His shirt and shorts were soaked with sweat. White stubble covered sagging cheeks.

"It's only ten o'clock. The bus isn't here yet," I said, realizing he was referring to the tour bus that would arrive after the Lady of the Lake ferry docked at Stehekin.

"I was just leaving," he said as he tried to push himself upright.

I helped him stand up, handling him cautiously because he looked very fragile. "I'll only be a minute," I assured him as I helped him to a bench near the outhouse.

My friend and I had driven a boat fifty-five miles up Lake Chelan early in the morning and hiked the three and a half miles from Stehekin to the bottom of Rainbow Falls. We wanted to hike up along the falls before the tourists arrived in the tour bus.

We were both in our early thirties in 1970, and we still believed we could hike up any mountain or to the top of a three hundred and twelve-foot waterfall.

I finished at the outhouse and hurried to join my friend. He had already started up the mountain. We had a great time exploring during the middle of the day, and the tour bus had come and gone by the time we returned to the base of the falls and the outhouse.

Curious, I opened the door to the outhouse again. The old man was sleeping on the floor.

"Sorry," he said. "I didn't hear the bus." He started to try to get up again.

"You don't need to get up," I said. "I just wanted to see

if you need any help."

"No, I'm just resting today. I'll start setting traps in the morning."

"Are you a trapper?" I asked, confused, knowing the trapping season wouldn't start for several months.

"Certainly, I trap this whole valley clear to Cotton-wood Camp and up to Trapper Lake."

He seemed not to notice the puzzled look on my face. Eighteen miles separated Rainbow Falls and Cottonwood Camp, and Trapper Lake was on top of a dangerous bluff overlooking Cottonwood Camp. I had been there, trapped at the lake in a snowstorm and fortunate to survive the climb down the icy bluff.

This man was in no condition to hike to Cottonwood Camp or climb a bluff.

"You aren't trapping there now, are you?" I asked even though the answer was obvious.

"No, I'm resting today. I'll set some traps tomorrow."

"Do you have a place to stay?"

"I have a cabin here, somewhere. I'm still looking for it."

"Are you sure it's near here?" I asked.

"I built it near the bottom of the falls. This is where my trap line starts, so it has to be here somewhere. I'll look for it tomorrow."

"Do you have food?" I asked, concerned because I hadn't seen any supplies.

"There're berries on the hillside if I get hungry."

"Have you eaten today?"

"I'll eat later if I get hungry. I'm resting right now."

"Are you ready to go?" my friend yelled. He was in a hurry to hike back to Stehekin so we could drive the boat to Lucerne and hike to Domke Lake to catch a mess of fish for dinner and camp for the night.

I felt obligated to stop at Stehekin Lodge to ask about the old man in the outhouse.

"Are you aware an old man is living in the outhouse at

Rainbow Falls?" I asked a woman at the lodge.

"My goodness, is he still there?"

"He was an hour ago. He doesn't seem very coherent, and he refused the candy bar and apple I offered him."

"He has been there for over two weeks," she said.

"Has anyone done anything?"

"We received a notice from a Seattle Police officer asking us to be on the lookout for him after he walked away from a nursing home. When we notified them he was here, they said a family member would come to get him."

"Did the police say why they believed the man might come to Stehekin?"

"They said this was his home before World War One. He trapped all up and down the valley. He told his roommate at the nursing home he wanted to go home to die."

"He told me he built a cabin near the bottom of Rainbow Falls."

"The government burned all the old trapper cabins two years ago when the area became a national park."

Then I realized what was happening. The old man had returned to his cabin to die, and no relative was coming to get him. His family was going to grant him his wish of dying with his memories at a place of his choosing.

I thought about the old man in the outhouse during the six-mile hike up the mountain to Domke Lake that evening and for a long time thereafter.

Might the confused old man die with more dignity alone in a hot outhouse inundated with vibrant memories of his trap line and cabin, I wondered, than in a cold nursing home with unfamiliar sights, sounds, and detached caregivers?

Who had the right to make the decision, if not the old man?

Stehekin

The northern end of Lake Chelan is accessible by boat, ferry, or seaplane.

Ferries travel to Stehekin from Chelan and from Fields Point on the south shore. The LADY EXPRESS, the smaller and faster of the two ferries, operates at least three days a week year around. The 100-foot long LADY OF THE LAKE II ferry makes the trip daily during summer months.

Chelan Seaplanes offers a thirty-minute flight to Stehekin flying at 1,000 feet over the lake for a spectacular view of the mountains and shoreline.

Stehekin has overnight accommodations at NORTH CASCADE LODGE, cabins, and a ranch. A bus provides tours to Rainbow Falls and High Bridge, a gateway to the North Cascade National Park and the Cascade Trail. You can hike to Canada or Mexico!

Make reservations for transportation and lodging on the internet at *www.lodgeatstehekin.com* and *www.LadyoftheLake.com*. Arrange for a flight by contacting *www.chelanseaplanes.com*.

Photo: Lady II loading passengers at Fields Point on Lake Chelan. This ferry can carry up to 350 passengers.

The Reluctant Groom

Ron Walker relished the solitude and contentment he felt as he maneuvered a hay mower around the alfalfa field. His life was simple and enjoyable. At least, it had been until his mother issued her ultimatum.

"I'm moving your father to Wenatchee at the end of the month to live closer to the hospital," she said. "And I'm going to sell the ranch if you haven't married before we move."

Ron didn't see a problem with his parents moving to Wenatchee. He had managed their ranch along with his for the last five years since his father had his first heart attack. He had also worked Sadie Sampson's ranch since her parents died in a car accident. In fact, he was mowing one of her fields right now. He could easily handle all three ranches.

His mother did see a problem. "I'll not turn this ranch over to an unmarried son," she insisted when he asked for an explanation. "If you aren't going to marry and have children to keep this ranch in the family, I might as well sell it right now."

Her unreasonable demand made no sense to Ron, so he ignored it. He believed she'd change her mind when she realized he wouldn't comply.

Then, after supper last night, she told him she had found an apartment to rent in Wenatchee near the hospital, and she restated her ultimatum. There was no way he could mistake her resolve this time after she added, "I've had the ranch appraised, and a real estate agent has a buyer ready to sign a contract."

Ron realized for the first time that she wouldn't change her mind. He also realized the end of the month was only three weeks away.

He knew what his mother was thinking. She had wanted him to marry Sadie Sampson, the neighbor girl, ever since he returned from Korea eight years ago. She likely believed her ultimatum would close the deal.

"Aw, nuts!" he mumbled, realizing he had been daydreaming and lost track of time. A quick glance at his watch confirmed what he suspected—he was already five minutes late for supper.

His mother always had food on the table at exactly six o'clock. She expected to see him and his father seated in time for grace when their grandfather clock finished chiming the hour.

Driving to the farmhouse will take ten minutes. Washing my hands and face on the back porch will take two. Mom's not going to be happy.

He realized his late arrival wasn't his only problem when he approached the farmhouse. Sadie had parked her car in the driveway.

Mom must think I don't know what she's trying to do. She keeps inviting Sadie for Saturday supper, hoping I'll take her to the dance.

Sadie had asked him to take her to the dance in Manson last Saturday, but he needed to keep an all-night watch on a sick calf. He knew she would ask him again tonight, but he needed to finish mowing before it rained. He could use the headlights on the tractor and mow all night if necessary.

He kept his head down to avoid eye contact as he entered the dining room. As he expected, they had started supper without him. Sadie sat directly across the table from his chair. He felt like a fool when he noticed her smile as she watched him slink to his chair like a misbehaving child.

A large platter of fried chicken sat in the center of the table. Fried chicken was his favorite food. He knew Sadie had most likely arrived early to prepare it.

"The way to a man's heart is through his stomach," he had heard his mother say many times. She must've shared her folklore wisdom with Sadie. They had fried chicken every time she joined them for supper.

"Sorry I'm late, Mom. I was at the far end of the field when I realized it was suppertime."

His mother responded by passing him the fried chicken. She pursed her lips but didn't say anything. He was thirty years old, a decorated combat-veteran, and successful rancher. She had long since given up reprimanding him verbally. Now she simply pursed her lips to show her displeasure.

He noticed his father ducked his head to hide a grin.

Dad knows what Mom's doing. He knows she's determined to have Sadie for a daughter-in-law.

Ron buttered a thick slice of his mother's homemade bread and tried, unsuccessfully, to concentrate on the meal. Unpleasant memories distressed him anytime he encountered Sadie, however, causing him to avoid her whenever possible and refuse to talk to her.

They had almost married, ten years earlier. He had proposed when he received his draft notice in 1951. The wedding was to take place when he returned from boot camp, but the army sent him directly overseas to Korea. He had no opportunity to return home during the remainder of his two-year commitment.

No one told him until he returned that Sadie married a migrant worker a few weeks after he reported for duty. She received an annulment when her husband skipped town a few weeks after the wedding.

He was sure Sadie would notice the scowl on his face, and she would know what he was thinking. They had been best friends since grade school. She was the only woman he had ever loved, and she betrayed him.

No way in hell will I give her a chance to betray me a

second time!

As usual, no one spoke during the meal. When they finished eating, his father pushed his chair back, extracted his pipe from a vest pocket, and held a match to it.

His mother glared at his father as a cloud of smoke engulfed the dining room.

Ron stifled a smile. His mother was as unsuccessful in getting his father to quit smoking as she was in getting him to marry Sadie.

Sadie watched the nightly routine, watched him, her eyes pleading.

No! Hell will freeze over before I take you to a dance where people can see us together and laugh at me behind my back.

He stood up to open two windows to let a cross-breeze remove the dense smoke. "Thanks for supper, Mom," he said, as he lifted the bottom half of a double-hung window. "Weatherman says we might have rain tomorrow. I need to finish mowing Sadie's field after I milk the cow and finish the chores."

"Can't the mowing wait until Monday?" Sadie asked, as he walked toward the door.

"No," he mumbled. He heard her voice as the screen door closed behind him, but he couldn't understand what she said.

Mowing the hayfield took longer than Ron expected. Clouds obscured the moonlight, making him dependent on the tractor's dim-headlights.

He noticed a car parked in front of Sadie's farmhouse for a few minutes before nine o'clock and again shortly after two in the morning. He was careful not to turn the tractor toward the farmhouse where the headlights would shine on the car.

What she does isn't any of my business.

He was exhausted when he finished mowing the field

at three in the morning. He drove back to the farmhouse, yawning to try to stay awake. There would be little time for sleep. He would need to start the farm chores at seven to be ready to take his folks to eleven o'clock church services.

I can catch a catnap during the sermon and a long nap in the afternoon while we listen to the Wenatchee Chief's baseball game.

His mother was placing bacon, eggs, and hotcakes on his plate at the kitchen table when he wandered in from the barn at nine o'clock.

He set the milk bucket on the drain board. Then he washed his hands in the kitchen sink and sat down at the table to wait for his mother to say grace. Just the two of them would eat breakfast. His father needed more rest due to his heart condition.

"We need to leave early today," his mother said. "We need to stop at the Apple Cup Cafe before ten-thirty."

Ron couldn't think of any reason they would stop at the restaurant in Chelan.

"The Greyhound Bus drops passengers off in front of the restaurant," she reminded him. "I hired a young lady from Davenport to work as a housekeeper and caregiver. She's going to help me take care of your father for the next three weeks until we move to Wenatchee. She'll arrive on the bus at ten-thirty this morning."

He wrinkled his brow. "This is kind of sudden."

"I've talked to her on the phone several times in the last month and checked her references. She comes from a large farm-family and has experience helping her mother care for young siblings and her ailing father. She has also worked as a cook in a restaurant. She's just what we need here."

While the idea of a housekeeper and caregiver was rather sudden, it did make sense when he thought about it for a moment. His mother had her hands full taking care of the house and his father.

"Makes sense," he said.

"Her name is Amanda Glassine, and she is 26. She has an ad in the Spokesman Review seeking a housekeeping position for a gentleman of good reputation with the possibility of matrimony, if compatible."

Ron didn't need to hear any more to know what his mother was thinking, but she told him anyway.

"Since you've rejected Sadie, I called Amanda last night to give you another option. You only have three weeks."

"Mom, this is crazy. Marriage to Sadie was never an option. Now you're talking about marriage to a woman I've never met."

"I know Sadie loves you, and you love her."

"I'm *not* going to marry Sadie."

"No, you're not. You've missed your chance. She called an hour ago to tell me Joe Wilson took her to the dance at the Manson Community Hall last night. After the dance, he proposed marriage for the fourth or fifth time. They're getting married in two weeks."

Ron stopped the car across the street from the Apple Cup Cafe at a quarter after ten.

His father was half-asleep in the front passenger seat. He raised his head and looked around as if he had no idea why they stopped.

"We're early," his mother said.

"The bus doesn't run a very tight schedule," Ron replied. "Never know when it might be early or late."

Waiting for the bus gave him time to think, which was not easy. He had gotten very little sleep after mowing alfalfa most of the night, and his mind had reeled in turmoil since breakfast when his mother told him about Sadie's wedding plans.

Two things he knew for sure. Sadie still loved him—she had told him often enough despite his attempts to avoid her. And she didn't love Joe Wilson.

He had heard friends talk about the forty-year-old bachelor. Joe was an honest, hardworking rancher who courted and proposed to every available female. Everyone knew he was desperate to find a wife to keep house, cook, and care for his invalid mother.

Sadie's marrying him out of spite. Just what I'd expect after she betrayed me once! If this housekeeper doesn't look like a dumpster with a black beard, I'll marry her.

The bus arrived on time, putting an end to his troubled thoughts. He stepped out and opened the car's back door to help his mother cross the street to meet the housekeeper.

Four passengers exited the bus in front of the cafe. He recognized three of them. The other passenger was an attractive female. She appeared to have dressed in her Sunday-best clothing in anticipation of accompanying them to church services.

His mother stepped toward the woman with a welcoming smile.

"Amanda, I'm so grateful you've arrived. I'm Ann Walker, and this is my son, Ron."

Amanda gave Mrs. Walker a quick hug and turned to hold her hand out to Ron. She smiled, looking him directly in the eyes as she reached for his hand.

Startled, he shook her hand lightly. *When did women become so forward and start shaking hands?*

She maintained eye contact and was slow to relinquish her grip.

He sensed she was letting him know she was sizing him up to see if he measured up to her expectations, and she knew he was doing the same. Despite her aggressive boldness, her infectious smile made him like her immediately.

"I'll carry that," he said after the driver retrieved an old suitcase from the bus undercarriage.

"Thanks," she said.

"We're parked across the street," his mother said. "We need to hurry, or we'll be late for services."

Amanda was still smiling, maintaining eye contact with him. She stepped closer.

He sensed she wanted him to hold her arm or hand to escort her across the street. He picked up the suitcase and pretended he didn't notice her subtle hint, fearing he might've misinterpreted her intent.

The parking lot was nearly full when Ron coasted to a stop near the church entrance. He helped his father out of the car, so his mother and Amanda could help him into the chapel while he drove to the far end of the lot to park.

His parents were sitting in their usual place when he entered the church. Amanda sat between them. They had left a space for him between Amanda and his father.

Sadie Sampson and Joe Wilson were sitting in the pew just in front of his parents.

He noticed curious stares as parishioners observed the unusual seating arrangement. Sadie usually sat on one side of his parents, next to his mother, while he sat on the other side, next to his father. Amanda was a stranger. This was the first time Joe had attended their church.

Ron could hear a dim murmur of comments. He knew tongues would wag in earnest when the service concluded.

He sat between his father and Amanda, looking at the back of Sadie's head until she turned to glance at him.

Never one to hide her emotions, Sadie's face briefly reflected shock when she noticed Amanda. Her chin started to quiver as she quickly turned back toward the podium where the minister was preparing to start the service.

Amanda squirmed beside Ron, causing him to turn his

head toward her. She was looking him directly in the eyes again, questioning, making him wish he were on the tractor at the far end of a field. She turned to glare at Sadie when she sneaked another quick look at them.

The sermon seemed to last twice as long as usual. His father's head bobbed several times before he settled into a comfortable nap. He could feel Amanda's body stiffen every time Sadie turned to glance at him. Joe seemed not to notice anything out of the ordinary was happening.

Ron didn't know how to react to the hurt he witnessed in Sadie's eyes when she turned to look at him. His first impulse was to flaunt Amanda in front of her as payback for betraying him ten years ago. Deep down, he knew he had never stopped loving her, and he didn't want to humiliate her.

No one spoke during the drive home. After he packed Amanda's suitcase to an upstairs bedroom, his mother served the cold lunch she had prepared after they finished breakfast.

After lunch, he and his father listened to the Wenatchee Chief's baseball game while his mother showed Amanda around the house. His father dozed almost immediately. He drifted into a troubled sleep during the second inning.

His mother woke him at four o'clock to start the evening chores.

Supper was on the table when he returned with the milk bucket and a basket full of eggs a few minutes before six o'clock. He washed and sat down at the dining room table.

His mother finished grace before the clock chimed six times.

Amanda sat across the table from him. She smiled when he dared look up from his food.

She won't be hard to look at across the table every morning. Her ad said she's interested in marriage. Why not? I'll marry her.

Ron rubbed the sleep out of his eyes as he walked downstairs the next morning on his way to the barn to start the daily chores. He stopped in the kitchen to get the milk bucket, but it wasn't on the end of the drain board where it belonged. His mother always placed the bucket there after she washed it. A quick search convinced him the bucket was missing.

The implication panicked him. He had started milking the cow after his father's first heart attack, but the strong-willed man still objected vehemently.

Darn it Dad, you've no business trying to milk the cow again.

He bolted out the door to run toward the barn. When he arrived, he could see the cow munching hay in a milking stall and hear milk squirting into a bucket. He recognized the head pressed against the cow's flank.

"What're you doing?" he asked in disbelief.

"Milking a cow," Amanda said.

"You know what I meant."

"I grew up doing farm chores. Early morning chores are rather invigorating, don't you think?"

"Mom didn't hire you to do farm chores."

"I know why your mother hired me. She needs help caring for your father, but mostly she hopes you'll ask me to marry you. I knew we'd have a chance to talk if I helped with the morning chores."

Her straightforward manner left him speechless for a moment. He was used to modest, reserved females—farm girls. Amanda made no pretense at acting coy. She acted like a city girl. Flustered, he said the only thing that came to mind. "Your ad said you want to get married."

"That's why I came here," she responded, as she looked him straight in the eyes again, unnerving him even more.

"You'd marry someone you've just met?"

"If you're asking if I have to be in love before I marry, the answer is no. I'll marry an honest, hard-working man. I'll learn to love him just as my mother learned to love my father. My parents met two days before their wedding, and they love each other very much. Each of my ten siblings will tell you the same thing."

He smiled, regaining confidence. "You'd marry me then?"

"This ranch and your neighbor's ranch are well maintained. You're obviously a hard worker and very responsible. Your mother says the *Cattleman's Association* has nominated you for their *Rancher of the Year* award."

"So, you'd marry me?"

"No, I won't marry you."

"I don't understand," he stammered.

"I'll marry a man I can learn to love as he learns to love me. You'd never learn to love me because you're hopelessly in love with Sadie Sampson."

He stared at her, opened-mouthed, as she patted the cow on the side. Then she stood up with the milk bucket and walked toward the barn door. She turned at the door to give him a sympathetic look.

"Your mother said I can use the car to run an errand this morning. We'll talk again after I visit with Sadie."

Amanda drove away in his folk's car before Ron finished the chores.

He took a lunch with him when he drove to the alfalfa fields. After he attached a windrow machine to the tractor, he spent the day raking alfalfa into rows so the hay could finish drying.

Amanda was helping his mother place food on the table when he returned to the farmhouse in time for supper. No one talked during the meal except for his mother's comment that Amanda prepared the fried chicken.

He knew what his mother was suggesting—Amanda could cook his favorite food.

Amanda smiled knowingly at him when he made the mistake of looking up from his plate.

When he finished eating, he thanked his mother for the meal. Then he walked to the barn with the milk bucket to start the evening chores.

Amanda arrived while he was milking the cow. She stood and watched him until he was nearly finished. Finally, when he didn't look up or say anything, she said, "Don't you want to ask about my visit with Sadie?"

"I assumed it was none of my business."

"Of course it's your business. We were talking about you."

He had no idea why they would talk about him. Curious, he said, "What did you decide?"

"We decided to have a double wedding."

Ron thought she was joking until he looked up.

"I don't understand."

"She convinced me I was mistaken. Apparently, she doesn't love you, and you don't love her. So, you and I are free to marry. Sadie suggested we make it a double wedding."

Amanda looked him directly in the eyes again as she waited for a reaction.

He knew she was telling him something important that demanded a response, but all he understood was, "She doesn't love you." The words flashed through his mind like rolling thunder. *"She doesn't love you. She doesn't love you."*

Did I misjudge Sadie's feelings?

Amanda continued looking at him, boldly, waiting for him to say something.

Then he recalled the rest of what she had said.

Whoa! Wait a minute. Things are happening too fast. Don't remember actually proposing.

Now, he realized, it was too late. Amanda had already arranged a wedding, a double wedding—with Sadie and Joe. Finally, confused and overwhelmed with emotion, he nodded his head without knowing if he was indicating comprehension, disbelief, or agreement.

"There's a stipulation, however," she continued, interpreting his head nod as agreement. "We need to get to know each other better before our wedding, and I need to get to know Sadie and Joe since they'll be our neighbors."

He sat on the milking stool, looking up at her, having no idea what she was suggesting.

"You're going to take me to the dance at the Manson Community Hall the next two Saturday nights before the wedding," she said. "We're going to have dinner with Sadie and Joe the next two Wednesday evenings. Sadie suggested we all go on a picnic after church services next Sunday. We don't have much time to get to know each other because our wedding is only two weeks away."

Ron was too stunned to comprehend most of what she said. The one thing he clearly understood alarmed him—he would have to watch Sadie and Joe together at dances, dinners, and a picnic.

The next two weeks were a swirl of activity that left Ron breathless and confused. His only solitude came during daylight hours as he baled alfalfa hay.

He realized he had never seen his mother happier as she helped Sadie and Amanda plan their weddings. His father simply watched and smiled.

When he overheard Amanda and his mom discussing which of the bedrooms would make the best nursery for a newborn, he quickly turned and walked outside.

There's nothing subtle about this woman.

The two Saturday night dances, Wednesday night dinners, and Sunday picnic were all of a kind. Disasters! He watched Sadie and Joe interact like teenagers. Joe was a good dancer, and he could carry on a conversation without getting tongue-tied. He knew Joe would be a good catch for any woman.

If she loved him.

Amanda frequently initiated changing partners as they danced. He would end up with Sadie as a partner, which upset him. They would stumble around the dance floor at arm's length. The women compounded his discomfort by insisting they eat dinner at Silvia's Diner on Wednesday evenings where they could dance in the lounge to music from a jukebox.

Amanda and Sadie quickly became good friends, judging by the amount of time they spent together. He noticed Amanda accompanied Sadie when she took Joe's mother to a doctor's appointment and to the Chelan Senior Center for lunch.

He couldn't help noticing the way Amanda and Joe danced at the Manson Community Hall the night before the weddings. Amanda asked Joe to dance with her when the band played a slow waltz. They pressed firmly together, cheek to cheek, as they swayed with the music.

Has she forgotten whom she's marrying?

Ron was greatly relieved after the last Saturday night dance. The weddings would take place the next afternoon. Then he could forget all this foolishness and get on with his life.

His mother and Amanda had breakfast ready Sunday morning when he finished the chores. Amanda sat across the table from him with a big smile on her face, looking every bit the happy bride-to-be.

She's everything a man could want in a bride, and I'm going to marry her in a few hours. Why do I want to run and hide?

They didn't talk while they ate breakfast. After they finished eating, his mother excused herself to check on his father.

"You nervous?" Amanda asked.

Of course, I'm nervous. I'm about to marry someone I don't know and don't love.

"No. Why would I be nervous?"

"Thought you might be nervous since we haven't had much time to get acquainted. Do you realize we've never kissed?"

Ron was glad he had finished eating. He might've choked if he had a mouth full of food. He still hadn't gotten use to her directness.

"I guess I hadn't thought about it," he said, knowing he must sound like a fool.

"Well, I've thought about it, and I'm not about to marry a man I've never kissed. We need to take care of that right now."

Before he had a chance to protest, she grabbed his arm to pull him out the door toward the barn. Amanda giggled like a teenager as he tried unsuccessfully to pull away from her. After she pulled him into the barn, she slammed the door shut, and threw her arms around his neck. She looked up at him and batted her eyes provocatively.

"We can be more intimate if we climb up to the hayloft," she whispered, breathlessly.

His eyes widened and he stepped back, shocked by her aggressiveness. "That wouldn't be appropriate," was the only thing he could think to say.

"A tumble in the hayloft before marriage was appropriate with Sadie, but not with me?"

"What!"

"Have you forgotten what happened the night before you left for boot camp ten years ago?"

"There was no tumble in the hayloft. Not the way you mean it."

"No, but both of you went further than you meant to go."

"Did Sadie tell you that?"

"Of course. And she told me why she married a stranger after your trip to the hayloft."

"What're you trying to say?"

"I'm saying someone who grew up on a farm around livestock should understand the ramifications of frolicking in a hayloft."

"Oh my God! Are you saying she was pregnant?"

"Of course she was pregnant, you fool. What did you expect?"

"She never told me."

"How could she tell you? You were already on a ship on your way to Korea when she realized she was pregnant. She was a month shy of eighteen, and you'd just turned twenty. The authorities would've charged you with statutory rape if she'd admitted you were responsible. She told her parents a stranger raped her. She did everything she could to protect you."

"I'd have found a way to come back home."

"You'd have arrived too late to help Sadie. Her parents wanted to avoid a scandal. They arranged for her to marry a migrant worker in front of a judge in Wenatchee. Her folks paid the kid to marry her and leave town when the harvest was over. Sadie met her husband for ten minutes in the judge's chambers. Never saw him again.

"She miscarried in the fourth month. Her parents kept her home the whole time. No one knew she was pregnant—not even your parents."

When Amanda finished talking, Ron was sitting on a hay bale with his head in his hands, trying to keep from bawling.

"Why hasn't Sadie told me any of this?"

"When did you ever give her a chance to tell you anything? You've refused to talk to her for eight years."

"Oh my gawd! She must hate me."

"Don't be a fool. She has never stopped loving you and you know it."

"I don't know what to do."

"You can start by thanking me. I'm the best friend you'll ever have."

"Thanks," he mumbled as he wiped his eyes and looked up at her.

"Why did she tell you what happened?"

"She told me because I asked. She would've told you if you'd given her a chance. You can still talk to her if you're prepared to apologize for your stupid behavior. You might start by telling her you love her. Her reaction might surprise you."

"There's no time. You and I are getting married an hour after church services today."

"You still haven't figured it out, have you?"

He looked at her, confused.

"I'm going to marry Joe Wilson this afternoon."

"What?"

"Sadie's going to stand beside me. She may be my bridesmaid, but she'd rather be a bride."

"What!"

"We hope to have a double wedding, but that depends on what you do in the next hour. She's waiting... if you're finally ready to talk to her."

The Apple Cup Cafe is a local favorite that has stood the test of time.

Lakeside

Drivers on Highway 97A will discover Lakeside on Lake Chelan's south shore just before they reach downtown Chelan. Lakeside is actually a part of Chelan although it appears to be a separate town because of its location on the lakeshore.

The first thing a visitor will notice is Lakeside Park. This is a beautiful park for family use with grass, shade trees, picnic tables, and restroom facilities. It has a boat dock, a large sandy beach for swimming, a sand volleyball court, and a basketball half court.

A large motel fronts the park and a gas station, convenience store, and Subway shop are next door. Other motels are within easy walking distance from the park.

The beach offers views of Lake Chelan, Wapato Point, Chelan, and orchards on the surrounding foothills.

Visitors will encounter vineyards, winemakers, and tasting rooms along the lakeshore before and after Lakeside and find parasail, watercraft, jet skis, a slide water park, and boat rental businesses between Lakeside and downtown Chelan.

Every Saturday Morning

The popular girls hang out at the mall on Saturday morning. The rich girls shop at nice stores downtown. I walk to Walt's Pawnshop on the depressed, hungry side of town where storefronts are decaying, sidewalks have crumbled, and panhandlers are aggressive. I stop at the pawnshop every Saturday morning because I want to buy a dress for the junior prom.

The windows at Walt's Pawnshop are as dirty as the sidewalk and street out front, so it's impossible to see if Walt has a customer. I wait across the street. No way do I want to be alone in the shop with Walt. He's probably nursing a hangover, trying to remember if he beat his wife and tried to molest his daughter again last night. This is a small town. Everyone knows.

As usual, a vagrant approaches me, holding out his hand, demanding money. The beggars assume a petite girl will be easy pickings. I flash my knife. He backs away, calling me filthy names, the same ones my daddy calls me.

An hour passes. Then a woman parks her expensive new car down the street. The car has a decal for a popular Lake Chelan resort on the back window. She looks around before she quickly walks to Walt's Pawnshop and enters.

I cross the street, knowing it's safe to enter the pawnshop now. The woman is standing in front of the counter as the door closes behind me. She's showing Walt a necklace, giving him a sob story. She has lost her job, she tells him. She needs two hundred dollars to pay her rent. The necklace is worth a thousand.

I hear the same story every Saturday morning when I stop at the pawnshop. I know what's going to happen. Walt is going to rob her. She is wasting her time pleading with him.

Examining the necklace distracts Walt for a moment. He turns his back toward me, giving me time to reach behind the display counter. The watch I grab is worth a hundred dollars. I can sell it on the street for twenty.

When I look up, the woman is watching me with a startled expression on her face.

Walt is slow to turn around. The watch is in my pocket before he looks at me. He tells the woman he needs to take the necklace to a backroom to test it. He leaves her standing at the counter.

The woman is still staring at me, looking at the pocket where I stashed the watch.

I smirk at the woman as she walks toward me as if she is going to reprimand a naughty child. I grab her arm, roughly, and I tell her the truth. Walt's a thief. He's going to rob her. She needs to leave. Quickly.

I already know she won't leave. They never do.

She is desperate, she tells me. She is three months behind on her rent. The property-owner won't accept the four hundred she has saved. He demands six hundred to avoid eviction.

Tears run down her cheeks, but I know they're as bogus as the cheap necklace and her story. Only the new car she drives and the needle marks I felt on her arm, hidden under long sleeves, are real. She needs another two hundred dollars, but to buy the fix she has to have to get through the day and survive another night.

I glance toward the back room, knowing Walt will stay there just long enough to down a shot of booze. I reach behind the counter, grab two expensive watches, and shove them in her hand. Her eyes grow big as I tell her to take the watches to Chelan to a pawnshop. The watches are worth six hundred. She can get two.

She hesitates, appalled, but desperate. Finally, necessity prevails. She hangs her head to hide her shame as she drops the watches in her purse.

Walt suddenly charges out of the back room, shouting obscenities. He points toward a security camera as he picks up the phone. He says he's calling the police.

I start to cry. I beg him to put down the phone.

The woman starts bawling, real tears now. Her husband will divorce her if the police arrest her, she tells him. She couldn't face her children, her friends, and her pastor.

He hates shoplifters, Walt tells us. He's going to have us arrested. He's holding the phone as he shouts at us.

I quickly pull the watch out of my pocket and slap it on the counter, begging for another chance. I've learned my lesson. I'll never steal again. I promise him.

The woman seems too distraught to react, so I reach into her purse to get the two watches and drop them on the counter.

Before either of us can say anything, Walt points toward the security camera again. Then he starts punching numbers on his phone.

I sob even louder as I watch him, knowing he doesn't care that a night in a jail cell could be a death sentence for the woman, a secret addict like most of his customers. He's a thief. He wants money.

I pull two hundred dollars out of my pocket, all the money I have, and toss the money on the counter. I tell him I was saving the money to buy a dress for the junior prom. He can have the money if he'll put down the phone.

He glares at me. He glares at the woman.

Waiting.

Traumatized, she fails to understand I've shown her a way out of this mess. I grab her arm again and shake her to get her attention. I tell her she needs to pony up money, or Walt will send both of us to jail.

She looks at the money I tossed on the counter. Sobbing hysterically, she finds two hundred dollars in her purse and places the money on the counter.

Walt growls like a rabid dog as he puts down the phone and slams her necklace on the counter in front of her. He hates shoplifters, he tells us again. He's going to save the tape from the security camera to show the police if either one of us ever comes back to his shop.

I grab the woman's necklace off the counter, drop it into her purse, and shove her out the door. I tell her the truth. Walt is drunk. She needs to run before he loses control and attacks her.

When the door closes behind the woman, I turn toward Walt to give him a piece of my mind. I tell him he's a pathetic thief. She had four hundred dollars in her purse. He could've had all of her money if he was sober enough to work the swindle to completion.

I grab my two hundred dollars off the counter and half of the two hundred the woman placed there. I glare defiantly at him as I shove the money into my pocket.

Walt snickers drunkenly as he watches me. He reaches under the counter for a hidden pint of cheap rotgut-whiskey—the only kind my daddy can afford.

Are you coming back next Saturday, he wants to know?

Maybe, maybe not, I tell him as I walk out the door, disgusted with his incompetence.

I'll be back, though. I need another hundred dollars to buy a prom dress at a nice store downtown, like the rich girls. He knows I'll be back because I stop at Daddy's pawnshop for some easy money every Saturday morning.

Forty Twice

You may remember the dreadful day in the fall of '64 when pigeons fell from the sky. Dead pigeons littered streets in Chelan after they plummeted onto cars and startled shoppers. Bystanders were appalled as they watched birds gasp a final breath and crash.

If you didn't see the dead pigeons in person, you may have read about them in our weekly newspaper under my byline. The editor placed my superbly written story on page one under an inch-high headline. Readers screamed in anger when they learned why the pigeons died.

The pigeons were roosting on a storeowner's roof and bombing his sidewalk and customers with *fowl* gifts from heaven. The desperate owner hired a pest control company to remove the pigeons because shoppers were avoiding his store.

"I assumed they'd trap the birds," he told me. "Never dreamed they'd dump poisoned birdseed on my roof."

Now the owner had a bigger problem than bird droppings. Public outrage! No question, the storeowner and pest control company had stepped in *it*.

My feature article was the talk of the town for the next week. Then a tragic house fire grabbed headline space. The aftermath of the pigeon fiasco never made it into the newspaper, so you didn't get to read the rest of the story.

You probably didn't know Rose Ann McPherson. You'd have liked her even though she might not have fit into your social circle. She lived in an apartment above the store where the pigeons were poisoned. She rented number 207, across the hall from my room.

Rose Ann had spent most of her life on a ranch where she cooked for harvest crews until her husband passed. Even in her eighties, she still cared for those around her. She frequently resuscitated me with black coffee on Monday mornings, so I could find my way to the newspaper office.

She retained her lifelong habit of getting up early. Walking city sidewalks at first light to pick up litter replaced the farm chores that occupied most of her years.

You wouldn't have known Montana, Jake, or Crusty. They certainly wouldn't have fit into your social circle. They lived in a hobo camp behind a warehouse. I knew them because I frequently visited their camp, looking for ideas for the blockbuster novel I planned to write. In addition, it's fair to say I occasionally enjoyed a nip or two of the wine they passed around the campfire on a dreary night, a star-bright night, or any other night of the week.

You might wonder how a reporter found time to visit a hobo camp. Frequently there's nothing worth reporting in small towns. Then newspaper editors fill space with stories from Associated Press. On such occasions, I visited the camp to listen to stories, hoping for inspiration for my novel.

Did I mention I used to enjoy an occasional nip of their wine?

You might enjoy a glass of wine on occasion, but you probably haven't developed a taste for Thunderbird, the hobo's cheap, fortified drink of choice. Thunderbird's subtle bouquet, a hint of diesel fuel mixed with rubbing alcohol spilled on a cow pie, has failed to gain popularity with the more genteel social class in our community.

Several weeks before the pigeon disaster, Rose Ann met Crusty on the street—literally. He had passed out on the sidewalk sometime during the night.

Crusty was still clutching his bottle of life support when Rose Ann found him. This was a common occurrence for Crusty. Like many hardcore drinkers, he suffered from blackouts, which allowed him to retain some measure of self-respect by erasing any memory of his deplorable behavior.

Rose Ann stopped to help Crusty, unlike others who might've ignored him or shied away with a self-righteous snicker. She called a cab and persuaded the reluctant driver to help her get him off the street.

She knew where to take Crusty because she also occasionally enjoyed a nip of the drink of choice around a campfire. Crusty was still dead to the world when she delivered him to Montana and Jake's *summer home* behind the warehouse.

Hobos appreciated Rose Ann's visits because she would frequently bring food. She missed cooking for large harvest crews, so she'd use money from her social security check to prepare a pot roast or a casserole for friends in need. For some, like Crusty, the calories from her food might be the only ones consumed during the day that didn't come from a bottle.

If the men felt obligated to share a sip of their Thunderbird, it would've been impolite for Rose Ann to refuse. She might accept several nips, if offered.

"They remind me of the harvest workers I used to feed," she told me. "Montana harvested wheat on ranches in Montana. Jake was a choke setter on oil wells in Texas. Crusty is... well... Crusty is crusty. Never said where he's from or what he did. Probably can't remember. Now they're seasonal field and orchard workers."

I usually visited their camp shortly after dark, between happy hour and passing out time for the residents.

Stories, jokes, and songs followed one after another. The people around the campfire on any given night might include university graduates and high school dropouts. They had been doctors, lawyers, teachers, preachers, laborers, rich men, and poor men. They had but one thing in common—an overpowering addiction to alcohol over which they had no control.

Many an evening, I listened as we sipped until the bottles were empty. Then we would start the well-known hobo chant.

"What's the word? Thunderbird!
What's the price? Forty twice.
"What's the word? Thunderbird!
What's the price? Forty twice."

The chant would continue, progressively louder, until the group collected eighty cents and identified someone capable of walking, staggering, or crawling to the nearest store or bar to buy another bottle of their fortified drink of choice.

At the risk of becoming part of this story, I must confess I visited the hobo camp the day the pigeons took their *swan dive*. I submitted my story to the editor before the printing deadline. Then I celebrated with a huge steak dinner and a few social drinks at Silvia's Diner. I decided to cap off the evening by listening to some stories. I was still seeking ideas, of course, for the grand novel I planned to write.

Rose Ann was at the campfire with Crusty, Montana, and Jake when I arrived with two bottles of Thunderbird. I wanted to celebrate, knowing my front-page story exposing the despicable behavior of the storeowner and the pest control company would be the talk of the town the next day.

Everyone was happy to help me celebrate.

Rose Ann had cooked a casserole for the men. I regretted filling up on steak when I watched them attack her food. Must have been good. And salty. Made them thirsty. Had to walk to the nearest store once with 80 cents. Maybe twice? It was a foggy night. Got foggier the longer we celebrated.

My editor was waiting at the office door when I staggered to work the next afternoon.

"Associated Press picked up your story," he announced excitedly. "Your article will fill dead space worldwide."

Startled, I stumbled into my office, locked the door, and banged my swollen head against the concrete wall to try to jettison the lingering fog. I realized our little town was about to become famous, under my byline, for murdering innocent pigeons. No one would publish the magnificent novel I planned to write with this story on my resume.

Then my phone rang, triggering fireworks in my head. I had no idea why a doctor would call me from the emergency room unless he was psychic enough to know Thunderbird had fried my brain cells. Maybe he heard the echo from my head banging on the wall.

"Do you have a friend named Montana?" he asked.

A fast five minutes later, I ran into the hospital waiting room. A nurse grabbed me by the arm to rush me behind closed doors. The emergency room was a disaster zone.

Crusty looked like he was dead... a reasonably normal condition. Montana and Jake were puking up their guts. The place smelled like diesel fuel, rubbing alcohol, and fresh cow pies—or any hobo camp after sundown.

The nurse pushed a cup of a chalklike liquid at me, trying to force me to drink it.

I refused.

She yelled angrily at me as she pointed toward Crusty. "Ya want to look like *that?*"

"Even dead, I won't look like *that*," I shouted back at her.

She still had a firm grip on my shirtsleeve, nearly ripping it, as I made my way toward the front door.

"Easy lady," I howled, as I shook her loose. "I'm a reporter. I only own two shirts."

I realized I couldn't help my friends by staying at the hospital. I might help them, however, by finding out what had poisoned them. I was a reporter, after all, with finely tuned, fact-finding skills. Pickled brain cells be damned!

Rose Ann was feeding sparrows behind our apartments when I found her. I complimented her on her potpie casserole and suggested the recipe would make good copy for a newspaper story if she didn't mind sharing. You know how women love to share a recipe. I made her day, listening patiently as she described everything in detail, including the meat she used.

"Any type of meat will work," she assured me, "but I only make a potpie when I can use leftovers or get free meat. I was picking up litter at daylight when the pigeons started falling from the sky," she said. "Pigeons were always a nuisance in the barn at our ranch. My boys used to shoot them with their 22 rifles. Then I would make their favorite casserole—pigeon potpie. I wasn't about to let the pigeons on the sidewalk go to waste when hungry men need food."

I thanked Rose Ann for sharing her recipe and rushed to a phone to call the pest control company to inquire about the poison on the birdseed.

The doctor in the emergency room called the Center for Disease Control in Atlanta for treatment advice after I reached the hospital to share my information. An hour later, he was able to say my friends would survive their near-death experience.

I walked back to my office, locked the door, and pounded keys on a typewriter until I finished the first draft of this story. Then I buried my account of the pigeon fiasco in a filing cabinet to shield my friends from embarrassment and public scorn.

Last night, seven years after the pigeon disaster, I dug the story out of my filing cabinet to update it.

My friend Rose Ann has passed to her heavenly reward after a lifetime of service to the community and those in need. Montana, Jake, and Crusty have not maintained a *summer home* behind the warehouse for two years. Their whereabouts and circumstances are unknown, most likely by choice.

I stopped visiting hobo camps when I realized good friends had drawn me to the evening campfires rather than their drink of choice or any burning desire to author a best-selling novel. Now I hang out with respectable civic leaders in the cocktail lounge at Silvia's Diner, faithfully attend Rotary Club meetings, and always report for work on time.

Truth is life would be damned boring now were it not for the pigeons I watch from my office window. They've not changed one bit since I wrote the first draft of this story. They're still dropping their *fowl* gifts from heaven on unsuspecting shoppers.

Thank You, God! I love those pigeons.

My True Love

The one thing I know for sure,
  My true love will always be there,
    At the Lakeside Saloon.

Most things in life are uncertain,
  Few come and go like the tide.
We seldom know what's behind the curtain,
  It is not within our realm to decide.
Few things are as predictable as air,
  And dependability is very rare,
But, the one thing I know for sure,
  My *true love* will always be there,
    At the Lakeside Saloon.

I'm alone all winter on my trap line,
  Enjoying the beauty of an untamed land,
Knowing that back in town, everything is fine,
  And when I return my true love will be at hand.
There is no need to wonder when or where,
  My true love awaits me at my favorite lair.
The one thing I know for sure,
  My *true love* will always be there,
    At the Lakeside Saloon.

Come summer, I'm living free,
  All alone on my cramped boat,
Chasing fish to where they happen to be,
  While thoughts of my true love are remote.
But, when I get to shore, I'll hold her, if I dare,
  Knowing my true love will take me on a tear.
The one thing I know for sure,
  My *true love* will always be there,
    At the Lakeside Saloon.

Class Reunion

"Failure is the condiment that gives success its flavor."
Truman Capote

Mike Faraday searched his pockets for a dime as he walked into the only tavern in Manson. When he found a coin, he plopped it on the bar.

"I'll have a glass of beer," he said. As Mike ordered, he noticed a huge man standing near him with his back against the bar.

The man was glaring menacingly at silent customers cowering behind tables along the walls. He turned his attention toward Mike when he placed the dime on the bar, watching him with little pig eyes sunk deep in a fat face.

"Like hell, you will," he shouted at Mike. "Apple harvest is over. Time for you bums to get out of town." Spittle sprayed from a mouth full of broken brown teeth, wetting the bar and Mike's jacket sleeve.

"Make that Rainier, if you have it on tap," Mike said, ignoring the man. He realized the bully could easily mistake him for a transient due to the beard he wore to hide the scar on his cheek.

The conspicuous scar came from a close encounter with a Japanese bullet during the 77th Infantry Divisions invasion of neighboring islands leading to the taking of Okinawa in '45. Several years in the ring after the war and a permanently flattened nose, compliments of Jersey Joe Walcott during a sparring session, erased any admirable facial features he might've had when he left Manson to enlist in the Army ten years earlier.

The petite woman behind the bar hesitated for only a moment after she glanced at Mike, seemingly sizing him up. Then she glared defiantly at the bully as she filled a glass. She set the drink on the bar in front of Mike.

Mike picked up the glass to take a long sip of the cold drink. The beer was his first since he vacated his apartment and loaded his worldly possessions in his vehicle to return to his hometown for his tenth-year, high school, class reunion.

"Hard of hearing?" the bully shouted at Mike. "Looks like I need to toss you out of here on your ugly face."

Mike turned to look at the man for the first time. "If you feel a need to throw me out of here, you're welcome to try."

"Must be stupid. Don't ya know who I am?" the man smirked contemptuously, as he stepped toward Mike. He extended both arms to wrap them around him in a bear hug.

Mike brushed the man's arms aside as he stepped inside them. He sank a quick, left jab deep in the bully's fat belly, followed by a short, chopping, right uppercut to the jaw.

The man dropped to the floor, unconscious, as customers gasped in shock.

Mike grabbed the back of the man's bib overalls to slide him to the back of the room, next to the exit. The room filled with applause as he returned to the bar to finish his drink.

"One on the house," the barmaid said as she refilled his glass. "About time he met his match. He has frightened away half of my customers."

"Thanks," he said. Then he picked up the glass to move to an empty table in a back corner. The previously silent room was suddenly alive with chatter as customers moved to the bar for refills.

No more than a minute passed before a small man

approached Mike's table with a pitcher of beer.

"Have a word with you?" he asked.

Mike, perturbed by the intrusion, glared at the man. He wanted to nurse his beer and relax after the long drive from Seattle to Manson.

"My employer is looking for a man for a special project. Willing to pay handsomely. You could handle the job."

Mike sipped his beer as he studied the intruder. The man had a sharp face with close-set eyes. Made him think of a ferret. Dirty clothes and an unpleasant body odor suggested his employer wasn't very selective in choosing employees.

"What makes you think I'm looking for a job?"

The man grinned as he scooted the pitcher across the table toward Mike's glass.

"Watched you park your fifteen-year-old car and walk along the boardwalk, looking in windows. Didn't go in the restaurant to eat lunch. Had to search your pockets to find a dime to pay for your glass of beer. You don't have money to buy another beer, pay for a meal, or a place to sleep tonight."

Mike emptied his glass as he concluded the man was smarter than he looked. He was broke after spending the proceeds from his last fight to purchase the car and gas. Worse yet, promoters weren't anxious to book him again, and the headliners no longer wanted him as a sparring partner.

"You're too unorthodox and rough," they said. "We want a standup slugger with a classic Joe Lewis style."

He could only meet their standard until a solid punch loosened the tiger in him. Then he would lose control, resulting in brawling, clawing, and gouging. If he shaved his beard, fight fans would recognize him by his ring name, Mauler Malloy. Everyone knew Mauler Malloy wasn't a good loser.

"I'm only going to be in town for a week," Mike said, thinking he might not have to sleep in the car tonight if he could make a quick buck or two.

"Job won't take but a few minutes."

"Town doesn't have a bank to rob."

"Nothing like that. Boss wants to hire someone to remove three men from cabins on an orchard owned by a widow. Harvest is over, and they refuse to leave."

"Isn't that a job for the sheriff?"

"Court action is required before the sheriff can evict them. Could take weeks or months. Boss wants to protect the widow by having the men removed now."

"Who's your boss?"

"A Good Samaritan who wishes to remain anonymous. He's authorized me to make arrangements and pay for the eviction."

"How much is he offering?"

"He'll pay a thousand dollars if the men are gone before midnight tonight."

Mike picked up the pitcher of beer to refill his glass. He wrinkled his forehead as if he were giving the offer serious consideration. Actually, he was thinking a thousand dollars was more than he usually earned in a preliminary bout before a championship fight. It was a huge amount to pay for an eviction. There had to be more to this.

"You said three men. I assume you mean a thousand dollars each," he finally responded.

"No, that's not what he told me, but he might pay more if you can do it immediately."

"Two thousand paid in advance will guarantee the three men are gone before the sun sets tonight."

"Meet you at your car with the money in a half hour,

if the boss agrees."

Mike followed the directions the man gave him, driving up the hill out of Manson and past Roses Lake to the Wapato Lake Road. He recognized apple orchards as he passed them and remembered their owners.

He realized the orchard the widow owned, overlooking Wapato Lake, was close to the orchard where his folks worked until the freeze in '47 killed most of the apple trees. His parents quit orchard work and moved to the coast to work at Boeing.

He stopped the car in the widow's driveway for a moment to reminisce, remembering the summer he helped the owner build the three cabins. There was always work here when his dad's employer didn't need his help. The place felt like home. A foolish feeling, he realized. He didn't have a home.

Mike could see three men lounging in front of the cabins. He watched them as he drove down the driveway to the farmhouse where he parked next to a car and an old pickup.

The farmhouse door opened as he stepped up onto the porch. The woman who stepped into view surprised him. He hadn't realized the orchard had changed owners, or that he would recognize the new owner's widow. Her name was Melissa, the younger sister of his high school sweetheart. Melissa had been a sophomore when he and her sister were seniors.

Melissa had her sister's good looks. He hoped she didn't have her sister's disposition. If she did, he would drive back to town and return the two thousand dollars he had accepted for evicting the three men.

Mike realized his bitterness toward her sister should have passed after ten years. She was the only serious girlfriend he ever had, though, and she dumped him the day they graduated from high school.

"I've decided to go to college," she explained, "so I can find a rich boy to marry."

He hitchhiked to Wenatchee to join the Army the next morning.

Melissa looked at him, inquisitively, for several long moments and frowned.

He realized she was trying to place him. It was apparent, however, that she didn't recognize him as Mike Faraday. He was pleased to note she showed no sign of the revulsion attractive females often displayed when they looked at his facial scars.

She finally said, "May I help you?"

He started to identify himself. Then, suddenly, on impulse, he changed his mind.

"My name is Mike Malloy," he said.

When she didn't react to the name he used with boxing promoters, he continued.

"I'm in town for a week with no place to stay. Heard you have some cabins. Stopped to see if you might allow me to use one of them for a week."

He noticed she glanced nervously toward the cabins before she spoke.

"The cabins are already taken."

"Heard you asked the men to leave, and they refused."

"You heard correctly. They moved into the cabins after my crew finished picking apples—won't work, and won't leave. Just sit there, drink beer, and leer at me. I need to finish the work in the orchard before it snows, but I'm afraid to leave the house."

"May I propose a simple solution?" he said. "I'll remove the three men right now if you'll let me use one of the cabins for a week. I can help you finish the orchard work while I'm here. I need the exercise, and Manson doesn't have a gym."

"I can't ask you to confront the three Logan brothers. Everyone is afraid of them. The deputy I called wouldn't even go out to the cabins to talk to them."

"But, you'd let me use one of the cabins if they were vacant?"

"Yes, but I fear for your safety if you try to get them to leave. I've heard they like to gang up on people."

"I didn't catch your name," he said, to change the subject.

"I'm sorry. Melissa, Melissa Frederick," she said. "If you heard about the three men in the cabins, you may have heard I'm a widow. My husband was Allan Frederick."

Mike recognized the name, of course. He and Allan had been friends in high school.

"Mrs. Frederick, a cup of coffee would taste mighty fine right now, but I don't have the makings. I believe I can convince the three men to leave by the time you finish making a cup of coffee, if it's not too much to ask."

"Oh, my goodness," she said, as he turned and started walking toward the cabins.

The three men stood, glaring a challenge at him as he walked toward them. Each radiated contempt and meanness, although they weren't particularly imposing physically.

They were tall and slim like their father, Luke Logan. Luke sold whiskey and beer to teenagers when Mike was in high school. He remembered three undernourished boys at the shack the Logan family called home. They didn't look any better now.

One of the men, the oldest, he assumed, stepped in front of the other two. "What do you want?" he snarled, believing, apparently, that his threatening tone and posture would stop Mike.

Mike never slackened his pace before he threw a long overhand right that hit the man flush in the mouth. The punch bounced him off the front wall of a cabin. He ended up in the dirt, spitting blood.

His two brothers cursed as they balled up their fists and stepped toward Mike to attack him.

"Sit down," Mike snapped in a sharp, sergeant's voice. "You won't get hurt if you sit down and listen to what I have to say."

The brothers stopped abruptly. They looked from Mike to their brother, sitting in the dirt, wiping blood from mangled lips. After hesitating for several seconds, they sat on the bench in front of a cabin.

"I just rented these cabins. You're going to leave, so I can move into them.

"Three of us. Only one of you," the man sitting in the dirt growled.

"True, but you don't know how to fight. I do. Do you listen to boxing on the radio?"

"Big fights," one of the men said. "So what?"

"Ever listened to Mauler Malloy's fights?"

"Of course. He'll cripple a fighter if he's behind on points," the same man said. "So what?"

"I'm Mauler Malloy. Giving you a choice—leave now, or end up crippled."

"How do we know you're Mauler Malloy?" asked one of the brothers seated on the bench.

"You can find out if you'll stand up for a minute."

The three men drove away five minutes later, shouting curses at Mike.

Mike surveyed the wreckage left behind in the cabins. He opened the doors and the single window in each cabin to try to air them out before Melissa arrived.

"This cabin stinks," Melissa said, as she handed Mike a cup of steaming hot coffee.

"No worse than the other two," he said.

"I'll get a bucket of hot soapy water and a mop. We can try to make one of the cabins livable for you for tonight, but I owe you an apology. I didn't believe you would be able to evict the Logan brothers, so I didn't tell you that I won't own the cabins after tomorrow."

"I don't understand," he said, seeing she was on the verge of tears.

"It's a long story, and there's nothing I can do to change the outcome."

"I'm a good listener, if you don't mind sharing."

"I'll get the soap and hot water. We can clean this cabin while I explain. Hard work is the only thing keeping me sane since my husband's death eighteen months ago."

They stripped the cabin bare and scrubbed until it smelled of lye soap. Melissa talked in a monotone while she scrubbed with a stiff brush.

"Allan drowned in Wapato Lake," she said. "Then I discovered he'd signed a promissory note for two thousand dollars, using the orchard as collateral. Payment on the note is due no later than noon tomorrow."

Mike resisted the temptation to interrupt her narrative, despite obvious flaws. He wanted to hear the complete implausible story before he said anything. When she finished talking and sat down on the bed to wipe tears from her cheeks, he started with the matter of Allan's death.

"There were no witnesses, and he ended up in the

lake while you were gone. The coroner said he drowned. Did you ever swim in Wapato Lake with your husband?" he asked, knowing the answer before he asked the question.

All of the high school kids swam in Wapato Lake. He and Allan used to swim across the lake and back to impress the girls. No one who grew up in Manson would ever go swimming in Wapato Lake alone.

"Of course, but I wasn't with him this time. I drove to Chelan to get groceries while he worked in the orchard. The coroner said he must have fallen and hit his head on a rock. He had a deep cut on the back of his head."

Nonsense, he thought. *The swimming area has a sandy beach. No rocks.*

"You didn't know about the promissory note Alexander Grant holds until after the funeral?"

"I had no idea Allan had signed a note using this property for collateral."

"And payment on the note is due no later than noon tomorrow."

"Yes and the bank turned me down for a loan. I don't have any way of paying the two thousand dollar note."

"Tell me more about Alexander Grant," Mike said.

"He moved to town the year I graduated from high school. Tried to date me," Melissa said. "He'd already graduated from college. Claimed to have lots of money, but he's a creep. Threatened me when I accepted Allan's marriage proposal—said he'd get even."

"And he says he loaned Allan two thousand dollars to cover a bet in a poker game. Did Allan gamble frequently?"

"He never played poker, didn't like card games."

"But it's his signature on the promissory note."

"I recognized his signature. Someone typed the note

before he signed it."

Nonsense, he thought again, as he watched tears slip down her cheeks. *Who types a promissory note in the middle of a poker game? She doesn't know how easy it is to forge a signature.*

"I apologize for promising you the use of a cabin I won't own after tomorrow."

"I have an apology of my own to make," he said as he pulled two thousand dollars out of his pocket. He dropped the money on the mattress.

Melissa gasped when she saw the money. Then she looked at him, seemingly confused.

"A man paid me two thousand dollars to evict the Logan brothers from your cabins. He told me a Good Samaritan wanted to help you by having them removed from the cabins before midnight tonight. I watched the man go to an office to get the money. The office had *Grant Real Estate* painted on the front window. Does Alexander Grant own the business?"

"Of course. Why would Grant pay to have them removed?" she asked.

"Don't know unless he believed the three men might side with you when he tries to evict you tomorrow."

"Never thought of that. For a few dollars and a case of beer, they might have put a scare into him."

"I'm assuming you don't want to lose this place."

"Of course not."

"Good, I'd like to propose a solution. Use my two thousand dollars to pay the note."

"I can't do that."

"Sure you can. I wouldn't have the money if he wasn't trying to steal your home and orchard. Can't you see the justice in paying him with his own money?"

"I don't know how I'd be able to repay you."

"Simple. You can let me use this cabin and feed me for a week while I'm in town."

"I've a feeling there's more to this. Is there something you aren't telling me?"

"I haven't told you someone knocked your husband out before they dumped him in the lake to drown, or that he didn't borrow two thousand dollars from Alexander Grant. I suspect you already realize what's happening. Grant's making good on his threat to get even with you for rejecting him.

"You may need to pay the two thousand to save this property—even if the note is bogus. I'll show you how Allan's signature may have ended up on the note. You can have a witness test the signature to see if it was forged. You need to have at least three neighbors of good character here as witnesses when he comes to collect the two thousand dollars tomorrow."

"Is there anything else you need to tell me?"

"There is, but it'll wait until after I gather evidence against your husband's killer."

Mike drove to Wapato Lake late the next morning and parked across from the popular swimming beach. He walked west through brush and trees for fifty yards until he spotted several fishing lines snaking out into the water from the shoreline. Several minutes passed as he watched the lines. Then the slack suddenly disappeared from one of them. A man hidden in the brush set the hook and started reeling in a fish.

Walking quietly, Mike approached the man while he was distracted. He stepped out of the brush behind him as he released the fish from the hook.

"Good morning, Luke," he said.

Luke Logan jumped in surprise when Mike spoke. He

whirled around, wide-eyed, to study Mike for a moment. Then he seemed to relax, realizing, apparently, that someone other than a game warden had caught him fishing illegally.

"What're you doing here? This spot is taken."

"That's no way to greet an old friend."

"Do I know you?"

"You sold me home-brewed beer when I was in high school."

"If I did, you should know I only sell it after dark. You'll have to wait until tonight."

"That's not what I'm after. I need something more important from you this time. I need information."

"Why would I tell you anything?"

"I know you fish illegally using several lines. I don't want to report you. I just want information. You can start by telling me why your boys moved into Mrs. Fredrick's cabins and refused to leave."

"That's easy enough. If you know me, you must know my boys don't always reason things out. They believed the widow would want to marry one of them if they moved into the cabins."

"That doesn't make any sense."

"Like I said, they don't always reason things out."

"Can't disagree. You were here when they dumped Allan Fredrick's body in the lake. Tell me what you saw."

Mike was not surprised to see Luke's face instantly turn white.

Luke started to say something, stopped, and sat down to bury his head between his knees with his arms over his head. "Can't talk about that," he mumbled, sounding frightened.

"You won't need to tell anyone else. I'll expose the killers and turn the evidence over to the sheriff. No one will ever hear your name."

"Too risky," he mumbled as he moved his arms from over his head to look around as if he expected to see spies behind every tree.

"Allan was working in his orchard at ten in the morning when his wife left to go shopping. They found his body floating in the water across the lake from your hidden fishing spot at two o'clock. You're here every day during those hours. Telling me what happened will be less risky than having to talk to the sheriff after I tell him you fish here every day. He'll realize you witnessed someone dump the body."

"They'll kill you if you go to the sheriff."

"I can handle myself."

"Are you the one who smashed my boy's mouth?"

"Like I said, I can handle myself."

"There were two of them," Luke said, in a near whisper. "They'll kill me if they ever find out we talked."

"They're not going to know we talked."

Luke hesitated before he spoke. "The big man drove Allan's pickup with Allan laid out in the back of it. He packed him down to the lake and threw him out into the water like a sack of garbage. The small man drove a car and never got out. They left Allan's pickup parked here at the lake and drove away in the car."

"Who drove the pickup?"

"Don't know his name. He's always at the tavern, trying to start a fight. I don't go in there anymore."

"Has a fat face and wears bib overalls?"

"Heard someone knocked him out yesterday. You?"

"Said I can handle myself. Who drove the car?"

"That's harder. Never got out of the car, so I couldn't see him clearly."

"I'm guessing you know every car in town."

"A small man was driving Mrs. Grant's car. Can only assume it was Mr. Grant. He wouldn't have used his car because it has his business name painted on the door panel."

"Mr. Logan, you don't know me. We've never talked."

"And you don't know I fish here?"

"Never been here," Mike said, as he started back toward his vehicle.

The noon hour passed before Mike arrived back at the farmhouse to talk to Melissa. Her car and Allan's old pickup were the only vehicles parked in front of the farmhouse. She was waiting for him on the porch, with a smile on her face.

"Your two thousand dollars is on the kitchen table," she said, as he walked up the steps to the porch.

"The signature was traced?"

"Using the technique you showed me. Before he arrived with the note, I showed my neighbors how Alexander might've traced the signature. Mr. Stanford rubbed the signature when Alexander showed him the note. Smudged just as you said it would.

"Mr. Stanford ripped the note to shreds. Mr. Chandler and Mr. Sorensen threatened to do the same to Alexander if he didn't get off my property and leave me alone."

"You had a good morning thanks to good neighbors."

"You also had a good morning. You have your two thousand dollars back. Did you find out anything?"

"Had a productive morning, I believe. I identified your husband's killers, but I don't have a confession. Considered confronting one of the individuals to force him to sign a confession, but realized it wouldn't stand up in court.

"I'll stop in Wenatchee to talk to the sheriff when I leave next week. He can use the information I give him to confront one of the men to get the evidence needed for convictions. I believe the man will talk when he hears there is a witness."

"Are you going to tell me who killed Allan?"

"I think you already know."

"Yes, I know."

The next few days were the most enjoyable in Mike's memory. He had forgotten how much he enjoyed working in an orchard. The productive physical labor in the fresh air beat the tedious workouts he had endured in stinky gyms.

Melissa worked right alongside him as they picked up props and boxes to stack them out of the weather. She mowed the weeds in the orchard while he cut the summer suckers out of the trees and flushed irrigation lines.

By the night of his class reunion, the orchard looked as tidy as any orchard in the area, and Mike had made two decisions. He was going to skip his class reunion, and he would look for an orchard he could buy. Melissa had insisted on feeding him all week, so he still had the two thousand dollars to use for a down payment.

He washed himself at the cabin when they finished working in the orchard, changed out of his work clothes, and walked to the farmhouse for dinner. He planned to ask permission to use the cabin for another week while he looked for an orchard to buy.

When he knocked on the screen door, Melissa yelled for him to come in. He was surprised to find her sitting at the kitchen table sipping a glass of red wine. She had her high school annual open on the table in front of her.

She looked up and smiled as he sat down across from

her. "Since we've finished the orchard work, and you're getting ready to leave, this would be a good time for us to share some secrets. Then we're going to do something special," she said, as she poured him a glass of wine.

Mike felt a knot form in his throat when he glanced at the high school annual on the table in front of Melissa. She had it open to the senior class photos. He could see a photo of Mike Faraday circled in red ink.

He'd felt guilty all week for his failure to properly identity himself when he arrived. He'd started to tell her several times, but he couldn't think of a way to do so without looking like a fool. Now she had caught him in a lie.

"Since the cat has your tongue, I'll start by telling my secret first," she said. "I loved Allan, and we had a good marriage, but he wasn't my first love. My sister used to date a boy in high school, and I was madly in love with him. He was a perfect gentleman, like you, so he would've been shocked to learn how I felt about him."

He tried to swallow the lump in his throat so he could say something, but his mind had suddenly gone blank.

"Mike, you look like you're about to have a stroke. Don't you think it's time to tell me the truth and get it over with?"

"How long have you known?"

"Took a few days. Your appearance has changed, but you're still the gentleman I knew in high school."

"I apologize for not telling you the truth," he said as he swallowed the knot in his throat. "When I recognized you, I believed you might run me off because of the falling out I had with your sister. Then, when I realized you were Allan's widow, I felt obligated to remove the three brothers from the cabins. As you know, Allan and I were good friends."

"Allan often spoke of you. I know what happened between you and Mabel wasn't your fault. She wanted someone with money, so she married the first man who offered her an expensive ring, a big house, and a Mediterranean cruise for a honeymoon."

"I'm not surprised."

"She was. The ring turned her finger green, they live in a small apartment over his office, and a trip up Lake Chelan on the ferry is as close as she has ever gotten to a Mediterranean cruise."

Mike suppressed a chuckle. Then he said, "Melissa, I enjoyed the orchard work this week. The work brought back good memories and helped me make a decision. I'm going to try to buy an orchard using the two thousand dollars as a down payment. There should be someone between Wenatchee and the Canadian Boarder willing to sell an orchard on a contract."

"There is, Mike. I realize you helped me this past week as a favor to Allan because he was your friend. Now, I'm going to ask for another favor, just for me this time. I don't have funds to hire help or pay operating expensive next year, and I can't work this orchard by myself. If you really want to buy an orchard, please buy a half interest in this property. I need a working partner?"

"I only have two thousand dollars."

"I would be lucky to get four thousand for the orchard if I have to sell it right now."

"You just found yourself a working partner."

"Good. Now it's time to do something special. We're going to your class reunion. I assume that's why you came back to Manson."

"Yes, but I've decided not to go to the reunion. Your sister will probably be there, and I really don't want to see her again. I've let her rejection eat at me for ten years. It's time to let it go.

"Besides, you must realize people will talk if you go to the reunion with me. You've been a widow for eighteen months, but that won't keep gossips from spreading rumors."

"Don't you realize everyone in town is already talking about us? Going to the reunion together will give us an opportunity to tell people we're working partners. They can take that to mean anything they want while we figure out what it means to us, and please quit blushing. We're adults. We don't have any reason to be embarrassed."

"You're right, of course, but I'm still not anxious to run into your sister."

"You've never met Alexander Grant, have you?"

"No."

"That's Alexander and his wife in the photo on the wall. They're standing beside my parents and Allan and me."

Mike noticed the photo on the wall for the first time. The photo was hanging where there had previously been a wedding photo of Allan and Melissa. The wedding photo was gone.

The group in the photo stood in front of a Christmas tree. Mike recognized her folk's living room in the photo. He had been there many times when he dated her sister.

The small man in the photo was Alexander Grant, apparently. A grossly obese woman stood beside Grant, holding his hand. She wore a wrinkled dress that was large enough to cover a John Deere tractor. Mike frowned, wondering what Grant and his wife were doing in Melissa's family Christmas photo.

"Have you guessed whom Mabel married?" Melissa asked, as she started giggling.

Mike had made the mistake of taking a sip of the red wine as he studied the photo. His mouth was still full when he realized the face buried deep in rolls of fat belonged to Mabel, his high school sweetheart. His explosion of laughter sprayed red wine across the tablecloth and down the front of his shirt.

Melissa was laughing just as hard as he was as she pounded him on the back to try to help him catch his breath. "Grant might find prison a welcome change," she laughed, as she tried to catch her breath.

Orchard Cabins

The orchard cabins the author remembers from the 1940s and 1950s are long gone but for a few abandoned examples. Housing for orchard workers today will likely resemble the duplexes and homes in town and have the modern conveniences available to renters and home-owners. The workers depicted in most of the stories in this book did not have such luxuries, but neither did most of the orchard owners.

Fire in the Night

The room was dark when I woke up to the smell of smoke. Flames leaped toward the sky outside my bedroom window.

I jumped out of bed to shake my younger brother awake. When we ran from our bedroom, Dad had already gathered up my baby sister, and he and Mother were at the front door. Within seconds, we were all standing outside in three inches of fresh snow, watching the roaring fire.

It was obvious at a glance we couldn't control the blaze. It was also obvious the fire was not an accident. A strong gasoline odor was nearly as overpowering as the heat and thick black smoke coming from the siding and tarpaper roofing.

Why someone would do this, I didn't know. Then I thought back to what happened during the summer and more recently.

Dad had decided we needed a bathroom in our house. My thirteen-year-old brother and I thought a bathroom was a strange idea since we had never lived in a house with any indoor plumbing. We understood Dad's reasoning, however, when he explained having a bathroom would make it easier for Mother to take care of our little sister.

While Dad installed fixtures and pipes, my brother and I dug a deep hole for a cesspool and lined it with rocks. After we connected a sewer pipe and placed a cover over the hole, the fun started. My brother and I dashed out to the hand pump at our cistern to pump water into a bucket. Then we ran back into the house to dump the water into the toilet to flush it. The toilet worked! We were amazed.

The novelty of indoor plumbing soon wore off, and we

resumed our normal routine until Dad realized my brother and I were still using the old outhouse. When confronted, my brother voiced what I was thinking.

"Dad, you don't really expect us to do *that* in the house do you?" He did. But we were just too embarrassed to do *that* in the house. We kept right on using the outhouse outside my bedroom window.

Our use of the outhouse came to an abrupt halt on the night of our first winter snowfall when someone poured gasoline on the outhouse and torched it. The fire had nearly burned itself out, and the smoldering remains had collapsed into the hole before Dad would look at us boys. The sheepish expression on his face confirmed what we had already guessed.

Caution!

The hills and mountains surrounding Lake Chelan are very dry during the summer. A spark from a cigarette, firecracker, or campfire can quickly start a fire you cannot control.

Lightning causes many regional forest fires, but valuable forestland, wildlife, homes, outbuilding, and livestock are lost every year due to human negligence.

In July of 2014, over a quarter of a million acres and 300 homes burned just north of Chelan in the Methow Valley and along the Columbia River, and over 22,000 acres burned just south of Chelan in the Entiat Valley.

Please be cautious. Build fires only in designated sites. Extinguish fires and smokes. Leave the fireworks at home.

Angel in Pink

Mary McGuire gritted her teeth and prayed no one would notice her quivering chin as she entered the stadium to meet her husband.

She maintained a firm handgrip on her two sons, as seven-year-old James tried to drag her toward a concession stand, while eight-year-old Mark tugged her toward a souvenir booth. An inner-voice pulled her in yet another direction, telling her to flee back to Chelan, 150 miles from the 1994 Washington State Track and Field Finals in Cheney.

"There's Dad," Mark shouted. "He saved us a place at the finish line."

Mary had no choice but to follow as both boys impulsively surged up the bleacher steps toward their father, forcing her to face the situation she had hoped to avoid.

Robert McGuire, the girl's track coach at Chelan High School, qualified a sprinter for the 100-meter dash. His intense interest in the girl, a ninth grader named Angel, distressed Mary, bringing back painful memories.

When Robert asked her to bring their boys to the state meet if Angel qualified for the final race on Saturday, she agreed, assuming a ninth grader couldn't possibly survive the preliminary heats on Thursday and Friday against more experienced sprinters. Then, when she checked her answering machine for messages after her Friday afternoon classes, Robert's words stunned her.

"Angel just qualified for the finals," he shouted excitedly. "She'll race at eleven o'clock tomorrow morning for the state championship. I'll save seats for you and the boys at the finish line."

Robert hugged Mary and both boys when they reached him. Then, as soon as they were seated and comfortable, he turned to look toward the 100-meter starting line.

Mary could see her husband was oblivious to her distress as she sat beside him, fighting back tears. She had never shared her secret with him. He didn't know hearing him talk about a girl named Angel amplified the agonizing regret and shame she felt daily.

"Will Angel win today?" Mark asked, interrupting her thoughts.

Robert chuckled before he responded.

"No, Mark. One of the seniors ran a 12.29-second race in the prelims. If Angel can improve on her 12.52 personal best from yesterday, it'll be a victory.

"You want her to win, though, don't you?"

"I believe Angel has the inborn capacity to win the state championship someday. She has a bright future ahead of her if I can keep working with her to help her improve her technique."

Robert squeezed Mary's hand as he spoke, failing to recognize how his words alarmed her.

"Second call for girl's 100-meter sprint," blared from overhead speakers.

"Angel's walking toward the starting blocks," Robert said. "She's up right after the boys' race."

"Where is she?" James asked.

"There, at the other end of the track," Mark shouted as he pointed to the area behind the starting blocks. "She's wearing pink racing shoes. Can't you see her?"

"See her now," James said.

Mary didn't see Angel. Tears blinded her as she

thought about the bill she paid for the pink shoes Robert charged to his credit card. He talked constantly about his new track star, so she knew all about Angel and the expensive shoes.

"Her parents died in a car accident when she was a baby," he said when he showed her the bill. "She lives in a foster home. Doesn't have money to buy the shoes she needs to be competitive. The state moves her every few months. They'll move her again when they can find someone willing to take her."

Mary ignored his hint. She hoped the state would move Angel back to the Seattle area before she had to deal with the problem. She couldn't become a foster parent for a girl whose name brought back painful memories and increased the regret and shame she felt.

A blast from the starter's gun for the boy's race startled Mary.

Robert and both boys jumped up to shout encouragement along with all of the people in front of her, blocking her view of the race.

Her mind quickly drifted to the events that triggered her reaction to Angel, forcing her to relive the experience again.

"Come on, Mary, don't be a wet blanket," her friend pleaded when she asked her to go to a sports bar after a Friday faculty meeting in Seattle in 1979, her first year of teaching. She remembered wrinkling her nose and giggling when she sipped the wine her friend ordered.

The wine, like everything else in the big city, was new to her after growing up in a strict home while attending a parochial high school and university where she was an honor student and track star.

When she woke up grimacing in pain the next morning, she couldn't remember leaving the sports bar. There was plenty of evidence to show what happened to her, however. Messages on her answering machine identified the individual responsible for her condition.

Robert and both boys shouted even louder as the boys crossed the finish line, causing Mary to look up. After the final yell, everyone in front of her sat down, and she could see the track again. She was looking at the finish line where eight boys were shaking hands.

"Final call for girl's 100-meter sprint," blared from the overhead speakers.

"Angel's race is next," Mark shouted.

"I hope she gets a good start," Robert said. "She's been slow coming out of the blocks because she's afraid she'll jump and be disqualified. She always has to come from behind."

Mary glanced toward the eight girls at the far end of the stadium. A slim girl, wearing pink shoes, stood in lane two at the starting line. She was too far away to make out any other details.

When the starter allowed the girls two minutes to adjust the starting blocks and finish warming up for the race, Mary's mind jumped back 14 years to the messages on her answering machine.

All of the messages were from Paul Green, a teacher who accompanied them to the sports bar. Paul was a former collegiate track star and a decorated war hero. He had an outstanding reputation as a teacher and planned to become an elementary school principal.

The first message from Paul was simple. "I'm so sor-

ry about what happened last night. Please call me. I need to try to explain.”

The second message was more informative. “This wasn’t your fault, Mary. You fell asleep at the sports bar and never woke up after I carried you up to your apartment.”

By the end of the third message, she had all the details.

“A stranger bought a round of drinks, and wanted to drive you home after you sipped the drink and went to sleep,” Paul said. “I volunteered to take you home because I believed he might’ve drugged you. I wanted to protect you, Mary. I didn’t mean for this to happen.”

A tearful apology and a plea for forgiveness followed his confession.

She remembered crawling into the bathroom and sitting under the shower to scrub her body raw as scalding hot water washed away tears. Then she filled the tub with hot water and soaked for most of the day. She ignored Paul’s repeated phone calls as she tried to decide what she should do, knowing the information on her answering machine would destroy him and devastate his family.

Mary was still lost in thought, wiping away tears, when the gun sounded for Angel’s race, drawing her attention back to her surroundings.

Everyone shouted and jumped up again, blocking her view.

“Good start, good start,” Robert shouted,

“Faster, faster, run,” screamed James.

“She’s passing her,” Mark yelled. “She’s in sixth place now.”

"She's not done," Robert shouted. "Catch her, catch her, kick, kick, Angel, kick," he screamed.

Mary sat on the bench, watching her husband and her two boys. She could see they adored Angel. She knew Robert wanted them to become foster parents for the girl. She expected him to ask today, after the race, and she knew her answer would come as a shock to him.

Just hearing Angel's name forced her to relive the experience. Even now, she couldn't stop the fleeting memories.

She recalled soaking in the tub for hours. She decided to wait until Monday morning to contact the police, hoping to gain some control over her tears before she talked to someone.

She ignored Paul's attempts to contact her and called in sick Monday morning. Then, before she could call the police, she heard the newsflash saying a local teacher committed suicide Sunday evening.

Paul's suicide note expressed regret and an apology for an unforgivable transgression but didn't mention any specifics. Students were heartbroken. The community grieved. His parents blamed their son's death on combat-related, posttraumatic syndrome.

Mary realized she was the only one who knew about Paul's criminal act. She knew, intellectually, she wasn't responsible for his death. Emotions were another matter. She knew Paul Green would be in jail, alive, if she had acted promptly, and she knew she would live with the shame she felt for her role in his death for the rest of her life.

When she realized she was pregnant, two months later, she hid her head under her pillow, crying uncon-

trollably. She suspected no one would believe what had happened to her since she had already erased the messages on her answering machine. Her tears didn't stop until she convinced herself she could live with the difficult decision she had to make.

She avoided people for the remainder of the school year, told her parents she was going out-of-state for summer school, and resigned her teaching position on the last day of school. Then she drove to Ocean City to spend the summer with a birthing nurse at her seaside home.

Her baby was born August 10, 1980. She could still hear herself sobbing, "Please protect my little angel" as they carried her baby from the birthing room. Giving up custody to allow adoption, she believed, was the best thing she could do for the baby, knowing her parents would be mortified if she returned home with Paul Green's offspring. She didn't anticipate the way giving up her little angel would affect her.

A few days later, she drove to Chelan to sign a teaching contract. She married Robert in 1983, electing not to share her secret with him, fearing he wouldn't understand. She didn't go to confession. She didn't feel she could confess the trivial transgressions of her daily life while hiding the shame she felt for Paul's death.

"She did it, she did it," Robert yelled as Angel crossed the finish line.

"Fifth place," Mark shouted as he jumped up and down. "She took fifth place."

"Amazing, against the best sprinters in the state," Robert said. "I believe she has another personal best."

Spectators finally sat down in front of Mary. Now she

could see the finish line where eight girls were congratulating each other. They were closer to Mary at this end of the track, so she could see the girl with pink shoes up close for the first time.

"Good Lord, no!" Mary gasped, clamping her hand to her mouth to keep from shouting the words. She was looking at a beautiful girl with a bronze complexion and jet-black hair. Despite the features inherited from her father, the girl was a mirror image of her mother when she competed as a high school sprinter.

Mary stood up, stunned, knowing instantly what she had to do. She realized tears were streaming down her cheeks as she turned to look at Robert, searching his face for a reaction, questioning if he might've guessed.

Robert, who was still jumping up and down, grasped her in a bear hug.

"I know just how you feel. I'm about to cry myself. Angel just ran the best race of her life," he said, indicating he didn't understand why she was crying.

Mary finally freed herself from his grasp to get his attention.

"Robert, does Angel know she was adopted?"

"Of course she knows. And she knows no one has wanted her since her parents died." Robert stopped talking, seemingly confused.

"How do you know she was adopted? That's confidential information."

"I can't explain right now, Robert. I need to leave. Will you please bring everyone home with you?"

"Mary, I know we're only a few mile from Spokane, and you deserve a chance to go shopping, but you've only been here for thirty minutes. Can't you wait until after we have lunch?"

"I'm not going shopping, Robert," she said as she held his hands, searching his eyes for some sign of understanding.

"I'm leaving to find a priest. I need to go to confession to try to get myself right with God. If God will forgive me, I'm going to ask the same of you for my failure to trust a good man with the truth. Then we're going to have a family conference."

Robert stepped back to look at her for several long moments before he responded.

"Just like every Sunday morning at breakfast before mass—you, me, and the boys?"

"No, Robert. I want the whole family there this time."

"I don't understand."

"Bring Angel."

"Does that mean we can be foster parents for her?" he asked, excitement creeping into his voice.

"Absolutely not."

"I still don't understand, then. I suppose adoption is out of the question?"

"Absolutely. Angel's mother is going to claim her little angel as she should have fourteen years ago."

"Mary, I don't understand what you're trying to tell me."

Before she could respond, she heard someone behind her say, "A personal best, Coach, 12.43 seconds."

As Mary turned around, both boys let out a wild squeal and started hugging Angel. Robert thrust his hand out to shake Angel's hand to congratulate her.

Angel seemed not to notice the hugs and handshake. She was staring at Mary, frowning as if she was looking at someone she believed she should recognize, seeing herself in twenty years.

Mary tried to control her tears as she studied the girl. When she could speak, she said, "Your birthday is August tenth. You were born in 1980 at Ocean City."

Angel continued staring at Mary for several seconds, apparently confused. Then, hesitantly, she nodded her head in agreement.

"I'm so sorry, Angel," Mary said, looking through flowing tears at piercing, brown eyes that seemed to bore into her eyes, searching for an explanation.

"I thought I was doing the right thing, giving my little angel a better life. Can you ever forgive me?"

Angel stared at Mary, obviously bewildered. Then, slowly, her eyes brightened. She understood. "Yes," she cried, as she rushed into Mary's open arms.

Robert hesitated for a moment, shocked, seeing Mary and Angel together for the first time. Finally, he realized what Mary had been trying to tell him.

"Oh, my goodness. Yes. Yes. Yes," he mumbled as he wrapped his arms around Mary and Angel, tears of joy streaming down his cheeks.

Mark and James were still clinging to Angel, jumping up and down, and chanting, "You were fifth... You were fifth..."

Several hundred spectators watched the McGuire family, amazed, having never witnessed a family get so emotional over a daughter's fifth place finish at a track meet.

Josie's Revenge

"What're you doing here?" Josie demanded to know as she stepped out onto the porch after Jasper parked her father's ranch pickup in front of the Martin farmhouse.

"Good to see you too, Josie Martin."

"Don't get smart with me Jasper Wilkin. You're supposed to be at Sheep Camp for another two weeks."

"Hate to disappoint you, but your father wants to talk to me."

"Whatever gave you the notion my father wants to talk to you?"

"Frank rode into Sheep Camp last night. Said your father wanted to see me just as quick as I could get here."

"That doesn't make any sense. Dad hasn't talked to Frank Hilliard in a week. Just put supper on the table for Dad. Get in here and pull up a chair. You can eat while you explain yourself."

Too danged bossy for a seventeen-year-old girl, he thought, as he followed her into the house. It ruffled his feathers some when she acted as if she ran the place. In truth, he supposed, she did now that her father couldn't get around much because of his rheumatism.

"Good to see you, Jasper," Blake Martin said, with a warm smile.

"Dad, did you send Frank to Sheep Camp to get Jasper?" Josie asked, as she placed a cup of hot coffee in front of Jasper and refilled her father's cup.

"Haven't seen Frank in a week, Josie. He's supposed to be cutting alfalfa."

"Frank told me Claire delivered the message for you," Jasper said.

Jasper noticed Josie's quick glance toward her father, seemingly communicating with him without words. He had a good idea what they were thinking, having lived in their home during his last two years of high school and in their bunkhouse thereafter.

He was the same age as Blake's older daughter, Claire, and her worthless husband, Tom Billing. He had gone to high school with them until they all graduated six years ago. He could only hope her father hadn't heard the stories about Claire and Tom that he had heard.

"Must be some mistake," Blake said. "Haven't seen Claire in two or three weeks. She doesn't come around much since her mother passed away."

"Except to borrow money," Josie blurted out, sounding disgusted.

Jasper looked out the large kitchen window at the driveway and barn, embarrassed for Blake. Claire believed only a fool would live or work on a ranch. She never hesitated to beg money from her father, however, since Tom couldn't keep a job, and she refused to work.

As Jasper looked at the barn, his gaze settled on something peculiar protruding from the corner of one of the windows. He studied the spot for several moments before he realized he was looking at the muzzle of a rifle barrel.

"Look out," he shouted, just as flames, smoke, and a bullet shot toward him. The large window in front of him exploded, showering the room and the kitchen table with glass fragments.

Jasper fell to the floor as sharp fragments hit him.

Josie fell on top of him, screaming.

They watched in horror as her father fell to the floor. Blake Martin's back had been to the window. The bullet hit him in the back of the head, killing him instantly.

Jasper covered Josie's mouth with his hand to stifle her scream. "Run. Hide. Josie. Shooter can't leave witnesses."

"Dad?"

"Dead, Josie. Nothing you can do for him right now. Run."

"Can't leave him."

"No choice. Need to hide. I'm right behind you."

"Pump house," she said as she shook off glass fragments. Then she started crawling toward the hallway, suppressing sobs as tears streamed down her cheeks.

Jasper started to follow Josie, but stopped when he heard a vehicle approaching on the driveway from behind the barn. He hesitated, thinking a neighbor might've heard the shot and stopped to investigate.

He crawled to the window, with glass shards cutting his knees, and peeked over the windowsill. Claire and Tom were getting out of a new 1952 Ford coupe in the driveway. They stood and looked at the shattered kitchen window for a moment. Then Claire ran toward the porch. Tom followed along behind her.

Jasper was sitting on the floor in front of the window when Claire rushed into the room.

She screamed when she nearly tripped over her father's body.

"Father," she cried as she slumped to her knees beside him.

"What happened?" Tom demanded to know, after he followed Claire into the room.

"Someone shot Blake from the window in the barn," Jasper said. "Shooter might still be there."

"Nonsense. We just drove past the back of the barn. Would've seen a shooter if there was one there," Tom said. He glared at Jasper with his fists balled.

"Father treated you like the son he wished he had," Claire said. "Took you in when your parents died. Why would you lie about how he was killed?"

Jasper noticed no tears accompanied the crying sounds he heard. "Shot came from the barn," he repeated as he glared a challenge at Tom and Claire, daring them to accuse him of the murder.

"Where's Josie?" Tom asked.

Jasper gripped the windowsill to pull himself to his feet. Suspicion seeped into his brain thicker than tadpoles in a stock pond. He looked at Claire's tearless face and turned to look at the barn again. Nothing added up, as it should. The timing was all wrong.

Questions flashed through his mind. The entry road

from Grade Creek to the farmhouse passed behind the barn. They knew he was coming to the farmhouse to see Blake. Might they have parked the car in the barn before he arrived? Why were they driving a new car when they were broke?

"Where's Josie?" Tom asked again, more demanding this time.

"Don't know. Here a minute ago," he said.

"Going to call the sheriff," Claire said, as she walked toward the phone at the end of the kitchen counter.

"Good idea," Jasper said. As he turned to watch her pick up the phone, he heard Tom moving behind him, but a vicious blow hit the side of his head before he could react.

Jasper could hear voices, but his head hurt too much to make any sense out of the words.

"Have to find her," someone said.

"We've looked everywhere. She's not here."

"Nonsense, I saw her through the window when we were in the barn. Has to be here."

The voices drifted away as Jasper floated in and out of consciousness. Shadows darkened the room when he heard the voices the next time.

He realized he was lying on the kitchen floor at the Martin farmhouse, near Blake's body. He recognized Tom and Claire's voices. They were talking out on the porch, in front of the farmhouse. Everything slowly came back to him as he listened.

"Should've shot her first," Claire said.

"Should've done it yourself. Then I wouldn't have to listen to your bellyaching."

"Dad was too crippled to get away. You could've shot him last."

"Doesn't matter. Blame Jasper when you call the sheriff's office. Say Josie helped him."

"Police aren't going to believe she helped him," Claire said.

"Sure they will. You stole her diary. Showed me what

she wrote about Jasper. *'We're going to grow old togeth- er, in love forever, side-by-side, living and working here on the ranch.'* Give the diary to the police."

"They'll know she is just a silly teenage girl, dreaming like all girls do in their diaries. You need to kill her, or she is going to claim half of the ranch. There's no way she'll let us sell this place," Claire said.

"You might be right about silly girls dreaming. I've not forgotten your high school yearbook. You had Mrs. Jasper Wilkin and Claire Wilkin written all over it. That was before Jasper turned you down when you asked him to take you to the prom. He had to move out to the bunk- house to get away from you."

"Oh, for Pete's sake. Grow up, and give it a rest. Jas- per's just a sheepherder, and I married you."

Jasper realized he needed to do something, but the fog was still drifting in and out of his head, confusing him. He tried to stand up with no success. His legs wouldn't work. Tom must've hit him on the head, stunning him, he decided.

Tom and Claire were still arguing on the front porch when something touched Jasper's arm. He felt a hot breath on his ear and heard a whispered, "Quiet. I'll get you out of here."

Someone helped him stand up, ducked under his arm to support him, and helped him wobble down the hallway toward the back door. When they reached the door, the fog in his head lifted enough for him to realize Josie had come back to get him. She helped him out the back door, across the lawn, and through tall weeds to the pump house.

"They'll look in here," he mumbled as Josie pushed him through the small door into the dark interior. He ended up sitting next to a water pump connected to a large irrigation pipe. Josie had to push against him to make room for two of them in the small structure.

"They won't come near this pump house or the stock pond. Too many weeds, and they're both afraid of rattle- snakes."

Something she said didn't sound right to Jasper, but the fog in his head was still too thick for him to figure it out. He closed his eyes and leaned his sore head against the water pipe. The cold pipe felt good, like an ice pack.

He believed Josie was talking to him. Close to his ear. But he couldn't stay awake long enough to understand what she was saying.

Jasper woke with a start when someone clamped a hand over his mouth. Total darkness greeted him when he opened his eyes.

"Quiet," Josie whispered in his ear.

Then he heard the voices again, and remembered Josie had helped him hide in the pump house. He recognized Tom and Claire's voices.

"Wasting our time," Tom said. "They're long gone."

"You should've tied him."

"We aren't going to find them in the dark. All we're going to do is get snake bitten."

"We have to do something," Claire insisted.

"They won't get away for very long. I disabled the phone, so they can't call for help. We'll leave the pickup sitting right where it is with the horse in the trailer. You know how Josie and Jasper love stupid farm animals. They won't leave the horse there all night with no water or feed."

"How's that going to help us?"

"We can go home and get a good night's sleep. We'll discover your father is dead when we come back in the morning. Then you can call the sheriff in tears to say Jasper killed him and kidnapped Josie. You can write a ransom note, and leave it where the sheriff will find it."

"But, they'll have gotten away."

"Not for very long. They'll try to hide from us because they know we have to kill them. I know Jasper. He'll go back to Sheep Camp, thinking it's a safe place to hide from us. You know Josie. She idolizes the fool, so she'll insist on going with him.

"All we have to do is follow them to Sheep Camp in the morning, and kill both of them. The sheriff will believe you when you say we read the ransom note, and we followed them to try to rescue Josie. We can say Jasper killed her, and we killed him in self-defense."

"What about Frank? I told him to stay at Sheep Camp until Jasper returns."

"If he sees us, we'll kill him and blame Jasper."

Sometime during the conversation, Josie removed her hand from Jasper's mouth. Soon after, they heard Tom drive out to the paved road, a couple of hundred yards east of the farmhouse. A long silent pause followed before the frogs in the stock pond started croaking again.

"It's safe to go now," Josie whispered.

"You wouldn't be whispering if you knew that for a fact," he whispered back at her.

"We can't stay here all night. The rattlesnakes will come out looking for frogs now that they've started croaking again."

"I don't want to be mistaken for a frog," he said. "We need to get away from here before the moon comes up. Follow me."

"Are you sure you can walk?" she asked.

"I'm as fine as hair on a frog's butt," he said, having no idea why he would say something so stupid to a young girl. He blamed the fog in his head for clouding his judgment.

They found Blake Martin lying in a pool of blood on the kitchen floor where Claire and Tom had left him. Jasper allowed Josie a moment with her father to say a prayer.

"We need to cover him with something," she said.

"I'll get a blanket. Need to hurry. Notify the sheriff. We can stop at George Engle's ranch."

George was his best friend from high school. He knew George would be happy to help him settle matters with Tom and Claire. His ranch was just down Grade Creek Road from the Martin ranch.

While Jasper walked to a bedroom to get a blanket,

Josie opened the coat closet to get her father's hunting rifle and a box of shells. She chambered a round.

"You can make the calls at George's place while I go to town to find Claire and Tom. I'll make them pay for what they've done," she said, as tears slipped down her cheeks again.

"Authorities will execute you for murder. You need to take care of the horse while I talk to George," he said.

"I'll take care of the horse, but I'm keeping this rifle until I settle this with Tom and Claire."

Jasper tried to push the fog residue aside to formulate a plan as he drove to George's farmhouse. The first part of the plan he settled on was simple. After they arrived, he told George what had happened and what he was going to do.

To help, George agreed to call the sheriff in the morning to report the murder and identify the perpetrators. Then he would call the funeral home in Chelan. He also agreed to help Jasper during the next few days with the rest of his plan.

The last part of Jasper's plan exploded in a flash when he told Josie she was going to hide at George's ranch until a deputy arrested Claire and Tom.

"Where does a sheepherder get off thinking he's Sherlock Holmes," she shouted angrily at him.

"Ranch hand," he said, defensively.

"They started this. I'm going to finish it," she insisted as she defiantly held on to the rifle.

"Fine, but you're goin' to do it my way, or I'll tie you to a bed upstairs until they're arrested."

"You wouldn't dare."

"Try me."

"Get out of here," George shouted to interrupt the spat before they could come to blows. "I'll call the Sheriff in the morning and make follow-up arrangements like you asked. I can take the deputy to Sheep Camp in Horsethief Basin with extra horses to bring out the survivors, but I don't want any part of this little hellcat. She's not staying here with me."

"Fine. There's no way I'm going to stay here," Josie shouted. "And I'm not turning loose of this rifle until I settle this with those two murderers."

Jasper realized he was stuck with Josie. He had no choice but to take her to Sheep Camp with him to keep her from going after her sister and Tom with the rifle. What he planned for the two murderers at Sheep Camp would be more painful for them, he believed, than what Josie had in mind.

"I smell bacon cooking," Josie said, as they approached Sheep Camp.

Frank had a fire blazing and bacon cooking when Jasper and Josie slipped down from the tired horse a few minutes later—a half hour before daylight the next morning.

They had followed the primitive reclamation road in the hills along Lake Chelan and parked at the trailhead near South Navarre Peak. Then they rode the horse on the forest service trail to Miners Basin and up into Horsethief Basin to Sheep Camp. Josie rode behind Jasper during the long ride, clinging to him as her tears wet the back of his shirt.

"About time you got here," Frank said when they arrived just in time for breakfast. "I'm ready for a restaurant cooked meal and a soft bed."

"You're not going to like what I'm going to tell you then, or like what we need you to do," Jasper said. Then he explained what had happened at the Martin farmhouse.

Josie sat beside the fire in a somber mood, eating Frank's bacon and biscuits. She didn't interrupt as Jasper explained what he was going to do when Tom and Claire arrived at Sheep Camp.

Jasper could see she was listening, and believed she might've recovered enough to understand what he planned. Her eyes were still red rimmed, but she had stopped crying.

"Let me get this straight. You want me to drive the

sheep west, and hide them," Frank said.

"You can't exactly hide six hundred bleating sheep, but you can move them to the other side of the mountain where they're out of the way. Take the horse."

"You're goin' to owe me big time when this is over. I already smell like a sheepherder. They ain't goin' to let me in a tavern for a month."

An hour later, Tom and Josie sat high on the side of the ridge in the shade of several pine trees where they could look down at the campsite. Frank and the sheep-dogs were slowly moving the sheep out of Horsethief Basin.

"Tom and Claire won't get here until late this afternoon," Jasper said. "I need to get some sleep before they arrive. I'm going to be up all night."

"Are you sure they will follow us?"

"They have to follow us. They killed your father to get the ranch. The ranch has no value to them as long as you're alive. They know you'll never let them sell it."

"I'll be right beside you tonight and every step of the way until I settle the score with those two murdering skunks," she said. Then she rubbed her eyes and rolled over to go to sleep, cradling her father's rifle in her arms.

Jasper laid his head back on the gunnysack he filled with food at Sheep Camp and pulled his slouch hat down over his face to block light. He was just nodding off when Josie spoke.

"Jasper, did you call this Rattlesnake Ridge."

"You know as well as I do this is Sawtooth Ridge. But I always call it Rattlesnake Ridge because of the snake den at the top of the ridge. You don't need to be afraid though. The sheep have pushed all the snakes up higher on the ridge near the den."

"You know darn well I ain't afraid of nothing, certainly not a danged rattlesnake," she said in a huff.

Jasper chuckled. He had known her since she was eight years old. They lived in the same house after her father took him in so he could finish high school. She was like the little sister he never had.

He had lived in their bunkhouse, and worked for her father since graduation. He knew she was speaking the truth when she said she was not afraid of anything. She would jump on a half broken horse any man with good sense would be afraid to get near, or buck hay bales faster and longer than any hired hand.

She was tall for a girl and slim with her sister's good looks. He hadn't thought about that before, and realized he shouldn't be thinking about it now with her only seventeen years old.

He knew Josie would never be a stuck-up homecoming queen like her sister. She would more likely be a rodeo queen who would insist on riding a bull, roping a calf, and bulldogging a steer just to show the men she could do anything they could do.

He closed his eyes and started to drift off. Then it finally came to him, what Josie said back at the pump house about rattlesnakes. Tom and Claire were both afraid of rattlesnakes. He smiled, knowing he had a gunnysack, and he knew where to find the snake den on the ridge above them.

The sun was two hours short of dropping behind the ridgeline along Lake Chelan's south shore when Jasper woke up. He sat with his back against a large pine tree. The brown shirt he wore blended with the tree to camouflage him.

He waited impatiently, confident he was correct in believing Tom and Claire would follow them to Sheep Camp. Josie snored quietly beside him, curled up in a tight ball like a kitten.

Frank had pushed the sheep through the timber to get them behind Old Maid Mountain. Jasper couldn't hear sheep bleating or dogs barking.

Another half hour passed before he spotted two horses approaching the campsite. Tom and Claire were walking, hobbling actually, and leading the two horses. He recognized the horses from the ranch. They were Josie's pets. She kept them in a pasture next to the farmhouse, so she could groom and ride them.

He might've made a noise or moved because Josie suddenly sat upright, looked at him, and then down the hill toward the horses. She snickered.

"They're even dumber than I thought," she said. "They're fools to come here. Completely out of their element. Neither of them have been on a horse or walked a quarter mile since they married four years ago. They've gotten fat and soft."

"Guessed as much."

"They're walking because they have blisters on their butts. Now they have blisters on their feet."

"Don't sound sorry for them."

"Heck no, I heard what they said. They want to kill us. I was listening when you told George and Frank what you are going to do to them. I'm not going to miss a minute of this. I want them to know I helped you do it."

As they watched, Tom and Claire reached the abandoned campsite. They stood next to the fire pit, looking at the woodpile and lean-to shelter for a few moments. Then they looked all around as if they expected to see the sheep that had trimmed the vegetation around Sheep Camp and deposited droppings in great abundance.

Claire hobbled to the lean-to to lie down on her side on a pile of soft fir branches that served as a mattress in the shelter. She appeared to close her eyes and fall asleep.

Tom led the horses away from the campsite and tied them to a tree. He didn't remove the saddles or their gear from the horses, or water them in the nearby East Fork of Prince Creek. The horses stood with their heads down, tired and thirsty.

"Can we start now?" Josie asked. "Someone needs to take care of those horses."

"Be patient. Let's see what Tom is going to do before we start."

As they watched, Tom hobbled to the creek to get a drink. Then he returned to the lean-to and laid down next to Claire.

"He's not smart enough to know to boil the water before he drinks it," Josie said. "Creek is full of sheep droppings."

"He'll think he has the flu in a couple of days, but this'll be over before then," Jasper said. "Give them a few minutes to doze off. Then we'll make our move."

Jasper was impressed with Josie's ability to move quietly down the hillside behind him as she duplicated his cautious catlike movements. They took most of a half hour to cover a distance he could have walked in five minutes.

The two ranch horses raised their heads to look at Josie as she approached them. The horses knew her, so they didn't make any noise other than sniffing sounds as she held her hand out to them.

After Josie rubbed the horses' necks, she untied them from the tree. Then she led them away, parallel to the trail, so they were walking on pine needles.

Jasper stood between the horses and the lean-to shelter with his rifle at the ready to protect Josie if Tom or Claire woke up. He didn't realize until he caught up with Josie that Tom had left his rifle cased on one of the saddled horses.

They continued walking the horses parallel to the trail until they reached a small feeder creek, about a quarter mile from Sheep Camp, where they could stop to water the thirsty horses. Then they stepped up onto the saddles to ride the revived horses on the trail. When they reached the steep grade down out of Horsethief Basin into Miners Basin, they reined the horses off the trail toward a dense thicket.

"This is where I told Frank we'd leave extra saddles and supplies," Jasper said, as he dismounted and loosened saddle straps.

Josie followed his example as they stripped the two horses.

"Did I already say Claire and Tom are even dumber than I thought?" Josie commented, as she riffled through Claire's saddlebag.

"I'm keeping her silk blouse and designer jeans to wear when she sees me. Want her to know we took the horses."

"Ain't going to fit you," Jasper said, as he put food and two boxes of bullets to one side.

"Don't care. I want her to know I took them out of her saddlebag," she said as she helped him pile the saddles, bedrolls, rifle, and saddlebags behind a log and cover them with brush. Then they walked the horses out to the trail, being careful not to leave any boot tracks.

They pointed the horses downhill toward the ranch and slapped each of them on the rump to get them moving. The horses might take several days to get to the barn, but they knew the way. They would cross a creek every few miles along the way, and there was no shortage of good grass.

Darkness closed in on them as they followed a deer trail to return to their vantage point above Sheep Camp.

"They're still sleeping," Jasper said. "Didn't expect to get Tom's rifle away from him this soon. Know if they own any revolvers or pistols?"

"Tom owns a revolver he carries anytime he goes near the woods. He's afraid of bears."

"And rattlesnakes."

"They're both afraid of rattlesnakes."

"But you aren't."

"I'm not afraid of..." She stopped abruptly when she heard him snicker. "Oh, shut up. What would a sheepherder know about being afraid of anything?"

"Ranch hand. Sometimes it pays to be afraid. I'm afraid of a revolver big enough to kill a bear, so we're going to be darn cautious when we make our next move.

"Don't forget for a minute that they came here to kill us. We were lucky to get the horses and all their gear away from them."

"I'm ready."

"Wait until it gets darker. Then we'll wake them up. No one sleeps tonight."

While they were waiting for full darkness, a fire flickered to life in the fire pit at Sheep Camp. The fire grew in size until it reached bonfire proportions. The light from the fire outlined two people sitting on logs on opposite sides of the fire.

"Have you ever heard a cougar scream at night?" Jasper asked.

"Yes, a couple of times while I camped with Dad on hunting trips. Dad was my best friend," she said, fighting to keep her chin from quivering.

"He was my best friend too, Josie. We'll both miss him."

"He always took me hunting and fishing."

"Do you think you can duplicate the cougar scream you heard?"

"Sound like a cougar? I can try."

Jasper jumped half out of his skin when she suddenly let out a prolonged series of screams that echoed off Sawtooth Ridge and down across Horsethief Basin. The hair stood up on the back of his neck.

"Josie. Didn't mean for you to do it right now."

"Did I sound like a cougar?"

"Close enough to scare me. Tom and Claire are both standing up, looking around."

"I'll bet Claire wet her designer britches."

"If not, she will before morning. You asked to be a part of this, right?"

"I didn't ask. I told you. I'm part of this."

"Sorry, Miss Martin. Forgot for a moment. You're the boss. I'm just a ranch hand."

"Sheepherder."

"I herded sheep for your father because I liked him. From now on, I'm a ranch hand until I save enough money for a down payment on my own ranch."

"They're moving around down there. What're we going to do?" she asked.

"Two things if you're serious about being part of this. Take a frying pan and some bacon with you and circle downhill toward the fire pit. Let loose with your cougar scream every half hour or so to make them think the *cougar* is circling their camp and getting closer to them. Get behind a big tree before you scream because eventually

Tom is going to panic and fire a round at the *cougar* to try to scare it. Keep screaming on-and-off during the night. If you get tired, find a place to hide and take a nap. I'll block the trail they came in on to make sure they don't try to leave."

"Scream all night and cook breakfast for you?"

"They left all their food on the horses, so they're going to be hungry before morning. Start a small fire a couple of hours before daylight, and fry the bacon. Be sure the wind is drifting toward them so they smell the bacon cooking.

"Tom may come looking for the food. Be careful, and come back here before it gets daylight."

"With your breakfast cooked?"

"Only a fool would waste good bacon."

After Josie slipped away, Jasper worked his way down the hill to within a hundred yards of the fire pit. He listened as the *cougar* worked its way along the ridge, slowly getting closer to Tom and Claire.

Tom threw more wood on the bonfire every time the *cougar* screamed. He held an oversized revolver in his hand, pointing it at shadows as if he expected the *cougar* might pounce on him if he turned his back.

Claire sat on a log close to the fire with her hands covering her ears.

Jasper believed she was crying. He watched for a few minutes. Then he screeched like a Big Horned Owl.

The call caused Claire to jump up and stare into the darkness with her hands pressed even tighter over her ears. Then she helped Tom put more wood on the fire.

"Damn! They're goin' to burn all of the firewood I cut and stacked close to the fire pit," he mumble to himself. He moved a few yards and screeched again. A few minutes later, he scraped a serviceberry bush with a stick. He had no idea what the noise resembled other than a rutting elk polishing its antlers, but reasoned they wouldn't know there were no elk in Horsethief Basin.

Anyone with mountain experience would laugh at the strange noises echoing off Sawtooth Ridge and back down across Horsethief Basin during the night. He could see

Tom and Clair's facial expressions. They were terrified. He could see they were talking, so he crawled closer to the camp to listen to their conversation.

"Soak your feet in the creek," Tom said. "The cold water will make the swelling go down."

"Flashlight's in your saddlebag, and you let the horses wander off. Probably halfway to the barn by now. I'm not going to the stream in the dark unless you go with me."

"My feet are just fine," he said.

"You were the first one to complain about blisters. You're afraid of the dark."

"We don't know what's out there."

"No, but I know what's here, just you, and you aren't anything to brag about," she shouted.

"I'll bet you wish Jasper hadn't dumped you. He'd know what to do."

"He didn't dump me, you fool. There was never anything between us. You're sick with jealousy over a sheepherder. You need to see a shrink."

"Knock it off, Claire. Everything will be fine once we get title to the ranch and find a buyer. After a couple of months in Hawaii, you'll see my true colors."

"The only color I've seen so far is yellow, and it isn't very flattering."

"Oh, shut up," he said, just before the *cougar* screamed again—closer now. Tom whirled around and fired two rounds at a shadow beside a tree at the edge of the firelight.

Claire laughed at him until tears rolled down her cheeks.

"You're getting hysterical, Claire," Tom shouted.

Jasper lost track of time as he listened to them bicker and complain. Their feet hurt too much for them to stand, their saddle sores hurt too much for them to sit, and they were afraid to lie down in the lean-to. Mostly, toward morning, they complained of hunger. He smiled when he smelled the bacon cooking.

"Frank is fixing breakfast. I can smell bacon cooking," Tom said. "We need to find him when it gets light. He'll feed us."

"You fool," Claire said. "Have you forgotten we came here to kill Josie and Jasper? Frank and the sheep aren't anywhere near here, but Jasper and Josie are here somewhere. They parked the pickup and horse trailer at the trailhead, and we followed their horse tracks here. We saw their boot prints where they mounted up and stopped to water the horse. They're both here, and we have to find them."

"Don't know how we're going to find them with no horses. We're not going to walk any place with blisters on our feet."

"We can soak our feet when it gets daylight. Then we can look for them," she said.

Before daylight, Jasper retreated to the viewpoint on the ridge to join Josie. They ate bacon and the glazed donuts Josie had *liberated* from Claire's saddlebag.

After daybreak, Tom and Claire soaked their feet in the creek for an hour before they returned to the fire pit. Within a few minutes, Claire was sleeping in the lean-to while Tom sat with his back against a tree. He kept one hand on the revolver he cradled in his lap. His posture suggested he was on guard duty.

"They didn't get any sleep last night, so they're dead tired. Their feet are too sore for them to walk out of here. By tonight, they'll be too weak from hunger to do anything," Jasper said.

"We may be just as tired if we keep up this pace," Josie said.

"Not if we do this right. We're going to take turns sleeping today. One of us will sleep while the other one makes sure they don't get any rest or try to leave."

"I'll take dibs on sleeping first, if you don't mind," she said.

"I'll wake you when I come back for lunch," he said. He sat for a few minutes and watched Tom's head bob up-and-down, trying to stay awake. Tom was sound asleep with his head on his chest an hour later when Jasper cautiously approached the lean-to.

Jasper stopped on the way down the ridge to collect one of the heaping piles of bear scat that surrounded the camp. Bears frequently slept close to Sheep Camp, waiting for an opportunity to ambush a lamb.

He managed to scoop up a huge pile of the stinking scat on a large piece of bark and carry it to the campsite. After he watched to make sure they were both sleeping soundly, he cautiously stepped toward the lean-to. He dumped the scat on the ground two feet from Claire's head.

Once he was away from the camp, he tossed pebbles at the lean-to to disturb Claire. She woke up, discovered the bear scat, saw Tom sleeping instead of guarding her, and started screaming. Discovering Tom had allowed a *bear* to walk into camp and defile a spot two feet from her head pushed her over the edge into an uncontrollable rage.

As Claire berated Tom, Jasper cautiously walked a half circle around the camp. He stopped several times to break brush to try to sound like an aggressive bear.

Tom fired the revolver in Jasper's direction several times, but none of the shots came close to him. He could hear Claire crying hysterically when she wasn't screaming insults at Tom.

Finally, Jasper hiked up the ridge to join Josie. He needed to take a nap during the afternoon while she watched the distraught couple at the campsite.

Josie let him sleep until sundown. "They've been awake all afternoon. Stayed by the fire except to soak their feet in the creek," she said when he sat up. "What're we going to do next?"

"I'm going to hike up the ridge with the gunny sack. When I get back, we're going down to the camp for the last time. They should be about ready to cooperate. You can bring the two notebooks and the ink pens George gave me."

"And wear Clair's designer jeans and silk blouse?"

"Certainly."

"Can I write the notes? Claire will recognize my handwriting."

"You really do want revenge."

"Wouldn't you?"

"Your father was my best friend, Josie. Let's finish this."

Jasper returned just before last light with the gunnysack, heavily loaded. He opened the top of the sack.

Josie dropped the notebooks and ink pens into the sack, causing quite a buzzing commotion.

After Jasper tied the top of the sack securely, he attached the note Josie wrote to the outside of the sack with two safety pins she provided. Then they started down the ridge toward Sheep Camp for the last time, with Jasper cautiously holding the gunnysack at arm's length.

As they approached the camp in the dark, Josie walked to the bottom of a small gully south of the camp to scrape and break brush to draw Tom and Claire's attention in her direction. Tom fired two shots toward the noise.

Jasper approached the camp from the north, behind the woodpile. He stopped to remove the pigging string from the top of the gunnysack. Then he swung the sack around in a circle a couple of times, and let it fly toward the front of the lean-to.

The sack hit the ground with a thud, freeing a dozen buzzing rattlesnakes in the middle of the camp.

Claire shrieked as Tom started shooting at the buzzing snakes. Claire ended up standing on top of a stump as Tom fired at the snakes until his firing pin landed on an empty casing.

"That was my last bullet," he said as the snakes slithered away from the firelight toward the dark bushes surrounding the campsite.

"Kill them with a stick," Claire yelled at him as tears ran down her cheeks. "Didn't kill any of them with your gun."

"You kill them with a stick, damn it. You got me into this. Thought all our troubles would be over with your father dead."

"You pulled the trigger, so don't put the blame on me."

Jasper resisted the temptation to yell at them to shut up and read the note on the sack. He smelled bacon cooking. Josie was doing her job.

"I can smell bacon. Frank's cooking breakfast," Tom said.

"Good grief, Tom. You're so dense. Do you think a gunnysack full of rattlesnakes just fell out of an airplane? Jasper is doing this. Can't you see a note pinned to the sack?"

"I was busy protecting you from the snakes."

"You fool, see what the note says."

"There're still snakes in the sack," he said, as he approached the sack with the stick. After poking at the sack, he lifted the bottom of the sack with the stick. Two notebooks and pens spilled out on the ground.

Claire, who was still standing on the stump, said, "What does the note say?"

Tom picked up the gunnysack and turned the note toward the bonfire so he could see to read it aloud. "You can have food and a ride out of here if you follow directions. Start by throwing your revolver in the creek."

"Gun's no good without bullets," Claire said. "Throw it away."

"That isn't all. It says we're to use the notebooks to write a complete description of our involvement and our spouse's involvement in your father's murder, and leave the notebooks on the stump next to the trail. If we tell the truth, they'll give us food and a ride home. If we don't follow directions, they'll leave us here."

"Is it signed?"

"Get down off the stump and look for yourself."

"Shut up and hand me a notebook and a pen."

"You aren't going to write something, are you?"

"Why not? I didn't pull the trigger. I need to eat, and I'm not going to stay here to be eaten by a bear or bitten by a snake."

"They can't prove anything. I'm not about to admit what we did," Tom said as he picked up one of the two notebooks. He noticed each notebook had a note written on the front of it.

"What does the note say?" Claire asked when she saw him reading the note.

"The note says they've listened to everything we said at the farmhouse and here. They'll know if we aren't telling the truth."

"I'm going to tell the truth," she said. "A good lawyer will know how to get us out of this mess. We can still blame it on Jasper and Josie."

"You aren't going to write anything. I'm going to burn these stupid notebooks. Let them try to prove we did anything wrong. It's our word against theirs."

"You're so dumb, Tom. I don't know why I ever married you."

"You married me because Jasper wouldn't have anything to do with you, remember? He knows a leech when he sees one."

Claire shrieked, jumped down off the stump, and slapped him. Then she grabbed a notebook out of his hand. "Do what you want, but I'm going to tell the truth. I need to get away from here."

"Give me the notebook," Tom demanded. He grabbed one corner of the notebook and tried to pull it away from her.

"No," she yelled, as she lost her grip on the notebook. She retaliated by slapping him across the face again.

Tom reacted by dropping the notebook. Then he slapped her.

She screamed and started flailing at him with both hands, slapping him repeatedly as she shrieked hysterically.

Jasper realized things had gotten dangerously out of hand. He yelled, "Stop it" as he ran toward them to intervene.

Tom seemed not to hear Jasper yell at him as he protected himself from Claire's blows. He used his forearms

136

to deflect the blows until a stinging slap bloodied his nose. Then he lashed out with his fist, striking a sharp blow to her jaw, knocking her to the ground.

When Claire fell, her head smashed solidly against one of the large rocks surrounding the fire pit.

Jasper gasped when he heard the sickening thud from Claire's head hitting the rock. He ran toward her as blood sprayed all over the rocks from a head wound.

Tom looked down at her, slack jawed, and wide-eyed, seemingly in shock. When he noticed Jasper approaching, he started backing away from the fire.

"Just protecting myself," he stammered as he turned to run away. He disappeared into the darkness, running north toward the horse trail.

Jasper knelt beside Claire and watched, as she seemed to relax. Then her eyes slowly glazed over. He knew she was dead even before he checked her pulse and breathing. Then he noticed Josie on her knees beside him with tears flowing down her cheeks.

"I'm sorry, Josie," he said. "Never meant for this to happen."

"She looks so peaceful and innocent," Josie commented, sadly. "Hard to believe she was so manipulative all her life and a cold blooded killer."

Seeing signs of shock in Josie, he said, "I have a small coffee pot and some coffee in my pack. Would you please make a pot of coffee?"

He hoped making coffee would distract her while he moved Claire to the lean-to and wrapped her body in a blanket."

They sat near the fire a half hour later, in a somber mood, sipping hot coffee. "Wanted revenge for them killing your father. Never dreamed it would end like this," Jasper said.

"She deserved to go to prison for killing Dad. She has gotten off easy."

"Tom will go to prison for both of them."

"Tom's as gifted a liar as Claire was. He'll take the stand and try to convince the jury you killed father and kidnapped me."

"That's true, but the evidence won't lie. I wore gloves when I handled Tom's rifle. His fingerprints should be the only ones on it. George will make sure the deputy doesn't contaminate the evidence. The police will test the rifle. They'll determine the bullet that killed your father had to have come from Tom's rifle. I'm guessing they'll find Tom and Clare's shoe prints by the window in the barn."

"So, where did Tom go?" Josie asked as she wiped away tears.

"Too dark to know for sure, but he turned toward the trail to Surprise Lake. If he gets to the lake, he can hike down to Cub Lake and continue downhill to Lake Chelan. His only alternative is to go uphill over Deadhorse Pass and down to a forest service road to Twisp."

"You don't think he'll come back?"

"He has never been one to take responsibility for his actions. He'll try to escape. When they catch him, he'll try to blame us."

"What're we going to do?"

"George will be here with a deputy and several horses in the morning. We'll wait for them. I'll fire the signal shot sequence I arranged with Frank before we ride out of here. He'll herd the sheep back and stay here to watch them for a few days while we take care of everything back in town."

George and Deputy Harold Lane arrived early the next morning with extra horses. After hearing what had happened, the deputy decided he needed to track Tom. He rode toward Surprise Lake.

George helped Jasper and Josie take Claire's body to the trailhead at Navarre Peak. They stopped along the way to pick up the saddles, Tom's rifle, and the other items they had hidden near the trail.

Two deputies met them at the trailhead to take statements. One deputy transported Claire's body to a funeral home in Chelan while the other deputy waited for Deputy Harold Lane.

George and Jasper loaded the horses in George's stock truck. Jasper and Josie followed the truck in her father's pickup, leaving the empty horse trailer for the deputies to use.

"We need to go to Chelan to make arrangements at the funeral home just as soon as we get home," Jasper said. "Then you need to talk to your father's attorney."

"We aren't going anyplace until we stop at the ranch, so I can take a bath. I stink."

"Is that the reason you have the window rolled down?" he said.

"Yaw, but at least I don't smell like a sheepherder I know."

"I'm done herding sheep. I'm never going to smell like a sheepherder again."

"What makes you think you aren't going to herd sheep?"

"I only herded sheep for your father because I liked him."

"If you aren't going to herd sheep, you'll work as a ranch hand, though, won't you?"

"Of course. That's what I am, a ranch hand, until I get my own place."

"Good. You can be my ranch hand and foreman until I finish high school and turn eighteen next summer."

"Only because I liked your father, and it'll help me save money to buy a ranch."

"Jasper Wilkin. Don't you know you're going to marry me the minute I turn eighteen, and then you and I are going to have a ranch together?"

"Not sure I liked your father that much."

Chelan Falls

Chelan Falls has a 33-acre park (shown above) alongside the Columbia River with day-use facilities. It has a picnic shelter, restrooms, boat launch and short-term boat moorage, a large swimming area, and playground equipment.

A state park across the Columbia River has facilities for recreational vehicles and a swimming area.

Chelan Falls is located along the Columbia River next to the mouth of the Chelan River, three miles from Chelan. Columbia River riverboats docked here before the railroad arrived. Passengers rode to Lake Chelan in a stagecoach on a treacherous switchback road. A private ferry provided access to the east side of the Columbia River until Beebe Orchards, located on the east side of the Columbia, built a private free-swinging bridge across the Columbia River to deliver fruit to the railroad and pipe water from the west side. The bridge abutments are still visible in the river next to the new state highway bridge. The author remembers crossing the swinging bridge—a frightening experience for a youngster.

The Chelan River drops 350 feet from Lake Chelan to the Columbia. A dam at Chelan directs water into a tunnel that delivers it to a generator at Chelan Falls to produce electricity.

Saturday Night Dance

Let me make it clear. I'm not writing this of my own free will. A deputy sheriff has *detained* me—he insists on using the word *detained* instead of arrested—at the sheriff's office in the Chelan County Courthouse in Wenatchee.

Deputy Jorgensen says I'm free to leave as soon as I write down everything that happened at and after the Saturday night dance at the Manson Community Hall.

He has already searched me. I assume he has someone searching my pickup while he *detains* me. After they search my pickup, they'll know I don't have the missing money from the dance.

The deputy says he wants all the details, so I'll start at the beginning. I'm Rocky Seeger. Rocky isn't my given name, but I've used no other since the second grade when the bigger kids teased me about the name my mother gave me. My friends started calling me Rocky after I thumped the biggest kid, a fifth grader, alongside the head with a rock. The name stuck.

I'm 22 now. Presumably, the statute of limitations has expired, so deputies won't *detain* me for my crime of passion in the second grade.

I've been a migrant worker since my high school graduation in 1948. I work my way north following the harvest each spring and return home in the fall.

We picked the last apples Saturday morning at an orchard in Manson where I worked for three weeks. The orchardist gave me my final paycheck, and I packed everything I own in the back of my pickup for the drive to my folk's home in California. I planned to leave town at first light Sunday morning, after the dance.

The dance was a benefit dance for the McNally family to help them rebuild after they lost their home in a fire.

The dance promoter, Mr. Moore, opened an account at the bank in Chelan for the family. All of the money from the dance was to go into the McNally account. The band and Mr. Moore donated their time.

There was an overflow crowd at the dance when I arrived. Nothing out of the ordinary happened until I joined the line to buy a ticket.

Mr. Moore was standing near the door. When he saw me waiting in line, he rushed toward me with a worried expression on his face.

"Rocky, I was hoping you'd be here tonight," he said.

I just looked at him, surprised he knew my name. Mr. Moore was the promoter for the dances held every Saturday night at the community hall. I never missed a dance while working near Manson, but we had never spoken.

Mr. Moore's daughter was standing several steps behind him. We had danced several times.

Her parents named her Sugar. One look at her made me think of sugar, spice, and everything nice. She was the sweet outgoing type who easily engaged a person in conversation, so she may have told him a bit about me.

"Need your help, Rocky," Mr. Moore said. "My two regular helpers are out of town. Gonna have problems if I don't have someone in the hall to keep things under control."

The two helpers he referred to were his two sidekicks. They acted as bouncers at the dances, keeping the local boys and the migrant workers separated inside the hall and enforced the alcohol ban.

I still didn't say anything.

Sugar was shaking her head as if she knew what he was going to ask me to do and was trying to warn me not to agree.

Mr. Moore interrupted my thoughts by pulling his billfold out of his back pocket. He pulled out a wad of folding money.

"Normally pay my helpers a hundred dollars each for the evening. I'm asking you to do double duty here tonight. It's worth two hundred dollars, out of my own pocket, if you'll help me out of a tight spot."

Two hundred dollars would pay all of my expenses for the drive home, so I ignored his daughter. I took the money he handed me and shoved it in my pocket. Then I followed him into the hall.

I didn't pay for a ticket, but I don't believe that's the reason I've been *detained* here at the sheriff's office.

Once inside, Mr. Moore handed me an orange vest with SECURITY spelled out on the back of it in bold letters. The vest was two sizes too large, but it let everyone know I was the designated bouncer.

I didn't expect to have any problems and didn't have any. The locals lined up along one side of the hall, and the migrants lined up along the other side. They knew my reputation as a fighter although they had likely heard exaggerated accounts.

I had boxed for several years at events up and down the coast. I always looked good against the local talent. My straight right hand would knock an amateur on his backside for the count. They didn't realize my left hand couldn't pop a water balloon. I didn't need to fight a professional to know I wouldn't last two rounds.

In hindsight, the only thing out of the ordinary during the dance was the behavior of Mr. Moore's daughter. Sugar actually danced with one of the three Logan brothers.

The brothers all look alike, so I can't tell you which one mangled her toes during a slow waltz. I just remember everyone gawking at the beauty and the beast.

The three brothers usually stand at one end of the hall by themselves. No one goes near them unless they want to buy the rotgut whiskey and homebrew they sell outside the hall. I'm not trying to tell tales out of school here. Everyone knows deputies have *detained* them and their father numerous times for selling alcohol to minors.

As I said, nothing out of the ordinary happened at the dance. The band stopped playing at two in the morning, and folks left in an orderly manner. The two hundred dollars Mr. Moore paid me was the easiest money I had ever earned.

As the last couple left the hall, I removed the orange vest to return it to Mr. Moore.

He was still counting the proceeds, so I stood and watched him. There was more money on the table in front of him than I had ever seen outside of a bank.

When he finished counting, Mr. Moore placed the money in a deposit bag with a deposit slip made out to the McNally account. He looked tired which was to be expected as he was easily the oldest person in attendance at the dance and didn't look to be in good health.

"Rocky, you did a fine job tonight," he said when I handed him the orange vest.

"I have one more favor to ask that'll put another twenty dollars in your pocket."

I just looked at him, having no idea what he had in mind. The mention of another twenty dollars held my attention, however.

Sugar was the only other person in the hall. She stood behind her father, shaking her head again. I didn't say anything.

"This money needs to go in the night deposit at the bank in Chelan. I don't feel very well, and I'm concerned about driving along the narrow lakeshore road this time of night. My night vision isn't what it used to be.

"I'll pay you another twenty dollars, out of my own pocket, if you'll take this deposit bag to Chelan, and drop it in the night deposit for me."

I didn't have to think for more than a moment to make a decision. My pickup was packed and ready to leave for home. I planned to leave first thing in the morning. There was no reason I couldn't leave immediately. I could drop the money off in Chelan on the way south, and earn an easy twenty dollars.

I said, "Yes."

At Mr. Moore's request, I waited while he and his daughter gathered their belongings and locked the front door to the community hall. Mr. Moore handed me the deposit bag and thanked me again as we walked out to our vehicles.

I placed the bag on the front seat of my pickup and started driving toward Chelan.

I made it as far as the sawmill turnoff road along the lakeshore. Then I spotted an old pickup stopped in the middle of the road.

It was darker than Satan's underworld, but I recognized the three Logan brothers in my headlights. They were standing at the back of their pickup with a flashlight, looking at a flat tire as if they believed the tire might inflate itself if they stared at it long enough.

The pickup blocked most the road, so I had to stop. Besides that, I knew they were too dumb to figure out how to inflate a flat tire.

Fortunately, I had a tire pump in my pickup. The three brothers watched while I pumped air into the tire. I kicked the tire a couple of times when I finished, and assured them the tire would hold air long enough for them to get home.

They turned their pickup around and started back toward Manson without a word of thanks.

When I walked back to get in my pickup, the deposit bag was gone from the front seat. I cursed myself for not hiding the bag and for allowing the brothers to distract me with a flat tire. Only then did I wonder why they had driven toward Chelan when their father's house was near the road past Dry Lake on the other side of Manson. I'm embarrassed to admit this in writing, but the three dumbest people in Manson outsmarted me.

Apparently, it didn't occur to the Logan brothers that I would recognize them and know where they live. I was two minutes behind them when they parked in front of their father's place.

All of the lights were on in the old shack when I coasted to a stop behind their pickup and walked to the front door. I could hear Mr. Logan shouting at the boys.

I didn't bother to knock. They were standing around a table when I opened the door. The deposit bag was on the table.

Mr. Logan was swatting one of his sons alongside the head. He stopped and looked over his shoulder when he heard the door open.

I stood in the doorway with my fists doubled.

The three brothers were still staring down at the deposit bag. The contents had spilled out onto the table when one of them opened the bag.

I could see at a glance the deposit bag had contained nothing but newsprint cut to dollar bill size.

The brothers finally turned toward me. "You switched bags," one of them accused.

His father swatted him alongside the head again. Then he looked back at me.

"Do you want to tell me what these three fools have done this time?"

"They stole that deposit bag from me," I said.

Mr. Logan glared at his sons.

They backed against a wall, looking guilty.

"Whose bright idea was it to steal this bag from him?" he asked.

The three brothers looked at each other before one of them spoke. "She said we could keep the money if we stole the bag from him. She told me how to stop him and get the money."

"Who?" I shouted at them.

"The pretty girl at the dance. She asked me to dance with her," he said. "I don't know her name."

He was talking about Sugar, of course, whom I had witnessed dancing with him.

I had no idea why she would have them steal the deposit bag from me. The bag didn't have any money in it. Someone had switched bags after I watched her father place the money in a deposit bag.

I could see the anger in Mr. Logan's eyes before he spoke.

"You stole the deposit bag with the money, and you let my boys steal this bag to shift the blame to them." he accused.

"No sir, I didn't," I said. "Someone did steal the money though, and Sugar tried to shift the blame from me to your boys."

"Why would she do that?" he asked.

I didn't have an answer for him.

"I don't know why she'd involve your sons, Mr. Logan," I said, after a long pause to think about what had happened. "But, I'm going to find out."

Mr. Logan seemed to believe me. After some discussion, he gave me directions to the Moore residence.

Manson is a small town, so it didn't take long to find their house. The lights were still on at three-thirty in the morning, and I could hear voices as I walked to the door.

The people inside the house stopped talking when I

knocked. No one responded, so I tried the doorknob. They hadn't locked the door, so I took that as an invitation to join them.

Sugar sat with Mr. Moore and one of his helpers at a table in the center of the room. She gasped, seemingly shocked to see me.

Mr. Moore glare at me for a moment. Then he smiled, pointed to an empty chair at the table, and waved me into the room.

I'm embarrassed to admit what happened next. I stepped into the room without thinking about Mr. Moore's second helper. He must've been standing behind the door when I opened it. All I remember is a moment of intense pain when something struck me behind the ear.

I must've collapsed immediately because I have no memory of anything until I opened my eyes sometime later. Sunlight tried to force its way through a dirty bedroom window. I was on a bed, tussled up like a Christmas goose. The house was quiet.

My head throbbed, and I couldn't keep my eyes open. When I woke up again, it was dark outside the bedroom window. I realized I must've slept all day Sunday.

People were talking in the living room. A couple of the voices were loud enough for me to hear what they were saying.

Mr. Moore's voice caught my attention when he spoke. "Take him down to the dock, and hold him under the water. Leave him on the shore with the empty deposit bag and deposit slip in his back pocket. The police need to find him, and he needs to have the evidence on him."

They talked some more, but I couldn't follow the conversation. Several hours passed before they came for me. The two helpers picked me up, packed me out to a vehicle, and dumped me on the back seat.

I knew they were taking me to the lake to drown me. My imagination ran wild, and I was scared.

They stopped after a short drive. I heard waves beating against wood pilings. One of the men opened the back door, grabbed my legs, and jerked me off the back seat.

The back of my head bounced off a rock. I could see stars now, most of them in my head, and believed it would've been better if the impact had knocked me unconscious. Drowning while awake sounded like something I didn't need to experience to know it wouldn't be pleasant.

The men held me by my feet as they dragged me past a small tool shed near the dock. Gravel scraped against the bruise on the back of my head. Then my head thumped on each of the planks as they pulled me out toward the end of the dock.

When they stopped, I still wasn't prepared to accept my fate. My only chance to survive, I decided, was to convince the two men they shouldn't drown me. Yes, I was going to beg for my life.

I tried.

They laughed.

"Take it like a man," the biggest man said.

"Would you?" I said.

"I ain't the one butted in where he didn't belong."

"Why isn't Mr. Moore here?"

I have no idea why I asked the question. I guess I was stalling, although it seemed pointless.

"He doesn't like to get his hands dirty. That's why he pays us."

"What about Sugar?" I was definitely stalling now. I really didn't want to drown.

"Went to a party. She said we should drown you because you're too stupid to live."

His comment hurt, but I ignored him.

"Where's the money?" I asked, since they seemed in no hurry to finish their business.

"Do ya have a smoke?" one of the men said, ignoring my question.

"I don't know why you never buy your own," the other man complained.

A match flared to life a few moments later, discharging sulfur fumes.

I looked up as one of the men held a match to a cigarette. Then, I caught a glimpse of two people standing on the dock behind Mr. Moore's helpers.

The light from the match reflected off the revolver one of them held in his hand.

"Where's the money?" I asked again. I couldn't identify the two people behind us, but I wanted to solicit more incriminating information if there was any chance they might help me.

The smoker chuckled. "It's in Moore's safe where it belongs. Usually, he just skims twenty percent from a dance, but he decided this was our chance for a big payday. All we had to do was find a fool like you to take the blame."

Well, I didn't have a response this time. They had certainly found a fool.

I was so mad, I forgot about the two people standing on the dock behind us until someone turned on a large flashlight. The dock suddenly lit up as if it was midday in July.

"Hands in the air," someone shouted in a sharp command voice when the light flicked on.

"Keep your back turned toward me."

I knew the man wasn't talking to me because I was still hogtied. All I could do was look around.

The speaker wore a police uniform. I didn't know he was a Chelan County Deputy Sheriff until later.

When I looked up at Mr. Moore's helpers, they were

reaching for the stars. They didn't say a word as the deputy handcuffed them.

The glare from the flashlight kept me from identifying the person holding it. Everyone ignored me while the deputy handcuffed the two men and herded them off the dock. Then the light moved toward me, and I could see Sugar was holding the flashlight.

She knelt down to untie the ropes binding me.

"We about froze waiting in the toolshed," she said.

"I wasn't very comfortable myself," I snapped at her.

"What kind of appreciation is that," she snapped right back at me. "You'd be swimming with the fish right now if I hadn't gotten away to find a deputy."

"I'd not be here if you hadn't had the Logan brothers steal the deposit bag from me."

"I tried to protect you. You would've taken the blame for stealing the money if you'd deposited the bag my father gave you. I assumed you'd call the police when the Logan brothers stole the deposit bag from you. It never occurred to me you'd show up at my father's house."

"Never underestimate a fool's capacity for stupidity," I mumbled to myself, knowing I had made enough mistakes in the last twenty-four hours to last a lifetime.

Calling the police hadn't occurred to me. Like most migrant workers, I had learned to avoid anyone in a uniform with the authority to *detain* me.

When Sugar finished untying the ropes, she helped me stand up. My legs were numb, and I shivered as I hobbled off the dock. I checked my pockets, and was surprised to discover I still had the money Mr. Moore paid me.

As we approached the deputy and his two prisoners, I could see cars racing toward us with blue lights flashing on their roofs. After the officers arrived, they prepared plans to converge on the Moore residence.

I was shivering worse now. The breeze was cool coming off Lake Chelan, and I was wearing a short sleeve shirt.

Sugar held my hand and leaned her body against me.

I assumed she was cold.

A few minutes later, a deputy volunteered to take me to my pickup.

I had left the pickup parked in front of the Moore residence, but Sugar said they moved it to a vacant lot. She had my pickup keys in her pocket.

Sugar and I ended up in the back of the patrol car for the short ride to Manson.

"My father is going to prison where he belongs," she said. "I've tried to get away from him several times, but he always stopped me."

I didn't know what she was leading up to, so I didn't say anything.

Finally, sounding exasperated, she said, "I'm eighteen, Rocky. I can go anyplace I want without his permission."

I still didn't say anything. I noticed she was squeezing my hand tighter as she moved closer to me. I assumed she was still cold.

"Please take me away from here, Rocky," she said. "I don't want to watch them take my father to jail. I know you're going south. I have friends in Wenatchee. Won't you please take me that far?"

Now she was pushing up against me in the back seat as if we were at a drive-in theater watching the same movie for the third showing. I'm embarrassed to admit my response. All I could think about was the fact that I hadn't eaten for over twenty-four hours. I was hungry.

"I'm starved," I said, knowing that wasn't the response she expected.

"The Apple Cup Cafe in Chelan is open all night," she said. "I'll buy dinner if you'll take me to Wenatchee."

That sealed the deal.

The deputy said he had all the information he needed based on what Sugar told him before they rescued me, and what he heard the two prisoners say when they were talking at the end of the dock.

He had no reason to *detain* me.

I quickly checked my pickup. Everything was where I had left it, including my hidden savings from picking jobs. Ten minutes later, at two-thirty Monday morning, Sugar and I started along the shoreline toward Chelan where we stopped to eat. I had a chicken fried steak and two slices of apple pie.

Sugar paid.

We arrived in Wenatchee at six in the morning.

Sugar asked me to stop next to the Greyhound Bus Depot. She said her friend lived behind the depot.

She wasn't nearly as friendly now. She didn't say anything before she jumped out of my pickup.

I drove out of town, headed south.

Everything else I know is hearsay. I didn't know a locksmith had discovered Mr. Moore's safe was empty until a deputy stopped me on Highway 97, south of Yakima, to *detain* me.

The deputy gave me a choice. I could ride to Wenatchee in the back of his patrol car, or I could turn my pickup around and drive back to Wenatchee with him following me.

I drove.

The deputy told me Sugar was the only person with the combination to the safe other than her father. Mr. Moore's two helpers swore they watched her father lock the deposit bag containing the money in the safe before he took two sleeping pills and went to bed.

Mr. Moore was still sleeping soundly when the police raided his house.

The deputy also told me Wenatchee police searched all

of the homes near the bus depot. They couldn't find Sugar.

I don't believe they will find her in Wenatchee.

Buses left Wenatchee traveling in four directions within a few minutes after I dropped Sugar off at the depot. She could've taken any one of the buses, gotten off anywhere along the way, and transferred to another bus going in a different direction. She can go anywhere she wants to go with the deposit bag full of money from the dance.

I realize now, there was never anything sweet or nice about Sugar. I don't believe the police will ever catch her or find the money.

So, this is my full and complete statement explaining what happened at and after the dance at the Manson Community Hall Saturday night. You'll find me at my folks in California if you have no further reason to *detain* me.   Rocky Seeger

The Manson Community Hall mentioned in the short stories is now the Manson Village Center with gift shops and a wine tasting room.

Michelle's in the Well

Neighbors still talk about the day Michelle fell in the well. Some proclaim it a miracle only one person drowned. Others whisper scornfully as they question her father's actions during the rescue effort and dispute accounts of what actually happened at the bottom of the well.

No one disputes the events leading up to the tragic accident, however.

Ross and Lorna Templeton and their two children, Michelle and Allen, lived on the old McCormick homestead on the Grade Creek Road past Manson.

Ray Lennar purchased the property from McCormick's widow to expand his rangeland. The farmhouse sat empty until Ray let the Templeton family move in and cultivate the three-acre field adjoining it.

If any family ever needed a break, it was the Templeton family. Ross and Lorna had nearly starved to death before they abandoned their farm in Oklahoma. They worked their way west during the depression, arriving in Manson on the back of a friend's, 1932-model, Ford truck.

Resettlement didn't bring prosperity for Ross and Lorna. They lived in primitive orchard cabins and worked in local orchards.

Observers smugly assumed Ross lacked ambition, although they would allow he always had a job or was looking for work. They didn't know polio affected Ross. No amount of exercise or work would strengthen his weakened muscles or increase his stamina. His slow movements and the need for frequent rest breaks were easily mistaken for laziness, making it difficult for him to hold a steady job.

The family was struggling to survive when Ray Lennar offered them the use of the old abandoned farmhouse in 1950. The farmhouse was rat infested, and the adjoining three-acre field looked like a rock pile. Anyone less desperate for housing might've rejected the offer.

Ross and Lorna accepted Ray's offer with gratitude. The family replaced rotten floorboards with planks pulled from the side of an old barn behind the property. They replaced broken windows with glass from abandoned buildings.

A year later, people who stopped to purchase fresh vegetables could hardly recognize the old homestead. The three-acre rock pile had vanished, replaced by a flourishing three-acre garden that supplied fresh vegetables for the local community.

Lorna worked endlessly to keep their small vegetable stand stocked. Michelle and Allen pulled weeds. Ross, people noticed, sat in the shade of a pine tree and watched.

No one except Lorna realized Ross's physical condition was rapidly deteriorating. No one at all knew the boards covering an old abandoned well in the middle of the garden were deteriorating even more rapidly.

McCormick dug the well shortly after he homesteaded the property. The hole he dug was just large enough for him to work in. Water started seeping into the hole at twenty feet. He dug another eight feet to provide a reservoir.

After McCormick married, his wife insisted on having running water in the house and an irrigated garden. He responded by piping water from a creek to the house and garden. He abandoned the well, but prudently covered it with thick boards and dirt. The boards slowly rotted during the next forty years.

Michelle fell in the well on a hot afternoon while she was weeding the garden. Her folks and brother heard her shrill scream and a loud splash when she plunged twenty feet down into the water. Rotten wood and dirt fell on top of her.

Her family reached the edge of the hole to stare down the dark hole before the dust settled.

"Can you hear me?" her father yelled.

"Yes, yes, get me out of here. I'm going to drown," the frightened eight-year-old girl shrieked.

"Can you touch bottom?"

"No, Poppa, I'm going to drown."

"Allen, run to the barn. Get a rope.

"Lorna, we're going to need help. Get the neighbors. Have them call for help," Ross said.

"Hurry Poppa, I'm scared," Michelle cried.

"Can you hold on to something?" her father asked.

"No, Poppa. Hurry. I can't swim."

When ten-year-old Allen ran back from the barn a minute later with a rope, his father was gone. He glanced around for him for a moment, confused. Then he dropped to his knees beside the hole. He could hear his sister splashing water, but it was still too dusty and dark for him to see her.

"Can you see the rope?" Allen yelled as he dropped one end of the rope into the well.

"I can feel it."

"Tie the rope under your arms so we can pull you out."

"Wait a minute. I'm shivering so much I can hardly tie a knot."

Allen alternated looking around for his father and staring down into the hole as he waited for her to tie the knot. The dust cleared some, and his eyes slowly adjusted to the darkness. Finally, he could see his sister's head.

"I have the rope tied around me. Pull me up. Hurry, please, I'm freezing."

Allen pulled the rope taut as he continued glancing around for his father. He tugged on the rope with all of his strength, but quickly realized he couldn't pull his sister out of the well by himself.

"Poppa," he hollered. "Where are you? I need help."

Allen was still holding the rope, and frantically yelling for his father when the first vehicle arrived. He could hear the siren from a fire truck in the distance as his mother jumped out of a car to run toward him.

Lorna dropped to the ground next to Allen to peer down into the well. "Oh sweet Jesus, my baby is drowning." she cried. Then she glanced around.

"Where's your father?"

Their closest neighbors, Mr. and Mrs. Lameson, an elderly couple, hobbled along behind Lorna. Mr. Lameson dropped down beside Allen to look in the well.

"Her head's above water. She's still alive," Mr. Lameson managed to say. Then he had to stop for a moment to try to catch his breath before he could continue.

"We need to get her out of the cold water before she catches her death," he said.

"She tied the rope around her body," Allen said as tears flooded his cheeks, "but I couldn't pull her out of the water by myself."

"Where's your father?" Lorna asked again.

"I don't know where Poppa went."

"Ross, where are you?" Lorna yelled as she glanced around, confused by his absence. "I can't imagine where he has gone."

"I'll try to help Allen while you look for him," Mr. Lameson said. "We're going to need his help."

"You'd think a man would stay to try to rescue his daughter instead of running off," Mrs. Lameson mumbled, scornfully, as she watched Lorna run toward the house to look for Ross.

Mr. Lameson took hold of the rope with Allen. "We'll have to try to pull her out of the well by ourselves," he said as he pulled on the rope with Allen.

They quickly realized they couldn't pull her up out of the water.

"You could pull her out if her father hadn't run off and left her to drown," Mrs. Lameson said, as she watched Lorna leave the farmhouse to run toward the barn. As she spoke, the volunteer fire truck from Manson turned into the driveway. Cars and pickups followed the truck.

"What's happening?" a volunteer fireman yelled as he jumped off the truck to run toward the well.

"Michelle's in the well," Lorna screamed as she ran back from the barn to meet the volunteers. "Please help her."

A burly volunteer grabbed the rope out of Allen and Mr. Lameson's hands as men dropped to their knees to peer down into the well. One of the men shined a beam from a large flashlight down into the hole.

"She has a rope tied around her," Allen said, as a fireman pushed him back out of the way.

"They would already have her out of the well if her father hadn't run off and left her to drown," Mrs. Lameson announced, loudly.

Lorna started crying as the gravity of the situation overwhelmed her. Michelle might've drowned, and she had no idea why Ross had disappeared. She realized he might not have been able to help pull her out of the well because his muscles were too weak, but she couldn't imagine why he would run away.

"We'll injure the girl if she tied a slip knot in the rope," one of the men said. "Someone needs to go down and get her."

"I'll go," shouted several of the volunteers.

"Johnny's the one for this job," said a man wearing a captain's helmet.

"He's small enough to fit in the hole and has the strength needed to hold on to her while we pull them up."

Johnny quickly buckled on a harness connected to a stout rope, and they lowered him into the well.

As everyone watched the action, Mrs. Lameson's sharp tongue continued blistering the girl's absent father for running off instead of staying to help rescue her.

The firemen ignored her, but several excited spectators listened. Then they started looking for the derelict father.

Lorna sobbed as strangers invaded her home and the barn to look for Ross. She held Allen in her arms.

Mr. Lameson tried to console them. He ignored his wife as she continued to excite the crowd.

Angry comments from bystanders drowned out the captain's words as he tried to talk to Johnny when he reached the bottom of the well.

The man who owned the flask shouted, "When they get her out, we should use the rope to hang her father. What kind of a man leaves his daughter to flounder in a well? The pine tree beside the house will work nicely."

Several inebriated friends shouted agreement as they waited for another sip from the flask.

"I have her," Johnny yelled from the bottom of the well. "She's unconscious, but she might still be alive. Pull us up. Quick."

The crowd quieted as the volunteers pulled Johnny to the surface, clutching Michelle in his arms. The soaked, little girl was as limp as a rag doll when Johnny handed her to the captain. Men pushed others aside as the captain laid Michelle on a blanket beside Lorna and Allen.

Michelle's violent shivering showed she was still alive, but for how long was in question. Lorna shivered when she hugged her daughter. Her little girl felt like a fifty-pound block of ice from the local creamery.

"We need to get her warm," the fire captain said. "I'll carry her into the house, so you can remove her wet clothes, and wrap her in blankets,"

"Where's her father?" one of the more intoxicated bystanders shouted, as the captain carried the little girl toward the house with Lorna and Allen running along beside him.

"I have the rope when we find him," another man mumbled, slurring the words.

Several of his friends shouted agreement. Someone passed around a second flask.

"Hanging's better than he deserves," Mrs. Lameson shouted, just as Ray Lennar parked his pickup beside the fire truck.

"What happened here?" Ray asked as he approached the men standing beside the well.

"The little girl fell in the well," several men yelled.

"And her father run off and left her there," Mrs. Lameson shouted.

"They just packed her into the house. She's still alive," a fireman said.

"No thanks to her father," Mrs. Lameson added.

Ray Lennar seemed to realize her inflammatory comments were causing spectators to act irrationally. He said, "Mr. Lameson, please take your wife home. We need to fill this hole. I'd have filled it before if I'd known it was here."

"You should've known. All of these old homesteads have hand-dug wells," Mrs. Lameson shouted as her husband grasped her arm to tug her toward their car.

"You're right. I should've known, but I never gave it a thought. Since we have volunteers standing around with nothing better to do, we can fill the hole right now. The family has stacked enough rocks along the edge of their garden to fill this hole if everyone will help for a few minutes."

In the house, Lorna stripped the wet clothes from Michelle and wrapped her in warm blankets. The girl was lying on her sleeping pallet on the floor when she opened her eyes a few minutes later. Her mother and brother were sitting on the floor beside her, rubbing her hands and feet.

Michelle looked up at the worried faces surrounding her. "I'm alive," she said as if she didn't quite believe what she was saying.

"Yes," Lorna said. "These brave men saved you. They pulled you out of the well."

Michelle slowly shook her head, although it appeared to take a lot of effort. "No Momma. Poppa saved me," she said.

Her daughter's response alarmed Lorna. She believed harmful effects of the long wait in the cold water were causing her to hallucinate.

The volunteers surrounding the pallet gave each other worried glances.

"You're safe now," Lorna said.

"Did they find Poppa?" Michelle asked.

"I've not been able to find him," her mother said. "I'm sure he'll be here to check on you in a minute."

"Poppa saved me, Momma. The water was too deep, and I can't swim. I was about to drown. Poppa made me stand on his shoulders."

Everyone in the room gasped when they heard what her father had done.

The captain turned to run out the door. "Stop, stop," he shouted, frantically, at the men throwing rocks into the well.

Neighbors still talk about the day Michelle fell in the well. Some proclaim it a miracle only one person drowned. Others whisper scornfully as they dispute accounts of what actually happened at the bottom of the well.

Everyone remembers the generosity of the local church parishioners and service club members. They collected funds to pay for Ross Templeton's funeral and a headstone. Ray Lennar organized the group that filled in the old homestead well, painted the farmhouse, and built an attractive vegetable stand in front of the garden.

Ray modestly disclaimed any credit for the events, but couldn't deny his obvious involvement when Lorna Templeton opened a letter containing a deed for the farmhouse and three acres.

Michelle survived her narrow escape in the well with no apparent ill effects. She and Allen helped their mother grow vegetables for the community until they finished high school. Michelle married, and Allen joined the army.

Lorna continued gardening until she passed away in 2006. She rests beside Ross in the local cemetery at Manson.

Lucerne and Holden Village

The ferry or seaplane will stop at Lucerne so passengers can hike to Domke Lake or go to Holden Village. The village bus takes passengers eleven miles up the mountain to the old mining town.

The mine at Holden Village was a major copper producer until owners abandoned the mine in 1957 when it became unprofitable.

The Lutheran Church eventually acquired the town site and rebuilt it as a non-profit Christian wilderness retreat open to everyone.

Hiking trails from Holden Village lead to the Cascade Trail and the spectacular mountain views, lakes, and glaciers shown in the photo on the title page.

Contractors are currently cleaning up the old mine site. Due to their activities, travel on the road to Holden Village is currently restricted to weekends. This will change as the cleanup progresses.

Visitors can get information and program schedules by writing to Holden Village, HCO Box 2, Chelan, WA 98816 or ***www.holdenvillage.org***. There are no phones in Holden Village.

Photo: Cabins along the shoreline at Lucerne. Railroad Creek and the public dock are out of the photo to the right. Trees in this photo obscure the trail to Domke Lake and the road to Holden Village.

Then the Bottom Fell Out

There was a time back in the '60s when my friends and I still believed drinking beer was a competitive sport. We would meet at a local watering hole in Chelan after work on Friday to drink, tell jokes, and lament a week's worth of injustices visited upon us.

Participants at the weekly event varied in frequency of attendance. There were seldom less than a half dozen and often more than a dozen men and women present. We simply moved tables together as people arrived to join the group.

No fewer than a dozen of us crowded around the tables to witness a memorable event I'm about to describe. As near as I can recall, the group included orchard and construction workers, teachers, business owners, and an attorney. Ours was not an exclusive group. Arrival with a pitcher of beer was the only requirement for a seat at the table.

Nothing out of the ordinary happened on this particular occasion until Adam Novice, a first year teacher from a neighboring community, started complaining about Joey Airhead, one of his students.

You might guess I've changed participant's names to tell this story even though there are no innocent parties to protect. Truth is I may be the only one willing to confess to having witnessed the event.

Most of the participants may not remember all the details. The beer was flowing nearly nonstop, and the aging server was having a hard time keeping filled pitchers of beer on the table. No one, however, will ever forget what happened.

As I said, Adam Novice started complaining about a student named Joey Airhead. Joey was impossible in the classroom, according to Adam. He would bully other students, lie, cheat, and disrupt the class by making noises simulating body functions. You know what I'm talking about here. You probably remember a Joey Airhead from your school days.

Adam was a good storyteller with a few drinks under his belt, and we were easily entertained. Copious amounts of beer helped.

Occasionally, Adam—who was as new to the sport of competitive beer drinking as he was to teaching—would pause to refill his glass or visit the restroom. Then someone would fill the void with a story or a joke.

Two or three people drifted away as the evening progressed. Others joined our group with their prerequisite pitcher of beer. The server's legs were getting shorter by the hour as she rushed to keep the beer flowing.

Then a man I had never met sat down across the table from me with a pitcher of beer. Someone introduced him as Clyde. We all nodded a welcome as Clyde's pitcher of beer made its way around the table. It failed to make a complete round.

Clyde said, "Hello," as someone yelled for the server to bring a refill. Clyde was a large man with broad shoulders, cauliflower ears, and the flat face and nose common to experienced fighters. He looked like he could thump Mohammad Ali without breaking a sweat. He drank beer, laughed at our jokes, but didn't add anything to the conversation.

Adam continued to fill any void in our banter with stories about Joey Airhead. Some of the stories were so wild they sounded like he was exaggerating details.

I happened to know Joey Airhead, so I knew Adam Novice wasn't exaggerating. I could've validated all of his stories and added a few of my own, but I kept my mouth shut. Adam was the center of attention, and he was enjoying the limelight. I didn't want to rain on his parade.

Then the bottom fell out.

Clyde cleared his throat to get everyone's attention. The room was suddenly very quiet. Clyde turned to look at Adam Novice and said, "Everything you've said about Joey is true, but his mother and I love him, just the same."

Several weeks passed before I discovered Clyde wasn't Joey's father. Clyde didn't know Joey, but he knew how to teach a novice teacher a valuable lesson with a few well-chosen words.

I don't know if Adam ever learned Clyde wasn't Joey's father, but I'm confident he never again mentioned a student's name in public. Adam continued teaching for over 30 years. He became one of the better teachers I've known, but he never did amount to much as a competitive beer drinker.

The vineyard beside Lake Chelan Winery is one of many around the lake. Many apple growers have adopted vineyard techniques for planting apple trees, so visitors—and old-timers—may need to look twice to know if they are looking at grape vines or apple trees.

Visiting Lake Chelan

Getting there is half the fun. Lake Chelan is about 180 miles from Seattle, 150 miles from Spokane, and 40 miles from Wenatchee. Each city has an airport with rental cars available.

From Spokane, follow Highway 2 west to Wilbur. From Wilbur, continue on Highway 2 to Orondo and turn north on Highway 97 to Chelan Falls, or turn at Wilbur onto Highway 174 to visit Grand Coulee Dam in route.

From Wenatchee, follow Highway 97 or 97A north to Lake Chelan.

Canadian visitors can follow Highway 97 south to Chelan Falls and take the turn off to the lake.

From Seattle, follow Highway 2 to Wenatchee and Highway 97 or 97A to Lake Chelan.

Each route has numerous roadside attractions and points of interest.

Lake Chelan is on the **Cascade Loop Highway**. The scenic highway passes through the Snohomish River Valley, the Stevens Pass Greenway, the Leavenworth Cascade Foothills, and the Wenatchee Columbia River Valley to reach Lake Chelan. From Chelan, a traveler drives through the Methow Valley, the North Cascades, the Skagit Valley, the Fidalgo Islands, and the Whidbey Scenic Isle Way to complete the loop.

Check the internet at **www.cascadeloop.com** for maps, driving directions, and travel times for the Cascade Loop Highway. The website provides event schedules, lists attractions, accommodations, side trips, views, pullouts, picnic spots, and tells where to eat and drink in each of the towns along the loop. The 400-mile loop is appropriate for either a short or an extended vacation.

Lake Chelan Attractions

Lake Chelan has been a vacation destination for over a hundred years. The lake, weather, and amenities attract tourists.

Lake Chelan has 300 days of sunshine a year, and the shallow water at the south end of the lake is 78 degrees during the summer. Local communities and entrepreneurs have added the facilities and attractions needed to help Lake Chelan become an internationally recognized tourist destination.

Family Activities: Parks and sandy beaches surround the lake. Children can swim while adults sunbathe. Everyone will want to visit Slidewaters on the hillside between Chelan and Lakeside. Teenagers may want to rent a scooter, watercraft, race the go-carts, and stop by Lake View Drive-in for a hamburger. Kids of all ages will enjoy picking blueberries at Blueberry Hills Farm near Manson and fishing from one of the docks along Lake Chelan.

Don Morse Park at Chelan is one of many swimming beaches on the lakeshore.

Visitors use every imaginable type of watercraft on the lake. The water at the southern and northern ends of the lake is often calm enough to enjoy standing up on a paddleboard.

Adult Activities: Wineries are easy to find, and there is a popular Casino near Manson. Spas and health clubs are available as well as fine dining opportunities.

Mill Bay Casino *between Chelan and Manson features gaming, dining, and entertainment.*

Lake Chelan Winery *on the highway between Chelan and Manson is one of many wineries and tasting rooms surrounding Lake Chelan.*

Sightseeing opportunities abound. Take a trip on the Lady of the Lake or Lady Express to see Lake Chelan and visit Stehekin. Drive the back roads around Chelan and Manson to view orchards, vineyards, and wildlife. Take a walk in Riverside Park at Chelan.

Expect to see mountain goats along the shoreline from the Lady Express or Lady of the Lake. Bear feed on berries on the mountains sides in the late summer and fall. Mule deer are present year around.

The views along the shoreline between Chelan and Stehekin are spectacular. There are numerous waterfalls along the shoreline, but nothing like 312-foot Rainbow Falls at Stehekin, which visitors can view on a day trip. Recommended for first time visitors—take the Lady of the Lake up the lake for an overnight, or longer, stay at the North Cascade Lodge, and return on the Lady Express. This gives a visitor time to see and appreciate more sights and plan next years extended stay.   Photo: Rainbow Falls.

Recreational opportunities are available all year. Skiing and snowmobiling are popular during the winter months. Golf and fishing are options nearly year around and trails for hiking and biking surround the lake. The lake offers opportunities for boating, waterskiing, jet skiing, parasailing and paragliding. Visitors can hunt birds, deer, and bear in the fall.

Visitors will find venders all around the lake with all kinds of watercraft for rent. If it is appropriate for the lake, it is available. Photo shows rental crafts with the swimming area at Manson in the background.

Boy Scouts and leaders hiking to their campsite at Stehekin. Hikers can select easy day hikes or extreme longer hikes that fit their experience and time schedule. They can use trails near Chelan, along the lakeshore to access mountain lakes, or follow trails at the upper end of the lake to lakes and glaciers.

Special events occur year around at Chelan and Manson. The Manson Apple Blossom Parade in May is always popular. Visitors may enjoy the winter fest, wine and chocolate tasting, a hang gliding contest, golf tournament, car shows, trail run, summer concerts, art and craft shows, a rodeo, a slam-n-jam basketball tournament, running and bike marathons, a sailing regatta, hydrofest, and small town Christmas festivals just to name a few special events.

Riverwalk Pavilion is on the shoreline path behind the Chelan business district. The pavilion is home to special events and farmer's markets. The grassy area in front of the pavilion is a good place for a picnic after a walk along Woodin Avenue to view the shops or to relax after eating at a nearby restaurant. It is within easy walking distance to the museum where you can learn about the area's history and the chamber office where you can learn how to access all of the areas available resources.

Spring is a special time around the lake when apple and cherry trees bloom and residents prepare for the Manson Apple Blossom Parade.

Visitors Guide

With so many attractions available—for families, adults, sightseeing, and recreation—and a year around schedule of special events, it may seem difficult to decide when to vacation at Lake Chelan. Special event dates change each year and business phone numbers and locations may change, so any specific information provided in this publication will quickly be outdated.

Fortunately, the Chelan Chamber of Commerce has anticipated the problem. They publish a booklet each year called, **LAKE CHELAN – THE OFFICIAL VISITORS GUIDE OF THE LAKE CHELAN VALLEY**.

The booklet provides the up-to-date information needed to plan a Lake Chelan vacation. The booklet is available at **www.lakechelan.com** in a format that allows a viewer to read every page on line.

Their special events calendar will help a viewer decide on the best time for a visit. The section on accommodations provides current contact information and information for campsites, hotels and motels, resorts, bed and breakfast, condominiums, and private homes.

The booklet provides contact information for Lake Chelan attractions and shows their location on a map so they are easy to find. Separate maps show a wine tour for 23 winery and tasting rooms, boat launch sites, and winter and summer trails for hiking, biking, and snowmobiling.

Visitors may want to pick up a copy of this booklet at the chamber's Visitor Information Center, 216 E Woodin Avenue in Chelan, during their visit. It is a glossy color publication, full of Lake Chelan photos, suitable for coffee table display.

Man of the Year

Nor the demons down under the sea
Can ever dissever my soul from the soul
Of the beautiful Annabel Lee.
                              Edgar Allan Poe

Ted Norris's Learjet coasted to a stop at the Spokane International Airport in the middle of a fierce March rainstorm. Ted and Jerome were the only passengers.

They hurried through the terminal. Jerome carried Ted's briefcase and suitcase toward a limousine waiting just outside the front door. He cleared a path toward the exit and blocked reporters and film crews covering Ted's arrival for the evening news.

Ted ignored the reporter's questions. They already knew he was returning to Spokane to receive the Man of the Year award from the university where he earned a degree twenty years earlier. His other reason for returning for the first time since graduation was none of their business. They didn't need to know he was returning to settle an old score.

The pilot and copilot would have Ted's plane ready for the flight back to San Jose in a few hours. He planned to be back in his office at six in the morning, conducting business as usual at Norris International.

His twenty years at the helm, working sixteen hours every day, had made the startup business one of the nation's most successful computer software companies. Dedication to always honoring commitments had made him, the company's sole owner, a multimillionaire.

The limousine driver stopped in front of the newly refurbished Davenport Hotel in downtown Spokane where the manager and a bellhop waited at curbside to escort Ted to an executive suite.

When Ted stepped out of the shower a few minutes later, Jerome said, "Everything is ready, Mr. Norris, Your clothes are on the bed. I renewed the polish on your dress shoes."

"Limo waiting?"

"Yes, sir."

Ted dressed in the clothes Jerome had laid out for him, brushed his graying hair, and started for the door.

Jerome followed him to the elevator with the briefcase, assuming they would drive to the steakhouse where he had made a reservation for dinner.

As Jerome entered the limousine, Ted surprised him.

"Know the town?" Ted asked the driver.

"Of course, sir. Take you anyplace."

"Drive to 241 Emerson Street, just off Division."

"Know the street," he said, sounding peeved by Ted's hint regarding the street's location.

Jerome glanced at Ted, surprised. Making arrangements had been his responsibility for the last ten years. His employer rarely bypassed him.

Ted didn't explain the reason for the detour, or that accepting the Man of the Year award provided a legitimate reason for his trip to Spokane. Now he could take care of some private business.

He had let her betrayal fester for twenty years.

Now it was payback time.

Ted recognized the house at 241 Emerson Street when the driver parked parallel to the crumbling sidewalk. The house looked much older now. Paint peeled from clapboard siding. Missing shingles exposed bare wood. The yard was mostly weeds, surrounded by overgrown shrubs.

Jerome slouched down in his seat, embarrassed. The limousine looked out of place on a street crowded with ten-year-old cars and dirty pickups.

"Wait here," Ted said. He stepped out of the vehicle to walk to the front door, following the only lead he had to find Katie Ferguson, his college sweetheart.

They were in love, bound for eternity, they had agreed, before he left town after graduation to join the startup company he would own within weeks. She stayed in Spokane to finish her degree before their wedding.

He received the letter that destroyed his life a month later. According to the letter, she had eloped with her high school boyfriend,

He didn't know her married name. With no leads to her current location, he had no choice but to start his search for Katie at her mother's house, knowing her mother never liked him. She had just cause, he reasoned.

Katie had dropped out of school for a year to work to support him after his father's business failed in Chelan, ending his financial support. Her mother objected, claiming he would dump Katie after he graduated and no longer needed her.

He knew several husbands who filed for divorce after their wives worked to put them through school, so he understood her concern. Her anxiety amused him at the time, however, because he loved Katie. He wanted her at his side for eternity. It never occurred to him that Katie might dump him.

Now he was determined to find Katie and make her pay for her treachery. He had riches and fame, but he could never again experience love after her betrayal. They were committed for eternity. They had agreed.

He was still committed.

Ted's knuckles were sore from knocking on the weathered door before footsteps sounded from inside. He took a deep breath, preparing to face her mother's wrath.

The woman who answered the door looked as old and worn out as the house. She held a water glass full of an amber colored liquid. Nauseous whisky fumes escaped out the open door, surrounding him, stinging his nose.

Her slouched posture and loosely tied housecoat suggested this wasn't her first alcoholic beverage of the day. She stared blankly at him as he waited on the uncovered porch with rain pelting his bare head.

She wasn't Katie's mother.

"I'm looking for Katie," he said. "Her name was Katie Ferguson when I knew her. Don't know her married name. Her mother lived here twenty years ago."

The woman gasped, dropped the glass, and weaved as she started to slump to the floor.

Ted caught her just in time to keep her from doing a nosedive. She collapsed into his arms as he maneuvered her to a recliner.

She sank into the cushions, staring up at him, wide-eyed.

"Didn't mean to startle you," he said. "You all right?"

"No! Ain't nothing all right," she said, slurring the words. She paused a few moments to straighten her housecoat and run a hand through tangled hair before she continued.

"Remember you. Ted Norris, Katie's boyfriend. Don't remember me, do you?"

"I expected to find Mrs. Ferguson, Katie's mother, here," he said.

"Passed away two years ago. I'm Molly, Katie's sister."

He had to think for a moment before he could remember her. She was ten years older than Katie.

"Do you know where I can find Katie?"

"Refill the glass you made me spill, a touch of water for mixer, and I'll tell you. Bottle is on the kitchen counter. Help yourself. Glasses under the counter."

Ted wanted to scream at her. He didn't have much time. Her stubborn demeanor told him that she wouldn't talk until she had a drink in her hand, however. He quickly mixed a whiskey and water, heavy on the water.

He didn't mix one for himself. His busy schedule during the last twenty years allowed no time to acquire divertive habits.

"Well...?" he said, clearing his throat impatiently after he handed her the glass.

She guzzled half of the liquid before she spoke.

"Mother told me what happened. She regretted interfering."

He knew Katie's mother never liked him, but had no idea what Molly was trying to tell him.

"I don't understand," he said, trying to keep her talking. He believed she might sink into an alcohol-induced stupor at any moment.

"You'll understand if you look at some letters. They're in a box in the cabinet under the clock. You can read them if you'll get them for me. I'm a bit unsteady on my feet this time of day."

There was only one box in the cabinet, a shoebox. He set it on her lap.

She removed the lid, looked at the contents for a moment, and retrieved six letters bound with a rubber band.

"Look at these," she said.

The aged rubber band broke when he removed it. He recognized the letters immediately. They had Katie's name and address on them in his handwriting. He had written his Denver return address in the upper corner.

Katie hadn't opened the envelopes.

He glanced at the dates on the postmarks. They were the letters he wrote to Katie before she sent the rejection letter telling him she was married, and she never wanted to see him again.

"She never opened my letters," he said, hearing surprise and disappointment in his voice.

"She never got your letters."

"That's not possible."

"You underestimated my mother. She intercepted your letters," Molly said. She handed him a second bundle of letters before he could respond. There were over a dozen letters in this bunch.

The letters had his Denver address on them. He recognized Katie's handwriting. There were no postmarks on the letters, causing him to stare at them for a moment, confused.

"Have you figured out what happened?" Molly asked, before she took another long sip from the glass.

Realization came slowly as he stared at the letters in shock.

"Your mother retrieved the letters from the mailbox on your porch before the mailman arrived?"

"Lucky guess," she said, with a silly giggle. She raised the glass to her lips again. The glass was empty, but she didn't seem to notice.

"I don't understand why she wrote these letters after writing to say she was married, and she never wanted to see me again."

"Did she write the letter you received or type it?" Molly asked.

"Oh my, Lord! Are you saying she didn't write the letter?"

"Mom assumed you'd break Katie's heart by dumping her after you left town. She thought she was protecting Katie. She typed the letter, and apparently, you never realized it wasn't from Katie.

"Mom regretted sending the letter almost immediately, but it was too late then."

"What do you mean, it was too late?"

"Katie needed you. Quit school. Went to Denver to marry you. Your apartment was empty. The business where you worked had vanished. She couldn't find you."

She might not have been able to find him, he realized. The business declared bankruptcy within days after he received the rejection letter. The owner signed the business over to him when he agreed to assume all debts as payment-in-full for ownership. He immediately moved the business to the Silicon Valley near San Jose and changed its name to Norris International.

"Do I understand correctly?" he said. "Your mother sent the rejection letter I received. Katie didn't know about the letter, and she didn't elope with her high school boyfriend."

"Katie never had a boyfriend in high school. You're the only one she ever loved. Said you promised each other eternal love. You were bound for eternity. Then you abandoned her when she desperately needed you."

"I didn't abandon her."

"Need a refill. Bathroom stop," she said. "Read the letters. Then you'll understand. She had no way of knowing you didn't get them."

Molly disappeared for several minutes, giving him time to read the letters.

Now he realized why Katie traveled to Denver to marry him. He could feel her anguish as he read her words. Tears streamed down his cheeks for the first time since he read the rejection letter nearly twenty years earlier.

When Molly returned, she handed him a water glass before she sat down with her drink.

He sipped the foul smelling liquid without thinking about it.

The possibility that Katie could be pregnant when he left town had never occurred to him. He rubbed his eyes to clear his vision as he looked at Molly.

She anticipated his question.

"A boy," she said. "A healthy baby boy delivered eight months after you left town."

Emotions continued to overwhelm him. He had to find Katie. Needed to explain, if it wasn't too late.

"Has Katie married?"

"Said you're the only one she ever loved."

"Is the boy with her?"

"No, he has lived here with me since mother passed. He won't be home until late tonight."

"What did Katie name him?"

"Named him Ted Norris, after his father."

"Can I meet him in the next hour?"

"You'll meet him soon enough, if you're who I think you are."

"I don't understand. You know who I am."

"I know you're Ted Norris, but it just occurred to me you might be the famous Norris who owns Norris International."

"Yes. I own it."

"I have your programs on my computer. Never connected the name with you."

"What does that have to do with me meeting my son?"

"Two things," she said. "You're here to receive the Man of the Year award. Your son is sophomore class president at the university. If you'd read a program, you'd know he's making the award presentation tonight."

"And...?" he asked, after she paused with her eyes downcast.

"And he hates you. Mother told him you abandoned him and his mother. He promised to find you someday and make you pay."

"Didn't Katie tell him the truth?"

"Katie never knew the truth. She believed you abandoned her when she didn't get any letters and couldn't find you in Denver. Our mother raised Ted and filled him with hate toward you."

"Why did your mother raise him? Where's Katie?" he asked, embarrassed by the shrillness of his voice.

"Katie waited two years. Cried every day. When it was obvious you weren't coming back, she left us. Mom found the note. Gibberish. About loving you for eternity and such."

"Where'd she go?"

"Downtown. In March. Eighteen years ago during the flood season."

Molly stopped for a moment to take a deep breath and wipe away tears before she could continue.

"She jumped off the Monroe Street Bridge. Never

found her body."

Jerome gasped in alarm when Ted staggered from the house, looking like someone had kicked him in the gut. He had never before seen his boss cry.

"Find a park with a picnic table," Ted sobbed, embarrassed, but unable to control his grief.

Jerome relayed the message to the limousine driver.

The driver jerked the vehicle away from the curb to speed toward the nearest public park with picnic facilities. He parked next to the curb at Franklin Park on North Division Street.

Jerome watched solemnly as Ted took the briefcase from his lap.

Ted walked to a picnic table with a cover that shed the persistent, March downpour. He spent half an hour writing several pages on a legal sized notepad. When he was satisfied the letter to his attorney would explain his actions and the document he wrote would correct, financially at least, the injustice his abandonment had visited upon his son, he signaled for Jerome to join him.

As Jerome approached, he said, "Bring the driver."

The driver reluctantly departed the limousine to join them under the shelter at the picnic table.

"I've hand-written a legal document that requires signatures from two witnesses, verifying I signed it in front of them."

Ted signed and printed his name.

"Please sign and print your names and addresses."

When they finished, he placed the document in an envelope and sealed it. He wrote his attorney's name on the front of the envelope. As they entered the limousine, he handed the briefcase containing the envelope to Jerome.

"To the Monroe Street Bridge," he said, loud enough for the driver to hear him.

"That isn't the shortest route to the university," Jerome protested.

"Stop for a moment in the middle of the bridge," Ted added.

"It's nearly time for the award presentation." Jerome said.

"I'm going to get out when the driver stops on the bridge. I have some unfinished business to attend to while I'm in town. You're to go directly to the airport and return to San Jose. Deliver the document we just signed to my attorney when you arrive. Get him out of bed, if necessary."

"I can't leave you standing on a bridge, sir. You'll be late for the presentation, and it's raining harder now. The rain will ruin your suit."

"I'll be in good hands, Jerome," he said, as the driver stopped the vehicle in the middle of the bridge.

"I'm going to join someone I haven't seen in twenty years."

"But, Mr. Norris," Jerome protested, as Ted stepped out of the vehicle into a cloudburst.

Ted's attorney was waiting at the airport when Jerome arrived in San Jose. He had already heard the news.

Jerome told him Spokane Falls was nearly invisible from the Monroe Street Bridge when Ted stepped out of the limousine. Floodwater from the Spokane River poured over the falls, crushing floating logs and anything else in the water.

A jogger, crossing the bridge in the storm, was the only one who heard a man crying.

"Bound for eternity, Katie. We agreed," she heard the man sob, as he stepped to the rail.

Killing Rats at Silvia's Diner

Brian looked up from the stack of invoices on his desk when Jolene jerked his office door open at three in the afternoon at Silvia's Diner, a five star restaurant overlooking Lake Chelan.

"Hate to interrupt you Mr. Rat Killer. A man at table eleven insists on talking to the boss."

"Please. Tell me you didn't spill hot coffee on him."

"No sir. I didn't, but you might wish I'd dumped the whole pot on him when you see his friend."

Brian mumbled, "Nuts!" as he stood up.

He wanted to work in his office all day to complete the business records his attorney needed. Three months had passed since a car crash killed his father and stepmother, and he and his attorney were still dealing with legal and business problems created by his father's failure to write a will.

Jolene's concerned expression told him he must look as tired as he felt. He wasn't surprised since he had worked on estate issues with his attorney most of the previous night.

He ran a hand through hair too gray for a fifty-year-old and rubbed his red eyes. Then he walked out to meet two men seated at table eleven. He hoped they hadn't heard Jolene call him Mr. Rat Killer, a name his employees gave him due to his persistent war on rats behind the restaurant.

An older man, short and obese, held a coffee cup in a manicured hand protruding from the sleeve of an expensive suit jacket. His cuff links had more diamonds than most wedding rings.

The second man sipped a Coke. He resembled the

winos sleeping by the dumpster behind the restaurant, but he wasn't one of the local winos. Brian would remember someone with a tattoo of a rat on his forehead.

"I'm Brian Toomey," he said as he approached the table. "You asked to speak with me?"

"We have important business to discuss," said the man in the suit. He handed Brian a business card.

"I'm Clark Kola, attorney. My client here is Jason Amman."

"Rat," the second man shouted. "People call me Rat. No one's called me Jason since I was a little boy."

Brian could see the man looked to be fifty or older. The first name, Jason or Rat, didn't mean anything to him, but he recognized the last name. His stepmother's name was Amman before she married his father.

"Was Carol Amman your mother?" Brian asked, as he watched Jason twitch and jerk so much he spilled the Coke down the front of his dirty tee shirt. Needle marks and scar tissue were visible along the veins on both arms.

Before Jason could answer, Kola said, "That's what I'm here to discuss with you. May I suggest you and I move to your office, so we can discuss this matter privately?"

"Sure, but what about Jason?"

"Rat," Jason mumbled, as he pulled the wet shirt away from his decimated body.

"I speak for him. There's no reason for him to be there," the attorney said.

"Jolene, please bring Jason a bar towel, another Coke, and a hamburger with a side of fries," Brian said, as he pointed the attorney toward the office.

Jolene turned her head, rolled her eyes, and stomped toward the kitchen. "Stray puppies and kittens and now he's going to feed Rat," she mumbled.

When they entered the office, Brian sat behind his

desk. "What can I do for you?"

"I'm here to discuss your father," Kola said, after he sat down. "The coroner's report says your father died on impact when a delivery truck failed to stop for a stop sign."

"If you're here to ask me to sue the truck driver, forget it," Brian said. "He drove past the stop sign because he was having a heart attack."

"That isn't the reason I'm here. I already have a client. Are you aware your father didn't have a will?"

Brian was certainly aware his father didn't write a will. His father conducted business with a handshake, avoiding legal documents to any extent possible.

"He didn't feel he needed a will because I'm an only child," Brian said. "I've managed this restaurant and my father's other interests for the last ten years since my mother passed away."

"I'm guessing your mother's name was Silvia."

"Dad used Mother's name for the business. They ran it together when I was growing up. Dad was too broken up to manage the business after cancer took her, so he turned everything over to me."

"Then your father married Carol Amman."

"Not until eight years after Mother passed away. Carol lost her husband twenty years ago. She was a very nice person."

"I'm guessing your father didn't have Carol sign a prenuptial agreement," Kola said.

"He'd have considered such a request an insult."

"Do you know when Carol died?"

"Two days after the collision, in the hospital in Wenatchee."

"So, she died after your father died."

"Sat with her for two days, but doctors couldn't save her. She never regained consciousness."

"In that case, you must realize why I'm here?"

"I have no idea why you're here."

"Washington State is a community property state. Your father died without a written will or a prenuptial agreement, so his wife, Carol, inherited all of his assets. When Carol died two days later, her assets passed to her only heir. Rat is her only heir.

"I'm here to serve legal notice that Rat owns this restaurant, your father's condominium in Hawaii, all bank accounts, stocks, bonds, and your father's lakeshore home here in Chelan where you're living. You have thirty days to vacate the family home and this restaurant and turn everything else over to Rat."

Brian glared at the attorney, stunned. He had experience dealing with adversity at the restaurant, but never encountered anything of this magnitude. He realized he needed time to collect his thoughts before he reacted.

"I need to finish some important business before we continue," he said. "It will only take a few minutes. I'll have Jolene move you and Jason to the cocktail lounge where you'll be more comfortable. Jolene will provide any drinks you might like."

Brian noticed the attorney tried to suppress a smile when he heard drinks were on the house.

As Jolene escorted Kola and Jason to the lounge, Brian called Jack Wilson, his attorney.

He assumed the information Kola gave about the law was true, but he needed to know more about the attorney to decide how he should handle the situation.

When Jack answered his call, Brian said, "I have an attorney inquiring about Dad's accident. His name is Clark Kola. Do you know him?"

"Every attorney in the state knows Kola," Jack replied. "Law school professors use him as an example when they give lectures on ethics. His office is in Seattle, but he has subordinates studying files in courthouses all over the state. They look for evidence to use to sue people or blackmail them. He spends most of his time fighting disbarment proceedings."

"You're telling me he's a crook?"

"He's a crook wearing an expensive suit purchased with money stolen from widows' trust accounts. Get rid of him."

"Thanks Jack, I'll get rid of him and check with you later. Thanks again for helping me last night."

Brian's second call was to Scott Flanagan, a good friend. Scott was also a deputy sheriff. Brian called him when he needed to remove an obnoxious drunk from the lounge or a belligerent customer from the diner.

"Scott, I was in a pinch for a dishwasher this morning, so I hired a guy off the street," Brian said. "I thought I should check him out because his appearance is rather bizarre. Do you know a man named Jason Amman?"

"Rat! You're talking about Rat Amman, with a tattoo of a rat on his forehead. Every law enforcement officer in the state knows him."

"Well, I guess you do know him. Fortunately, our customers never see our dishwasher because he works in the kitchen."

"You put him in the kitchen where you can't see what he's doing! You messed up big time, Brian. He could be poisoning the food in your kitchen as we speak. His addiction makes him unpredictable."

"You sound serious."

"I am serious. He'll do anything to get back in prison. It's the only way he can get off drugs."

"You're scaring me. I'll get rid of him and check back with you later."

Jolene ran into the office as Brian hung up the phone.

"You need to do something quick," she shouted. "Sally just slapped the fat man, and his friend has passed out on the floor."

Brian didn't need to ask what had happened. He knew Sally would joke and banter with her customers in the cocktail lounge, but touching her inappropriately would bring immediate physical retaliation.

"How drunk is he?" he asked.

"Straight shots, doubles, as fast as Sally could set them up."

"What about the other one."

"He only drinks Coke. He went into the restroom. Two minutes later, he fell off his chair. I had the dishwasher check the bathroom for needles. He didn't find anything, so he must've swallowed or snorted something powerful."

"Oh, great! Have they disturbed our paying customers?"

"I put them at a table in the back corner, so no one has noticed them. I just hope a state liquor inspector doesn't pick today for an inspection."

"Send the drunk in here, and have someone move Jason into the kitchen out of sight."

Kola gripped a drink firmly in his fat fist as he stomped into Brian's office. He sat down, smirking confidently despite the red spot on his cheek.

"This is a nice restaurant and lounge with a beautiful view of Lake Chelan and the mountains, but you need to do something about your employee's manners."

Unlike Kola, Brian was thinking about all of his employees. Most of them had worked at the restaurant for many years. He was still absorbed in thought when the attorney spoke again.

"Your father reasonably expected you would inherit this business and his other assets, but the law is the law. I'm legally obligated to represent my client's interests. This mess could've been avoided if I'd been your father's attorney."

"I don't claim to understand the law," Brian said,

"but it's obvious your client is not able to manage this business, and twenty-six people are going to join the unemployed ranks if he tries."

"Having people lose their jobs would be a shame, but that seems likely given Rat's unfortunate condition," Kola said. "Fortunately, you're in a position to save your employees' jobs for them."

Brian frowned. "Keep talking," he said, realizing the anticipated shakedown was about to begin.

"You're a good manager. You were able to pay your father a very generous retirement income for the last ten years from profits here at the restaurant. Since I'm ready to retire, I have a simple proposal that will make this problem go away.

"I suggest you employ me as your attorney-of-record. That will obligate me to represent your interests rather than Rat's. As payment, I'll live in your father's Hawaii condominium and receive half of the amount you paid him each month. You can give yourself a raise with the other half. We'll both be winners if you follow my advice."

"What about Jason?"

"Rat's completely addled by drugs. He doesn't know why my driver brought him here today, and he won't remember being here. He'll do something stupid in the next couple of days to end up in jail again. The arrangement I'm proposing will be just between the two of us. We need to come to an agreement right now, so I can have my driver dump Rat back in the rat infested alley in Seattle where my aides found him."

Brian smiled, knowing now what he had to do to make the problem go away. He nodded his head to let Kola know he understood his terms.

"I'll have Jolene order dinner for you in the lounge while I make final arrangements for you."

"Sounds good to me," Kola said, with a smug smile.

Brian realized he wasn't a first class chef, but he had worked in the restaurant since he was a teenager. He knew his way around the kitchen.

He decided this would be a good time to give his chef and the kitchen staff an hour break, so he could personally prepare a special dinner for the attorney.

Kola quickly downed several free doubles while he waited for dinner. He could barely hold his head up when Jolene delivered a large platter heaped with an especially prepared fettuccine alfredo.

The intoxicated attorney eagerly wolfed down every bite of the meal.

The volunteer ambulance crew stopped working on the man on the floor when a doctor, a frequent customer at the restaurant, pronounced him dead.

The other man on the floor hadn't moved from his fetal position, so the ambulance crew rushed him to the hospital.

Brian waited to call his attorney until the city police and Deputy Flanagan arrived.

"Jack, I just messed up big time," Brian said, when his attorney answered his call.

"I hired a temporary dishwasher today, and he poisoned one of my customers."

"Is the customer dead?"

"Oh, yeah. He's as dead as the rats in my dumpster."

"Are the police there?"

"The city police have secured the scene. Deputy Flanagan is standing outside my office door, waiting to talk to me. I feel awful about hiring this dishwasher. He found the poison I use to kill rats in the alley. Apparently, he dumped most of the powder in a customer's fettuccine alfredo. Then he spilled the rest of it on his own shirt and pants."

"I'm on my way. Don't talk to Flanagan until I get

there. Did you get rid of Kola, like I told you?"

"Yeah, I made that problem go away," Brian said, as he hung up the phone.

Deputy Flanagan walked into the office when Brian opened the door.

"I told you to get rid of Rat before he did something stupid," he said, angrily.

"I know what you told me," Brian said. "Jack told me not to talk to you, but you already know this is my fault, so I'm not going to hide behind my attorney. I had an emergency and forgot about Jason. I'll have Jack represent him in court, and I'll make sure he gets medical help and support for his addiction. Do you mind waiting until Jack gets here before you question Jason?"

"I don't have any choice. They couldn't wake him up before they rushed him to the hospital. He's full of dope. Don't know what kind. He probably won't remember what he did."

"That seems likely," said Brian, shaking his head sadly.

"No harm, no foul, I guess," the deputy said. "Rat will be happy in a warm jail cell with free meals and a cot."

"Definitely. No harm, no foul," Brian agreed, thinking his employees would get to keep their jobs and Jason would finally get the help he needed. Now he could finish the business records he needed to update so his attorney could untangle the mess created by his father's failure to write a will.

Pleasant Memories

Manson looks very different today than it did when I lived on an orchard at the south end of Roses Lake over seventy years ago. Manson was a block long with wood sidewalks in front of most of the stores. Manson Community Hall at the end of the business district hosted civic events, dances, and served as a school gym.

Most farmhouses were small by today's standards. Our home for my parents and three boys had a kitchen, living room, and one bedroom. Dad built a larger house after Mom surprised us with a little sister. Orchard cabins for seasonal workers had one or two rooms.

Our water came from a cistern filled with irrigation water during the summer. The cistern, with a hand pump on it, was in front of the house near the cellar where we kept our icebox. The outhouse was behind the house.

We walked to school, to town, and to our friends' houses to play. The community supported many youth activities, including 4-H and a Boy Scout troop that provided valuable life lessons and experiences.

We swam, fished, and camped at Wapato Point, Wapato Lake, and Willow Point. We hiked along roads looking for bottles we could sell for two cents, and collected newspapers to finance our adventures.

I don't recall ever hearing friends say they were bored. We were products of a generation of adults working from 'can see' to 'can't see'. We were too busy to be bored.

Photo: Roses Lake near Manson, surrounded by orchards and vineyards, with Slide Ridge in the background.

Blood Brothers

Nihil boni sine labore.

Alan and the other six-to-nine boys were pulling weeds in the garden the day Sister Mary brought the new boy to St. James in Fresno, California. They stopped to watch her car pass with the boy in the front seat.

"New kid looks mad. Might be my age, maybe eight," one of the boys said.

"He's carrying a paper sack," someone said, when the boy stepped out of the car.

Lucky kid, Alan thought. *That's more than I had when I arrived.* He was just guessing, of course, since he had no memory of his arrival. He had been too young to remember—didn't even know his name.

"Found you in an alley behind a restaurant in Stockton, eating out of their slop bucket," Sister Mary told him when he was old enough to ask.

Sister Mary gave him a home at St. James. A judge gave him a name—Alan Perez. They couldn't give him a friend, however. Not someone he would trust with his life. Not until the day the new boy arrived.

Alan watched the boy follow Sister Mary toward a door that had *Nihil boni sine labore* engraved above it. She stopped at the door and turned to summon Alan from the garden.

Alan glanced at the inscription above the door as he followed Sister Mary and the new boy inside. He knew the Latin words said *nothing good achieved without hard work*. The sisters made sure every boy understood hard work was their ticket to a successful future when they were old enough to leave the orphanage.

"This is Mike Martinez," Sister Mary said. "Mike's

going to live with us. Please take him to the dormitory, and find a bed for him."

Alan could see the new boy was slim, looked under-nourished—had an overgrown crop of black hair. *Sisters will get rid of the long hair first thing. Lice control!* Then he noticed the only thing that set the two of them apart in appearance. Mike had green eyes, unlike his, which were dark brown.

He hesitated for a moment as he tried to decide which of the three empty bunks he would give Mike in the dormitory for six-to-nine boys. Up close, he could see Mike looked nervous rather than mad. *Of course he's nervous, coming to a place like this. Got a black eye and scuffed knuckles. Good! Might fight the older boys when they torment us.*

"You a fighter?"

"Want to try me?" Mike asked, as he squared himself into a fighting pose.

"You can have this bunk, next to mine," Alan said, pointing at a single, metal-frame bed with a thin cotton mattress rolled up on one end.

Mike adjusted the mattress to fit the bed. He sat down, removed a large bible from his paper sack, and placed it on the stand beside the bed. He dumped the rest of his worldly possessions, dirty socks and underwear, onto the floor.

"You an orphan?" Alan asked.

"Got an uncle. Don't want me," Mike replied. "You?"

"Don't know," Alan said.

"Any friends?"

"Just one. You," Alan replied, with a broad grin.

And they were—immediately. Two against the world. Inseparable.

Six months later, they became blood brothers after they watched an old western movie in the dining hall. Each of them cut a finger with a sharp knife *borrowed* from the kitchen and mixed their blood together, imitating the fake Indian and mountain man in the movie.

During the next ten years at the orphanage, they were always together, protecting each other. Then they joined the army and served in Korea until '52 when the army released them from a military hospital with Purple Hearts.

They followed the harvest from California to Washington State for the next seven years using the skills they had learned working on farms in the San Joaquin Valley while they were teenagers at St. James.

They kept in contact with Sister Mary and used the orphanage as their mailing address. They spent winters working close to Fresno where they could visit the only home they had ever known, and Sister Mary, the closest thing to a mother either of them could remember.

Alan and Mike returned to an orchard near Yakima, Washington in the fall of '59 to pick apples. They had become very proficient at picking fruit, so the size of the paychecks they received at the end of the workday on Saturday didn't surprise them.

They followed their usual Saturday-night routine. Mike started a fire in the wood-burning stove in their orchard cabin while Alan retrieved the number-two washtub they kept in the back of their pickup. He placed the tub on top of the stove and filled it half-full of water.

After the water heated, they placed the tub on the floor to take their weekly bath—each in turn with fresh water. Then they dressed in their Saturday night clothes and drove *Sweetheart,* their pickup, to town. The vehicle was so named because it was the closest thing to a sweetheart either of them had ever had.

Mike called Sister Mary to give her their current address, so she could send accumulated mail to the orchard where they were working. Alan found a mailbox to deposit a letter addressed to a bank in Fresno. The envelope contained their paychecks, one attached to a deposit slip for their joint checking account and one attached to a deposit slip for their joint savings account.

"Ketchup with your fries?" the cute waitress asked when they stopped at a restaurant to enjoy the first meal they hadn't cooked themselves in a week. "Mustard on my hamburger," Mike said. "Drown it." Satisfied after a leisurely supper, they walked to a nearby tavern for a couple of beers to complete the evening.

"Even more people here tonight than last Saturday night," Mike said, as he followed Alan to a table in a back corner.

The music from a jukebox was turned to full volume to compete with conversation in the crowded bar. Drinkers reacted by talking louder.

"A pitcher of beer," Alan shouted to augment the hand signals he used to place an order with a barmaid.

More people arrived. No one left. Two women ended up at Alan and Mike's table when they couldn't find a table by themselves.

"We must look harmless," Mike commented, so only Alan could hear him.

We are harmless, Alan thought. He noticed the women were likely in their late thirties, possibly older. They were the usual sort of women they encountered in bars where migrant workers were welcomed. He glanced at the crude markings on their fingers and arms. *Prison tattoos!*

The women ordered Rainer and introduced themselves.

"I'm Irene," said the woman in a bright red outfit.

"And I'm Ellen," said the woman wearing a blue dress.

Alan didn't hear their names clearly due to the noise. *Irene, maybe, and Helen or Ellen?* He noticed the woman in red moved her chair closer to Mike after she loudly proclaimed, "I like husky men with green eyes."

He wasn't sure why the woman in blue moved her chair closer to him. *Maybe she likes husky men with brown eyes.* He ignored her as best he could. He would admit to being shy around women. Growing up in a boy's orphanage hadn't prepared him for idle conversation with females. Except nuns, of course. Then he got his knuckles smacked with a ruler if he didn't watch his mouth.

Mike frequently teased him about his shyness. "You'll never find a sweetheart with more teeth then tattoos," he would laugh.

Alan believed he might be right. *Someday, maybe. After we save enough to get our own place. Then a sweetheart might give me a second look.*

Mike ordered another pitcher of beer and refilled all four glasses. The women giggled. Friendly now. Chatty.

Alan still couldn't understand most of what the woman in blue said to him, but what he could hear let him know what she had in mind. He shook his head to let her know he wasn't interested.

She pouted and tried again by placing her hand on his leg as she moved even closer.

The woman in red led Mike to the dance floor when *Your Cheating Heart*, Hank William's popular '52 hit, started playing on the jukebox.

Alan snickered, knowing Mike couldn't dance any better than he could.

As Mike and the woman stumbled around the dance floor, Alan filled the four glasses to empty the pitcher.

A barmaid rushed to the table to offer a refill.

"We're done," he told her.

She grabbed the empty pitcher and picked up the fifty cents change Mike had left on the table, glaring a challenge at Alan as she dropped the money into her pocket.

He shrugged. *Easy come, easy go.*

"I'm going home," the woman in blue said, angrily.

Alan ignored her. It was time to go home, but not to where she had suggested. He had a bed waiting for him in the orchard cabin—a single bed.

Mike seemed to notice the mood when he returned to the table. He quietly finished his drink, making it obvious he was ready to leave.

During the next pause between songs, the woman in red said, "Can you escort us to our car? Rough looking crowd tonight. Don't want anyone following us."

Her request surprised Alan. *She looks tough enough to handle drunk harvest workers—or bench press a buffalo.*

Nonetheless, the woman in red gripped Mike's arm tightly as they walked toward the door to leave.

Alan noticed the woman in blue lagged behind, ignoring him, as he followed Mike and the other woman out the door.

The cool night air had just hit Alan in the face when the woman in red screamed.

"Oh no! My husband," she shrieked, as she released her grip on Mike's arm.

Then shots rang out. Rapid fire. Six shots.

Both women screamed and ran toward the dark parking lot—gone.

The masked shooter turned and ran around the corner—gone.

Mike was down on the sidewalk, bleeding—going nowhere.

Alan spent Saturday night and all day Sunday at Mike's bedside in the hospital, listening to him moan painfully on the few occasions when he regained consciousness.

The doctor's report was discouraging. "Your friend

has three bullet wounds," he told Alan. "Two bullets passed through soft tissue, leaving nasty exit wounds. The third bullet lodged in bone dangerously close to his spinal cord, paralyzing his lower limbs. I need to deal with the flesh wounds before a surgeon can remove the bullet. Your friend will survive, but it'll take up to a year of physical therapy after surgery for him to walk again."

Alan returned to work Monday morning and visited Mike every evening. Two weeks after the shooting, the orchardist gave him a package from Sister Mary along with his paycheck.

Alan took the package with him when he visited Mike that evening. He found Mike was more alert now, although he still looked terrible and received pain medication through a drip tube.

"The doctor explained my medical situation," Mike said. "They're going to remove the bullet Wednesday morning. But I still don't know why someone shot me. What happened?"

"I'm not sure," Alan replied. "The woman in red indicated her husband was the shooter, but he wore a mask. Don't know how she knew it was her husband. He used a revolver, so there were no shell casings at the scene. People in the bar won't admit they know the two women. The police don't have any evidence and don't seem very interested."

After they discussed the shooting, Alan opened the package from Sister Mary and removed several envelopes. He read aloud the letter she addressed to the two of them.

"I'm praying for you. You need to be good boys, and remember to say your prayers."

"She thinks we're still in the six-to-nine dorm," Mike interrupted, clinching his teeth in pain when he tried to chuckle.

"She loves us," Alan said.

"Yes... she does."

Alan finished reading Sister Mary's long letter before he looked at the other envelopes. He set their monthly bank statement aside and inspected two letters addressed to Mike. One letter had a return address for a law firm in Chelan, Washington. The second letter was also from Chelan.

He showed Mike the letters. "You expecting a letter from a lawyer?"

"Probably an ambulance chaser," Mike grumbled. "They're quick. Smells a fee suing the bum that shot me."

"If they ever find him!"

"Open it. Maybe he'll pay any medical bills the VA won't cover."

"That would be nice."

Alan opened the envelope and skimmed the contents, finding big words he couldn't pronounce.

"Know someone named Frank Martinez?"

"My uncle. He didn't want me," Mike said.

"How do you know?"

"Mrs. Sherman told me. She kicked me out of her foster home when he refused to take me or send money for my upkeep after my mother died."

"Ever meet him?"

"No. Wouldn't know him if he walked in here right now."

"Well, he won't. He's dead. Did you know he owned an orchard in Chelan?" Alan Asked.

"No. I've never heard anything from him."

"Well, you have now, through his lawyer. If I understand what all these big words mean, you'll inherit your uncle's orchard in Chelan if you take possession before the apple trees blossom next spring."

"You're kidding me!" Mike said.

"Here. You read it."

"Ya know I can't read any better than you can. That

wasn't exactly a finishing school the nuns conducted at St. James."

Alan looked at the second letter as Mike spoke. He opened it, curious to know why Mike would get two letters from Chelan at the same time.

"You want to read this?" Alan asked.

"You read it. My eyes are blurry from all the dope they're pumping into me."

"Yeah... right!"

Alan noticed someone had handwritten the letter in a very neat style, unlike what he would expect from a man identifying himself as Frank Martinez's orchard foreman. He read the letter from Luis Garcia twice, becoming more concerned as he did so.

"Ya look like you swallowed a dill pickle."

"Didn't tell you what the lawyer said would happen if you don't take possession of the orchard before apple blossom. Your uncle's stepson gets it."

"That only gives me five months to get there. The doctor said I'll need a year of physical therapy to walk again."

"You can't wait a year or even five months according to this letter from Luis Garcia. The stepson's already there, cutting trees for firewood as workers pick the apples. He told the foreman to leave when the pickers finish because he's going to remove all the trees to sell the property to a developer. Luis says there won't be any orchard for you to claim if you don't get there right now."

An elderly woman glanced up from her True Romance magazine when Alan walked into *Homer and Associates*, located in an old house on a Chelan side street.

It was three in the afternoon, Monday, two days after he and Mike read the letter from the attorney. They had talked all day Sunday at the hospital, trying to decide what they should do.

"I'm Mike Martinez," Alan said. "I need to speak with Mr. Homer."

He watched for a reaction as he self-consciously adjusted the green-tinted sunglasses he had purchased before he left Yakima. They were too large—wanted to slide down onto his nose.

"Mr. Homer's out of town. You should've called for an appointment," she said, after she marked her place in the magazine with a finger.

"Can I see an associate?"

"You're ten years too late. Mr. Homer doesn't have any associates. He'll be back in a few days. You'll have to wait."

"Can you give me directions to the orchard my uncle owned?"

"Oh, my!" she said, as her eyes widened. "Your name didn't register for a moment."

She closed the magazine to study him more closely. She frowned, bit her bottom lip for a moment, and hesitated before she spoke. "You're Mike Martinez, Frank's nephew?"

"Yes. Can you tell me how to find the orchard?"

She stared at him for several moments, looking him directly in the eyes.

He adjusted the sunglasses again, acting cool.

"Did you get a second letter?"

"From Luis Garcia. Same day I received the letter from Mr. Homer."

She took a deep breath as she continued studying him. Then, seemingly satisfied, she said, "Luis is a good man. He and his family have worked the orchard for many years."

"He said there are problems at the orchard."

"Young man, if you don't already know, Frank Martinez was a terrible man. He was a drunken, gambling, womanizing, felon. He won the property in a poker game twenty years ago. He never went to the orchard except to collect the profits from Luis once a year. Frank's stepson is harassing the Garcia family as we speak."

"That's why I'm in a hurry to get to the orchard."

"Frank's stepson, Lon Bormann, is a dangerous man. He'll hurt you if you go there."

"I'm going, just as soon as you give me directions."

"I hope you know what you're doing, young man. The orchard is easy to find, but you'll likely decide you don't want it after you inspect the trees and records. If you want it, you'll need an attorney to probate Frank's will and transfer the deed. There are several good attorneys in Chelan. Ask around."

"I assumed Mr. Homer would be my attorney."

"I said a good attorney. I wrote the letter you received from Mr. Homer. He is addicted to drinking, gambling, and chasing women just as Frank Martinez was."

Alan accepted the map she sketched on the back of an envelope and turned to leave. He said, "Thanks Mrs..."

"Mrs. Homer. My husband can't keep a secretary," she said, as she opened her True Romance magazine.

Alan stopped *Sweetheart* at the edge of the orchard, on a hillside overlooking Lake Chelan. A farmhouse, directly in front of him, faced the lake, the south shore, and Slide Ridge. He recognized the features from the map he and Mike studied at the nursing home. A machine shed and several orchard cabins lined the driveway beyond the farmhouse.

Several workers picked apples along the west side of the orchard. Someone had cut down several trees near the pickers. Tree limbs, with wilting leaves, surrounded naked stumps.

A tractor emerged from a row of trees as Alan watched. A spry looking man drove the tractor to a loading dock beside the machine shed.

After the driver stopped the tractor, Alan drove the pickup to the machine shed, parked, and stepped out to walk toward the loading dock. He adjusted his sunglasses again to get them up off his nose.

"I'm Mike Martinez," Alan said as the man stepped down from the tractor. "Are you Mr. Garcia?"

"Call me Luis," the man said with a smile. "I'm very pleased you've arrived. We've been very worried."

"That I wouldn't come?"

"That they would kill you before you could get here."

"Lon Bormann?"

"Yes, Mr. Martinez. He and his crazy friend."

"Call me Mike," Alan said with a smile. "I'd like to look at the orchard if this is a convenient time for you."

"Absolutely."

They spent the next two hours walking around the property. Alan viewed well-maintained equipment, and a well-managed, but outdated, orchard. Pickers had to use tall ladders on old, overgrown trees producing varieties that were no longer profitable.

"How large is this vacant field," Alan asked, as he sifted sandy soil thought his fingers and noticed the southern exposure and natural drainage.

"Forty acres with water rights. Never been planted."

As they passed orchard cabins, Luis introduced Sam. "He lives here," Luis said, without further comment. Sam looked older than dirt. He nodded his head at Alan and smiled. Didn't speak.

"Frank Martinez never wanted to live here, so he told me to use the farmhouse," Luis said. "I'll look for a place tonight, so you can move in."

"That's not necessary. All I have is what you see in the pickup. The empty cabin next to Sam's cabin will work just fine for me."

"You sure?"

"I need to look at orchard records before we consider

any changes."

"My wife will have supper ready in a half-hour. You're invited. My daughter wrote the letter you received, and she keeps the books for the orchard. She can show you the records after we eat."

"Thanks. I'll be there in a few minutes."

As Luis walked to the farmhouse, Alan drove *Sweetheart* to the empty cabin and packed his duffle bag inside. He displayed Mike's family bible and billfold on the table before he followed Luis.

Luis met him at the door and introduced his smiling wife, Isabel.

Alan removed his sunglasses as Isabel escorted him to a chair at the dining-room table.

"I'm Lorna," an attractive female said before her father could introduce her. She smiled brightly, seemingly as happy to meet him as her parents were.

Alan returned her smile—tried not to stare. *Beautiful smile and teeth. No tattoos. I'll tell Mike I've met an angel when I call him in the morning.*

Sam walked in as the women placed food on the table. He smiled at Alan—didn't say anything.

Lorna was the only one who talked during supper. "Harold wants to take me to a movie Friday night," she announced. "I don't know what to wear," she added, looking to her mother for help.

Alan felt a hint of jealousy. *Foolishness! Don't even know her. Probably has tattoos I can't see—dozens of them.*

It occurred to him, painfully, that he had never been on a date. Known women of course, from bars, but never actually dated a sweetheart. Not someone he would introduce to Sister Mary. *Someday!*

Sam nodded his thanks when he finished eating and stood up to leave. He looked at Alan for a moment and smiled again as he walked to the door.

"I know you want to look at the orchard records," Lorna said. "We can do that right now. I work the early shift in the office at Campbell's Resort, so I'll be gone most of tomorrow."

Alan nodded his head to agree and followed her into an office. They spent over an hour looking at production records, bank statements, and warehouse receipts. Then Lorna opened a promissory note signed by Frank Martinez, pledging the orchard as collateral for a bank loan.

"Frank needed money for nursing home care," she explained. "Orchard profits can pay this loan off, but it won't leave anything to work with for the next five years. We've been making a small profit here, but nothing like we would if my father had updated the orchard."

"Why didn't he?"

"Frank Martinez wouldn't allow it. He always needed money to pay his gambling debts, so he took all of the profit rather than putting some of it back into the orchard. Are you going to do the same thing?"

"A friend and I have worked hard to save money to have a place of our own someday. We'll never have a better opportunity than right here. We'll invest what's needed and work to develop this property to its full potential."

"What're you going to do?"

"The first thing I'll do is listen to your father. I think he'll suggest replacing old trees with more profitable varieties and planting grapes on the vacant land. We can plant alfalfa as a transitional cash crop."

"I've listened to Father say the same thing since I was a little girl. You two will work well together if you keep him as your foreman."

"I need his help to develop a long-range plan for this property and to implement it. We can start after I talk to a lawyer in the morning to settle legal issues."

Two men were waiting for Alan when he walked back

to his cabin after supper. One was standing on his doorstep and one was sitting on *Sweetheart's* tailgate. There was no mistaking their demeanor.

"Waiting for me?" Alan asked as he watched the belligerent looking man on the doorstep glare at him. No one had to tell him this was Lon Bormann. He was forty-five or older, dressed as a city dandy in a suit and tie that looked like fugitives from a disposal bin.

"Don't know what you think you're trying to pull here. I'm Lon Bormann, and I'm going to own this orchard. You best get down the road while you still have some hide on you."

"I'm Mike Martinez. I own this orchard according to my uncle's will. You're trespassing."

The bulldog-faced man sitting on the tailgate pulled a revolver from behind his back and pointed it at Alan. "Mike Martinez is dead. Shot him six times. Bang, bang... bang, bang... bang, bang!" he shouted to simulate shooting Alan six times.

"Shut up, Ben," Lon howled.

"Shot him six times. He's dead, like you wanted."

"Shut your mouth, you fool," Lon yelled, louder.

"You shot the wrong guy," Alan said.

"Did not! Shot the bum with green eyes with my cousin," Ben said, ignoring Lon's shouting.

"Your cousin wore the red dress?"

"That's right. She found the bum with green eyes for me, and I killed him."

"Your cousin drank too much. She didn't notice when my friend and I switched partners as we walked out the door. You killed the wrong guy."

"Take off those stupid looking sunglasses and show us you have green eyes," Lon demanded. "You ain't fooling us with Mike's billfold and bible in the cabin."

"Which one of you is tough enough to take the glasses off me?"

"Don't matter. Mike Martinez is dead. Ben opened his fool mouth and told you he killed him, so we need to take you for a ride."

Alan realized he would die if they forced him into their car. The fight would have to happen here where they couldn't shoot with possible witnesses in neighboring cabins. He stepped to one side to get a better angle, hoping he could disable one of them before the other one jumped on him. As he assumed a fighting pose, a loud blast startled him, causing him to jump as buckshot shredded Ben's fingers, causing the revolver he had been holding to fly through the air before it landed in the dirt.

Ben shrieked in pain as Sam stepped to Alan's side, holding a double-barreled shotgun.

Lon held his hands out as a shield, as if that would stop buckshot from cutting him in half. He backed away from Sam and the shotgun.

Ben turned to stagger toward their car, howling like a wounded coyote. He clamped his right hand under his left armpit to try to control the bleeding.

"Only one shot left, Lon. It has your name on it," Sam said in a raspy, smoker's voice.

"We'll be back," Lon stammered as he continued to back toward their car. "We'll take you along for the ride."

"No, you won't," Sam said. "I'll have slugs loaded next time and shoot the minute you cross Mike's property line. You have a five-minute head start before I can get to a phone to call the sheriff. Then every officer in the state will be looking for you for killing Mike's friend."

Alan and Sam watched as Lon ran toward their car, following Ben.

"Thanks, Sam. That wasn't going to turn out very well."

"No thanks needed. Frank Martinez let me live in a cabin here to protect his interests. That's what I'll do until someone tells me to leave."

"You just saved my bacon. That earned you cabin-rights for as long as I'm here."

"My cabin is a palace compared to the six-by-ten cell I shared with Frank at Walla Walla. I have the cabin all to myself, enough retirement income to pay Isabel to feed me, and I can step outside to enjoy the sunshine anytime I want."

"You heard what they said before you scared them off?"

"Didn't need to hear what they said. Already knew you weren't Mike Martinez. Frank always bragged about his pure Spanish ancestry. Claimed everyone in his family had green eyes. Your green-tinted sunglasses didn't fool Mrs. Homer. She called Luis before you could get here. You must have made a good impression on her because she suggested we should give you time to tell us what happened to Mike. She said I might need to help you get rid of Lon and his friend."

"I owe her and you. They shot Mike, but he's alive. He asked me to take his place until he could get here."

"Figured it was something like that when I looked at Mike's bible and billfold in your cabin. Assumed you displayed them there so one of us would look at them. Never saw an entry in a bible for a blood brother before or a billfold stuffed with so many pay stubs. You're Alan Perez?"

"Yes. Mike's blood brother."

"You two know orchards, vineyards, and hay fields if the pay stubs are any indication."

"Not as well as you and Luis, but we'll learn. I'll explain what happened to Mike at supper tomorrow, so everyone knows why I'm here in his place."

"Good. After supper, you might want to ask Lorna to go to the movie with you Friday night. Her twin sister, Norma, replaces Lorna for the evening shift at Campbell's Resort. When Mike gets here, he might want to ask

Norma to go to a movie with him on her night off. They're both tired of soft city boys and deadbeats trying to court them."

"Lorna said she's going to the movie with Harold."

"Don't know much about women, do ya? She doesn't know anyone named Harold. Made that up to try to make you jealous."

"It worked. She got any tattoos?"

"What the...," someone mumbled from behind Alan's right shoulder.

"No tattoos you're likely to see anytime soon," a female said from behind his left shoulder.

Alan jumped in place, startled, and whirled around to face Lorna and her father. Luis held an old hunting rifle at port arms. Lorna was grinning.

Sam chuckled and turned to walk to his cabin. Luis started laughing as he turned to walk back to the farmhouse.

"Sorry," Alan said. "Got a bad habit of shooting off my mouth. Meant no disrespect."

"None taken," Lorna said, as she brushed hair out of her eyes. "They're showing a double feature at the Ruby Theatre Friday night, if you're interested."

Alan smiled and bit his tongue to suppress a giggle. "It's a date," he said.

Finally! A real date. An honest-to-god date with a sweetheart. Can't wait to call Mike.

The Widow's Red-Haired Baby

William and I swore a solemn oath. We would never tell what we did at the old abandoned mine behind the widow's property or reveal our shocking discovery.

We kept our secret for sixty years.

Last week, six grandsons carried William's casket to his final resting place, leaving me alone to keep the secret.

This morning, my doctor delivered his ominous diagnosis. "This has progressed to stage four, David. You need to think about hospice care," he said, making it clear I would soon join my brother in the Drixon family section of the cemetery at Chelan.

Now, our closely guarded secret would die with me.

Or would it?

Since William passed, I've had time to reflect on what happened in the summer of '49.

I have also thought about William's funeral.

His family and friends attended the services. The lovely widow and her red-haired baby were also there.

The widow's red-haired baby glared knowingly at me during the eulogy, letting me know he knew what William and I did to him sixty years ago.

At the risk of ridicule, I've decided it's time to admit what we did at the mine, and reveal our startling discovery.

The world has a right to know the truth about the widow and her red-haired baby.

"Be quiet, David. You sound like an elephant," William hissed as we crawled through the bushes under the living room window at our house.

"You should talk. Your feet are bigger than mine," I hissed right back at him as we pressed against the clapboard siding under the open window.

My brother had just turned thirteen, making him an authority on all subjects and old enough to think he was his brother's keeper. I was the brother, two years his junior and dumber than a box of rocks according to him.

"They'll skin us alive if they catch us listening," he whispered as we waited impatiently for our mother and our neighbor, Mrs. Thorold, to finish making coffee in the kitchen and adjourn to the living room to visit.

I knew we would need to listen to an hour of meaningless gossip to retrieve a few golden nuggets from their conversation. We would have no idea what was happening if we didn't listen to them.

"Did you see her at church services last Sunday?" asked Mrs. Thorold as the two women entered the living room.

"How could I miss her? Walked right down the center aisle to the front row, just like she always does," said our mother.

William and I rolled our eyes at each other.

We knew whom they were discussing because they obsessed endlessly over the widow, Mrs. Tiffany Sewell. She lived in the box canyon on Magic Mountain just behind our farm on Boyd Road, between Manson and Chelan.

I had no idea, at the time, why someone had named it Magic Mountain. The mountain looked no different from others surrounding Lake Chelan.

I knew everyone noticed the widow because she was always the most attractive woman in any group. Her youthfulness, deep tan, and poise made her a perfect target for gossips.

The thing that intrigued me the most was our mother

and her friend's insistence that the widow was older than they were—much older. We had heard Mother say the widow and her husband lived in the box canyon when she and Mrs. Thorold were young girls.

"You heard what the undertaker told Mrs. Volstead about the widow's husband?" Mrs. Thorold said.

"I suspect everyone has heard the story by now. Mrs. Volstead is the biggest gossip in town," my mother said.

William and I always smiled at each other when they badmouthed gossips.

"Her husband looked as young as she does until they put him in the casket after his tractor rolled over on him in their orchard. The undertaker told Mrs. Volstead they had to have a closed casket funeral because her husband aged to become a very old man during the night after his death," Mrs. Thorold said.

"I never heard of such a thing before."

"You remember him when we were little girls. We got older, but he and his wife never seemed to age."

"Tiffany doesn't look a day older now than she did thirty years ago."

"I'm sure my mother said she, Tiffany, and Tiffany's husband were classmates at Chelan High School," Mrs. Thorold said. "That doesn't seem possible because Mom will be sixty-five this next December. Tiffany looks like she is still in her twenties," she added.

William tugged at my arm to get my attention before he crawled away from the window.

I caught up with him in the apple orchard behind our house before we spoke.

"What's your hurry?" I asked.

"They're freaking me out with all that creepy talk about the widow's husband getting older after he was killed. They'll start talking about her being a witch in a minute," he said. "Have you forgotten it's Wednesday?

We need to go for a hike."

I knew what he had in mind. The box canyon behind our farm always drew us like a magnet on Wednesday afternoons.

We often ran through the tall brush and trees along the edge of the canyon to reach our concealed observation point overlooking the widow's property. Our visits were so frequent we had worn a trail. We could follow it at night under a full moon.

We had listened to our mother and Mrs. Thorold say the widow couldn't possibly earn enough money working in her orchard to support her lifestyle. They believed she must have another source of income.

William and I had decided her source of income was gold from the old abandoned mine behind her orchard in the box canyon. We had observed her entering the mine every Wednesday afternoon. She always stayed there for exactly fifteen minutes.

"Someday, she's going to forget to lock the door at the mine," William said. "Then we're going to go in and pack off some of the gold for ourselves. If the mine doesn't have gold in it, she wouldn't need to keep a big padlock on the door to keep people out."

We knew miners had taken gold out of the Cascade Mountains years ago, so we believed there might still be gold in Magic Mountain.

The hike to reach our vantage point toward the back of the box canyon took only a few minutes because we ran most of the way.

When we arrived, we looked first to see if the door to the mine still had the padlock on it. It did, as always. Then we watched the widow, Mrs. Tiffany Sewell, work in her apple orchard.

The widow was a tireless worker in the orchard, but she always followed the same schedule. She stopped working at three in the afternoon every Wednesday to go to the mine.

She kept a large skeleton key in her pocket to open the padlock to enter the mine. She would stay in the mine for exactly fifteen minutes, never a minute more or less. Then she would return to work in the orchard.

She never took anything into the mine with her other than a flashlight, and she never brought any gold out of the mine that we could see.

We concluded the gold was so highly concentrated she could pack enough in her pockets to support herself for the next week.

Her routine never varied. She might make a mistake and forget to lock the door to the mine someday, however. We wanted to be there if she did.

As luck, or fate, would have it, she did finally make a mistake, and we were there.

After she locked the padlock and started walking back toward the orchard, the big skeleton key fell out of her pocket.

I heard William gasp softly as the key dropped to the middle of the trail in front of the mine. He turned to look at me, wide eyed, as she continued walking toward the orchard.

The widow stopped next to an apple tree to take a drink from a water jug. Then she climbed a ladder to thin apples.

We watched her for several minutes.

We watched the key.

We nervously smiled at each other.

Finally, it was too much for William.

"Make a hawk call if she climbs down out of the tree and starts toward the mine. I'm going to get the key," he whispered.

Sure enough, before I could tell him I didn't know

how to make a hawk call, he snaked his way down through the brush toward the front of the mine.

He stopped beside the trail, reached out, and carefully picked up the key.

I watched as he studied the key for a minute. Then he took a slip of paper and a pencil stub out of his pocket and traced an outline of the key on the paper. He carefully placed the key back in the middle of the trail, and returned—after he erased his tracks.

"Thought you were going to get the key," I said, when he sat down beside me.

"Naw. She would cut the padlock off, and replace it with a new lock if she doesn't find the key where she dropped it. We don't need her key. There are several old skeleton keys in a drawer in the kitchen. We can file one of them to make a duplicate."

We watched the widow until it was time to run home for supper. We still hadn't seen any sign of witchcraft at the widow's farm.

A witch should have bats hanging from the eaves on her house, or a pot brewing over a fire in her front yard, we believed. If the widow was a witch, as gossips alleged, she hid the evidence.

After supper, Dad asked us to go with him to milk the cow.

William rolled his eyes at me.

I turned red, embarrassed.

We knew what was coming.

Dad was going to give us another one of his man-to-man talks. He always kept his head down, and mumbled words I didn't understand.

I always quizzed William later, hoping he would explain what I had missed.

"You'll understand when you grow up," he would say.

Years passed before I realized he had no idea what

Dad was trying to tell us.

Dad didn't say anything until milk started hitting the bottom of the pail. Then, he spoke without looking at us.

"Have you boys noticed a red-haired man lurking about the area?"

The question caught us completely by surprise. We both said, "No."

"A hired man just started working for the Klockmires. He's living in one of their orchard cabins just down the road. People are saying the man has a prison record, and he likes to chase young boys."

William and I looked at each other and shrugged.

I couldn't imagine why a man would chase us if we weren't bothering him. If he was old enough to go to prison, he was too old to play tag, kick the can, capture the flag, or any of our other games.

Dad interrupted my confused thoughts by saying, "If you see him, run home, and tell me. He'll hurt you if he catches you. Tell me if you see him on our property."

His warning ended our man-to-man talk for the evening, so we were able to slip away to modify a skeleton key in our father's workshop while he finished the evening chores.

The widow always drove to town to do her weekly shopping on Friday afternoon, and we wanted to be ready. If we could file an old skeleton key so it would open the padlock, we could explore the mine while she was gone. Then we would know if there was any gold in the mine.

We had no idea if our modified skeleton key would work on the padlock when we ran toward the mine Friday afternoon.

We also had no idea someone was following us.

The widow drove away from the front of her farmhouse at exactly two o'clock, right on schedule. She had never once varied her routine.

We knew she would return promptly at four-thirty. We had at least two hours to explore the mine and find the gold, if the key worked.

As we started to sneak through the brush toward the mine entrance, I heard a twig snap behind us. I whirled around, thinking Dad might've followed us for some reason.

William and I both gasped when a grungy looking man with a mop of red hair stepped out from behind a tall bush. He was big and dirty, and he leered at us the way I had seen men in front of the tavern look at women.

Chills ran up and down my spine as my mind shouted at me to run. My feet, however, were firmly rooted in place.

Fortunately, William grabbed my arm and gave me a violent jerk. That snapped me out of my trance.

I quickly followed him through the brush toward the mine entrance.

"Key better work," William shouted over his shoulder as we ran toward the door to the mine.

I followed in his footsteps only because I didn't have a better idea. We certainly couldn't outrun the big man for any distance, and I knew he would find us if we tried to hide in the brush surrounding the box canyon.

Luck was with us. The key fit perfectly. In a second, William had the door open. We ran inside and slammed the door shut.

Total darkness engulfed us for a second until I turned on the flashlight I had brought in anticipation of exploring the mine to find gold. I could hear the man's footsteps approaching rapidly as I waited for William to lock the door.

"There's no latch on the inside," William whispered, sounding scared. He had the big padlock in his hand, but there was no way he could use it to lock the door on the inside.

"Follow me," he whispered.

I turned with the flashlight beam toward a dark tunnel that seemed to snake into the hillside. The flashlight beam bounced around on the walls like cat's eyes, watching us as we ran into the tunnel. I could hear the door open behind us as we rounded the first curve, a hundred feet into the tunnel.

"We're trapped," I said as we continued running.

"He probably doesn't have a flashlight. He can't catch us if we can find a place to hide."

We ran several hundred feet before I noticed smaller tunnels angling off to each side from the main tunnel.

William grabbed my arm and jerked me toward one of the smaller tunnels. I dropped to my hands and knees to follow him into the opening. He stopped after we crawled to the end of the narrow tunnel, about a hundred feet.

"Turn off the flashlight," he whispered.

I turned off the flashlight.

Then something happened that nearly made me wet my pants in fright.

Very slowly, the mine's rock walls started to glow, an iridescent greenish color. I could easily see the tunnel walls, but fortunately, the rocks didn't give off enough light to illuminate the tunnel itself.

Then I noticed the heat. The tunnel walls were warm. I started sweating.

I couldn't see anything except the glowing walls in the dark tunnel, but I could hear footsteps. The man was slowly walking toward us in the main tunnel.

"Don't move. He can't see us if we don't move," William whispered.

I was too scared to move. I couldn't even breathe.

The man was walking even slower now. He stopped frequently as if he was listening to try to locate us. He should've heard my heartbeat because my heart was pounding like an Indian war drum.

Time seemed to stand still for the next hour or longer as the man felt his way along the tunnel, looking for us. He didn't have a flashlight, and the tunnel was so dark he couldn't possibly see anything except the glowing walls.

I believed my heart might explode in my chest before the man finally passed in front of the small side tunnel where we were hiding. Only the bottom half of his body was visible as he passed our side tunnel. His footsteps continued along the main tunnel.

"He thinks he has us trapped in the back of the mine," William whispered, as the man's footsteps grew so faint we could hardly hear them.

As William spoke, I realized the walls were glowing less brightly now. Then the greenish glow slowly faded to black, leaving the mine in total darkness.

"Follow me," William whispered. He jerked my arm to direct me toward the main tunnel. I bumped my head on the wall several times along the way and bumped into him when he stopped at the intersection with the main tunnel.

William helped me stand up after we crawled out of the side tunnel. "Turn on the flashlight and follow me. Run fast," he said.

I switched on the flashlight, and we started running toward the entrance. In seconds, we could see light from the door. The man had left it standing open.

We ran through the doorway.

William stopped, slammed the door shut, and snapped the padlock in place.

We were both out of breath when we reached our observation point on the hillside. We were also soaking wet from sweating in the hot mine shaft. We sat there for several minutes, letting the warm sunlight dry our clothes and us.

"Did you see any gold?" William asked.

"Forgot to look."

Then William stood up. "I need to go down to the trail to erase our tracks. We don't want the widow to know we were there."

"Are you going to let the man out?"

"He'll chase us if I do. We have to leave him there. The widow will let him out when she hears him banging on the door."

If he can find his way back to the door in the dark, I thought. I worried the man might tell the widow we had locked him in the mine. Then I realized he would have to explain why he was chasing us, and he would be in big trouble.

Our experience at the mine left me shaken after we ran back to our house. William was quieter than usual as we flipped through pages in the encyclopedia set Mother had purchased from a traveling salesman. We hoped to find a logical explanation for the glowing walls and the heat in the mine.

According to the encyclopedia, Zinc Sulfide found in mines in Franklin, New Jersey will glow for a minute after turning off a light. The glow would last longer if radiation or a heat source were available. We were a long way from New Jersey, and the hot mine walls in the box canyon had glowed for over an hour.

Mother was looking at us strangely, I noticed, as we studied the information in the encyclopedia set. I assumed she was surprised we had finally taken an interest in the books. Then she surprised us.

"William, stand by the door casing for a minute."

William dutifully walked to the door, slipped off his shoes and backed up against the door casing where mother always marked our heights with a pencil on our birthdays. She had made a mark for William not more than three months ago, so I was surprised she would repeat the procedure so soon.

"This is strange," mother said as she waved our father over to the door to look at the new mark.

Even from the table where I was reading a page in one of the encyclopedia books, I could see the mark was lower than the mark she made on his birthday.

"David, come over here, so I can make a mark for you," Mother said.

I hesitantly walked to the door, slipped off my shoes, and backed up against the casing. I stood tall, as usual, while she made a mark.

She frowned as I stepped away from the door.

When I turned around, I could see my new mark was lower than the mark she made on my birthday.

Mom was looking at Dad as if he should be able to offer an explanation.

William and I looked at each other and shrugged.

"Did they have their shoes on last time?" Dad asked.

"No," Mother replied. "We always do this the same way."

Despite the confusion, I forgot about the measurements as I continued looking at the books, seeking an explanation for what we had witnessed.

William and I retreated to the orchard after dinner to discuss the situation. We wondered if the red-haired man had gotten out of the mine. We couldn't think of any way of finding out without exposing what we had done. We decided to keep quiet.

I didn't think about the confusing marks on our door

casing again until church services two weeks later.

Our family sat in our usual spot, three rows back on the right side. We always arrived early, and the widow always arrived at the last minute. Our neighbors always glared at her disapprovingly as she walked down the center aisle to the front row.

This Sunday, there were loud gasps as the widow walked down the aisle. She held a bundle in her arms.

I could see a baby's red hair protruding from the top of the bundle.

We sang the usual hymns, and then Reverend Mossberg started his fifty-five minute sermon. He never missed the fifty-five minute mark by more than a couple of minutes.

William and I always timed him because we had a nickel bet on under or over the fifty-five minute mark. Timing him to see who would win a nickel kept us awake.

This time, we didn't need the nickel bet to keep us awake during the sermon. We had a baby staring at us from over the widow's shoulder. The baby had a full crop of red hair and big mature eyes that glared accusingly at us.

I recognized him immediately. Worse yet, his glare told me he recognized us. He knew we had locked him in the mine. I realized he must've been in the mine for a week before the widow found him.

William and I retreated to one of our hidden forts after church services to try to make sense out of what had happened. Finally, we concluded Magic Mountain really was magic, or at least the rocks in it were magic.

We decided we would never enter the mine again. We didn't want to lose another year's growth, or end up like the red-haired man.

Obviously, the widow knew the rocks had magical powers. She was taking advantage of that knowledge by spending fifteen minutes in the mine every week to retain her youth.

The widow and her husband had discovered something more valuable than gold. They had discovered an alternative to the fabled fountain of youth.

Now, sixty years later, the widow attended William's funeral with her red-haired baby. She still looks like she is in her twenties. The baby is still a baby, and he watched me, accusingly, with his big mature eyes.

William and I kept the widow's secret for over sixty years, but I'm relieved to have finally revealed the truth.

I'm not fool enough to think everyone will believe this improbable story. Many will assume I'm confused because I'm an old man, and I live in a nursing home. There will be naysayers, certainly.

Local gossips will probably smile condescendingly when they hear my story. They will still believe the widow is a witch and the baby is a midget.

Nonetheless, I can pass in peace knowing I have finally told the truth about the widow and her red-haired baby.

Picnic sites are crowded during the summer. You may need to share a table with ducks, geese, and deer.

Photo: Three mule deer bucks in the picnic area at Fields Point at Lake Chelan during the middle of the day. They ignore tourists with cameras.

The Gold Seeker

There is no risk too great to take,
No love too sweet to forsake,
 For the pursuit of gold.

Show the gold seeker a mountain
 And he will climb it.
Show him a raging river
 And he will cross it.
Show him a hole in the ground
 And he will explore it.
The pursuit of gold knows no bounds,
Either above or below the ground.

The gold seeker mined the Black Hills
 In the middle of an Indian war,
After stampeding across the California desert
 Hoping to make that one big score,
Then shipped out to the Yukon
 To try his luck just once more.
There is no place off limits to those so bold,
As to risk it all for the lure of gold.

The gold seeker will work all night
 And hide from renegades all day,
In the heat of the summer desert
 Or far north of the sun's last ray.
He will work to his dying breath
 And for only one thing will he pray,
"Let there be gold in this God forsaken place,
That my life not be a total waste."

The gold seeker has left it all behind him,
    The family and the secure life,
To dedicate his life to the pursuit of gold
    Despite the hazards and the strife,
With no one to trust, no one to lean on,
    No supportive companion or wife.
He is determined to make it on his own
Or litter the wilderness with his bones.

The gold seeker dreams of making the big strike
    And pictures life thereafter as milk and honey.
He fantasizes about how famous he will be
    And what he will do with all that money,
Little suspecting that habits are forming
    And life thereafter will not be so sunny,
For he is addicted to the pursuit of gold,
    And he no longer fits any other mold.

Photo: North Cascade's main lodge at Stehekin. The restaurant, store, and lodge are conveniently located by the ferry dock for ferry riders, residents, and hikers. Residents pick up supplies at the dock when the ferry arrives, and day riders rush to the bus to visit Rainbow Falls. A longer stay allows time to relax, see attractions, visit with tourists from all over the country, and meet hikers in off the trail for a hot shower, meal, and supplies.

Easy Money

Kelly Malison let out a joyful yelp as he accepted the paycheck the orchardist handed him. Then he kicked up his heels, doing a little jig in front of us.

I laughed along with everyone else. His playful display helped break the boredom as I waited in line to receive my paycheck.

His antics were fun to watch, but something about Kelly always disturbed me. He had never given me any obvious cause for my uneasiness, so it wasn't something I could explain. I would soon have reason to regret not having listened to my instincts, however, after I let him talk me into earning some easy money.

We were all young men, killing time, working at the apple orchard near Manson while we waited for the Army to catch up with us.

Escalating combat in Korea dominated the news. We knew we had a draft notice in our future that would obligate us to report to boot camp.

Our lives were on hold as we waited, and now we would be without work or a paycheck for three or four weeks. We had finished thinning the apples and propping up the tree limbs, but the apples weren't ready to pick.

"Scott Dailey," the orchardist shouted, disrupting my thoughts.

I stepped forward to get my paycheck. Mumbled, "Thanks." Then I started walking toward my cabin.

"Room for one more in the car," Kelly said, as he walked alongside me.

I had already turned down his first invitation to accompany him to the tavern in Manson to celebrate, but he was persistent.

"Friday night, Scott. Money in our pockets. Time to celebrate," he said.

"I have plans," I said, for the second or third time.

A couple of hours of daylight remained, giving me time to try to catch the monster trout I was after at Roses Lake. I was anxious to try new line, hooks, and the angleworms I'd dug the night before.

I wouldn't have minded a cold beer, but I knew one beer wasn't an option if I rode to town with Kelly. We didn't have to work the next day, so Kelly and the others would cash their checks at the tavern and stay until closing time. They would get rip-roaring drunk. Then they would be broke until the apples were ready to pick.

I was more interested in having another go at the big trout resting in deep water just off the rock bluff at the lake. The fish had eluded me twice.

"Gonna to be around tomorrow?" Kelly asked, as we approached our cabins.

He had parked his car in front of his cabin, which was directly across the dirt road from my cabin. Several friends stood beside the car, waiting impatiently.

"May go fishing early in the morning if I don't catch the big one tonight. Be here the rest of the day."

"Good. See ya about noon."

If your hangover doesn't kill you, I thought.

I fished until dark that evening and for two hours the next morning. The big fish wasn't interested in angleworms. I fried the smaller fish I caught for supper and breakfast.

Kelly didn't open the door to his cabin until after one in the afternoon the next day. He stumbled toward the outhouse.

Looks awful.

I was sitting on the bench in front of my cabin at four in the afternoon when Kelly opened the door to his cabin again. He looked a little better this time.

Might live.

I watched him walk to the irrigation ditch behind my cabin. I knew what he was going to do. A couple of our friends had already soaked their swollen heads in the cold water.

Water dripped from Kelly's hair and chin when he walked to my cabin.

"Have a cold beer you can spare?" he asked, as he sat down on a stump next to the bench where I was sitting.

I knew he was joking. Our cabins didn't have an ice-box or a refrigerator.

"Not today," I responded.

"Damn. I'm only one beer away from a miraculous recovery."

"Or dying," I suggested.

"No. Not today. Did I tell you about my mother?"

I didn't remember him ever mentioning his mother. I had no idea why he would mention her now, but he continued talking before I could ask.

"Called her from a payphone last night. She's sick. Doctor says she has to go into a nursing home because she's too sick to take care of herself. She doesn't have money to pay for a nursing home."

I had no idea why Kelly was telling me about his mother, but it did occur to me she might have some money if he hadn't spent his paycheck at the tavern.

"What're you going to do?" I asked.

"If ya'll help me, I'm gonna get the money she needs."

"Don't know how I can help. I'm making a dollar an hour just like you."

"Not askin' ya for money. Already know where to get it. Just need ya to help me."

"I'm not into robbing banks, even to help your mother."

"Don't need to rob a bank. My mother's brother already robbed the bank. I know where he hid the money."

"You're scaring me."

"Read this." He pulled a newspaper clipping out of

his pocket and handed it to me.

I unfolded the yellowed newsprint. It was the front page of a Lake Chelan Mirror newspaper published in the third week of July in 1931.

ROBBERY, proclaimed the bold inch high headline. *Mining Company robbed at gunpoint. $34,000 missing.*

The article under the headline said the robbery occurred at the Chelan Copper Mining Company office in Chelan. A masked gunman held employees at gunpoint and forced a security officer to open the safe.

The article quoted James Moore, company superintendent, as saying the company had the money on hand to pay for development costs at its Holden copper mine.

Kelly was smiling when I finished reading the article.

"Robbed a company safe instead of a bank," he said. "Made off with thirty-four thousand dollars."

Then he handed me a second newspaper clipping.

"Mom's maiden name was Gilliman," Kelly said, as I unfolded the weathered newsprint.

"Her brother was Ike Gilliman. He worked for the Chelan Copper Mining Company doing exploratory work at sites all around Lake Chelan."

As Kelly talked, I scanned the clipping.

The headline said, **ROBBERY SUSPECT KILLED IN SHOOTOUT**.

According to the article, a security officer recognized Ike during the robbery. The same security officer confronted Ike in Chelan a month after the robbery and killed him in a shootout.

The article concluded by saying Ike didn't have any money on him when he died. The location of the stolen money was unknown.

"Stupid of him to shoot Ike before they found the money," I said.

"Ike didn't have a weapon on him when he was shot, according to my mom. There was no shootout. The security officer executed him."

"How would your mom know he didn't have a weapon?"

"He'd just left her house to go to the company office to report on the exploratory work he was doing for them."

"Did your mom know he was the holdup man?"

"Sure, she knew. He told her about the holdup just before the security officer killed him. He wanted her to know where the money was hidden if anything happened to him. He put the money in his mine, and covered the entrance so no one would find it. He gave her a map showing the location of the mine.

"He was gonna keep working for the company for a few years. Then he'd resign his position and open his mine. He believed it'd be safe then to use the money from the hold-up. People would assume the money came from the profit from his mine."

"Didn't anyone check his mine for the stolen money?"

"No one knew he had a mine, except my mother. If he had filed a claim for the mine, it would've belonged to the mining company because he was working for them when he found it."

"You said you know where he hid the money."

"Mom gave me these newspaper clippings and the map Ike made for her the last time I visited her in Chelan. The map shows the location of the mine behind a lake. She has forgotten where the lake is located except that it's somewhere up Lake Chelan. I don't know how to find the lake. I've heard ya talk about fishing all the high country lakes around Lake Chelan. Thought ya might've been there."

"What lake are you talking about?"

"The mine is behind Trapper Lake."

"That's not good."

"Already know that's a problem. Ike told Mom it's nearly impossible to get to the lake. That's why she never tried to find the money. Have ya been there?"

"Been there and swore I'd never go back. Too dangerous."

"Would ya take me there for two thousand dollars? That's as much as ya'll earn all year working here in the orchard. We can be back in time to pick apples."

"You've no idea what you're asking. We'd need to get to the upper end of Lake Chelan. The climb to Trapper Lake starts at Cottonwood Camp, over eighteen miles up the Stehekin Valley from the head of the lake. That's the easy part.

"Trapper Lake is on a bench above Cottonwood Camp. Only way to get to the lake is to climb up a dangerous bluff."

"I knew the mine was up Lake Chelan, so I found someone with a boat," Kelly said. "He'll drive the boat for us. Knew we'd need help from someone with mining experience. Found a man who worked in the mine at Holden. He's eager to earn some money.

"They've each agreed to help me for a thousand dollars. If ya'll help me for two thousand, I can get the money my mom needs for a nursing home."

Foolishly, I ignored my gut instinct. I allowed Kelly to persuade me to become involved in his harebrained scheme. Helping his mother was the primary factor, of course. At least, that's what I told myself to rationalize my decision.

As Kelly talked, I was remembering the cutthroat trout in Trapper Lake. The trout didn't know a fish hook from a mayfly. I simply couldn't resist having another go at them.

I tried not to think about the obvious motive. The lure of easy money influenced my decision. Two thousand dollars was a fortune for someone making a dollar an hour working in an orchard.

We started up Lake Chelan early the next morning in a huge boat. This wasn't a typical fishing boat of the type

234

normally seen on Lake Chelan. This was a cabin cruiser with bunks, a kitchen, and a bathroom below deck.

Kelly introduced the driver.

"Scott, meet Ricky Reinforce," he said. "Ricky works for the folks who own this boat. He agreed to get the boat and drive it for us."

Right then, I knew I had made a serious mistake. Ricky was just a kid.

"He stole the boat?" I said.

"No such thing," Kelly snapped at me. "The rich owners are vacationin' in the Bahamas, so Ricky borrowed the boat. He'll return it before they fly back from their vacation."

Ricky smiled at me as he gripped the wheel to turn the big boat toward the center of the lake. He had a cigarette pinched between his lips.

Going to take more than a cigarette for you to pass as an adult, kid.

"Welcome aboard," he said, in a squeaky voice, after he flipped his cigarette stub over the side of the boat. "They use me as a deck hand when they cruise up and down the lake to show off their boat," Ricky said. "They let me drive it sometimes."

I nodded a greeting as I watched him adjust controls on the panel in front of the steering wheel. He seemed to know what he was doing.

When I heard a grunt, I turned to watch a large individual lumber up the stairs from below deck.

"Scott, meet Andy Krefeld," Kelly said. "Andy's our mining expert."

"The foreman at Holden wouldn't have fired me if I was an expert," Andy mumbled. He lifted a nearly empty fifth of whiskey to his lips and chugged the contents.

"That belongs to the boat owners," Ricky shouted. "We aren't supposed to get into their liquor cabinet. You promised, Kelly."

"They ain't here," Andy said, defiantly. He looked at

the empty bottle for a moment. Then he tossed it overboard.

"Another dead soldier," he mumbled.

"I'll replace anything that's missing when we return the boat," Kelly said.

Great! I'm on a stolen boat, driven by an immature kid. Our mining expert is a belligerent drunk. What can possible go wrong?

I retreated forward to the bow to get away from them.

Andy and Ricky continued arguing.

Kelly yelled at them to stop.

Andy stomped down the steps to go below deck.

Kelly joined me a few minutes later.

"Andy went below deck to take a nap," he said.

"To find another bottle," I suggested.

"Owners will never miss the booze. They're rich."

"Is Ricky going up to the mine with us?"

"Sure, why not? We'll need all the help we can get when we open the mine."

The kid didn't impress me as having enough strength to pick up a ten-pound rock, but he did know how to handle the big boat. He maneuvered it alongside the dock at Stehekin before noon without any damage to the boat or the dock.

Kelly walked to the lodge to rent a vehicle.

Ricky opened the deck lid and dropped down into the cargo hold to hand items up to me.

I stacked our supplies on the deck. Food, camping equipment, mining tools, a small box of dynamite, and rope ended up in a large pile.

Andy stood and watched me as he sipped from another nearly empty fifth of whiskey. He grunted and glared at me malevolently when I suggested he could stack the items on the dock.

After he emptied the bottle, he tossed it overboard and started packing items to the dock.

I retrieved my fishing rod and blanket roll from below deck when Kelly parked a rental pickup near the dock. We loaded our supplies into the back of the pickup and started the slow eighteen-mile drive on the primitive road to Cottonwood Camp.

Andy sat in the back of the pickup with our supplies, sipping from another bottle. The clinking sounds coming from his pack suggested he had *liberated* several bottles from the liquor cabinet.

We reached Cottonwood Camp in the afternoon with plenty of time to hike up the bluff to Trapper Lake. Kelly was anxious to get started, but Andy fell flat on his face when he crawled down from the back of the pickup.

I suggested we stay at Cottonwood Camp for the night. "We can pack most of our gear up to the base of the bluff before dark, and climb the bluff first thing in the morning."

Kelly agreed, knowing Andy was done for the day.

There was no sign of a trail to the base of the bluff, so we had to hack our way through vines and trees on the rockslide below the bluff to find a crevasse we could climb.

Andy slept all afternoon while Kelly and I packed our supplies to the base of the bluff. Ricky tried to help, but he couldn't carry more than a few pounds. Kelly suggested he stay in camp and gather firewood.

We were sitting around a fire after supper, relaxing, when Andy finally woke up, holding his head like it was fine china.

He glared at Ricky for a moment.

"Bring me a bottle out of my pack," he said.

"We took your pack up to the base of the bluff," Kelly said.

This bit of news caused Andy to howl and storm around the campsite, raging like a wild bull for several minutes. He looked like he might throw up when I offered him leftovers from the supper I had cooked two hours earlier.

He glared at me for a few moments, seemingly weighing the odds of whipping me. Then he crawled under his blanket and went to sleep.

We climbed the bluff the next morning without incident, after I anchored two ropes at the top of the bluff. Ricky was too weak and Andy was too clumsy to risk climbing with a pack on their backs. Kelly and I each made several trips up and down the bluff to get all of our supplies to the top.

We set up our camp on the backside of Trapper Lake. Kelly wanted to be close to where the mine entrance was marked on Ike's map.

Trees and vines had overgrown the area in the twenty years since Ike caved in the entrance to his mine. We spent the afternoon clearing brush and trees.

Andy suggested Ike had used dynamite to bring rocks and dirt down over the entrance. He was convinced he could see an outline of the original entrance, so we started moving rocks.

I excused myself after the sun went down. I wanted to catch our dinner. The fish cooperated, and we had a fine feast of fresh pan-fried trout for supper.

We were late starting the next morning because Andy was sick with a hangover, and Ricky was in tears because of Andy's bullying.

We had to break up some of the bigger rocks using the dynamite Andy supplied. It took all day to uncover the mine entrance. As darkness fell over us, we could see an opening that was about five feet high and three feet wide. We decided to wait for daylight to determine if it was safe to enter.

Ricky had stayed at our campsite in the afternoon to avoid Andy's bullying. When we returned, he was standing beside a large bonfire, watching a bear eat berries on the far side of the lake. He was scared and upset because we didn't have a gun.

Andy's muscle and experience helped during the day, after he sobered up. He moved rocks Kelly and I couldn't budge, and he knew how to use dynamite to break up the rocks we couldn't move. Now, however, he was ready to celebrate with a bottle of whiskey. He sat beside the fire, downed whiskey as if it was soda pop, and badgered Ricky.

"Bears smell fear," Andy proclaimed. "They sneak in-to camps at night to carry off anyone with the scent of fear on them."

Ricky crowded closer to the fire as Andy spoke.

The moon was up early, and I could see dimples in the water when the fish started feeding. The bear had disappeared, so I used a dry fly along the shoreline while Kelly cooked our supper.

Andy continued tormenting Ricky while I was fish-ing.

I caught a nice mess of fish for breakfast, and started cleaning them on the shoreline. Before I finished, the bickering in camp turned to fighting.

As I turned to watch, Ricky lunged toward Andy to exchange blows. I didn't realize, until Andy collapsed, that Ricky had a rock in his hand.

One sharp blow to Andy's temple ended the fight.

Kelly cussed and Ricky started crying as I walked back to the fire.

Andy was on his back with blood soaking the side of his head, but the blood was the least of his problems. He jerked violently for several minutes as if he was having an epileptic fit. Then his body stiffened straight as a board for a long minute before his muscles relaxed.

Then there was no movement at all. None!

"Oh, Jeezes, Ricky, ya killed him," Kelly said.

"Accident," Ricky sobbed. "Didn't mean to..."

"Well, ya did, damnit," shouted Kelly. "Ya killed him."

I just stood there, stunned. Not in a million years

would I have believed Ricky could kill Andy, but he did.

Then, before Kelly could do anything but cuss, Ricky let out a crazy sounding shriek that echoed off the mountainside. He turned and ran blindly away from us, toward the lake.

I heard a loud splash when he hit the water. Moonlight reflected off the lake, so I could see him.

Ricky swam toward the bluff side of Trapper Lake as if he was trying to escape from us. Then he slowly sank out of sight near the center of the small lake.

Kelly continued cussing as Ricky disappeared.

I just stood there, knowing the freezing cold water came from glaciers on the mountains behind the lake. I couldn't help Ricky.

It was deadly quiet. Kelly and I stood there for a long time, willing Ricky to resurface, knowing he wouldn't. Neither of us spoke.

We ended up sitting beside the fire for most of the night. I had no idea what Kelly was thinking, but I was cursing myself for getting involved. Had I not helped Kelly find Trapper Lake, Andy and Ricky would still be alive. My motives for helping seemed flimsy in that light.

I must've dozed at some point. The fire had burned down to coals, and it was getting daylight when I jerked awake to look around.

Kelly sat across from me with his head on his chest.

Andy's body was a few yards from camp where we had placed him under a blanket.

Ricky's body had floated to the shoreline next to our campsite.

Kelly woke up when he heard me stand up.

I walked to the shoreline and pulled Ricky's body out of the water. He was white and shriveled up—looked like a twelve-year-old.

Kelly blew on coals to get the fire burning again. He placed a pan over the fire to fry the fish I caught the previous evening.

My stomach reminded me we didn't eat the supper Kelly cooked the night before.

"What now?" I said when we finished eating.

"We get the money and get the hell out of here before something else goes wrong," he said.

"What about them?"

"Can't pack them down the bluff."

"Bears will eat them if we leave them here."

"Thought of that. We can put them in the mine with the mining tools and camping equipment. I'm gonna bury the stuff in the mine before we leave. We ain't leaving here with anything but money."

His suggestion repulsed me, but I didn't have a better idea, so I didn't object. Neither Andy nor Ricky had any family in the area, according to Kelly, so the mine would be as good a resting place for eternity as any other. I honestly didn't know what else we could do.

We entered the mineshaft with flashlights right after breakfast. The money was in an unlocked toolbox close to the entrance.

Kelly started cussing again after we packed the box out and counted the money.

"Should be thirty-four thousand here," he howled, amid a prolonged cussing fit.

We counted the money a second time, but it was obvious. There was twenty-five thousand dollars in the box.

"This explains why the security officer shot Ike on sight," Kelly said. "The officer must've pocketed nine thousand dollars after the robbery and blamed it on Ike. He had to shut Ike up, so the police wouldn't discover what he'd done."

I didn't know if that accounted for the missing money or not, and I didn't care. Ike might've spent the money or given it to someone. I just wanted to get away and try to forget what had happened.

Kelly was still cussing.

"I don't care about the money. Don't want any of it," I

told him. "Twenty-five thousand should be more than enough to take care of your mother. She's welcome to all of it."

Kelly seemed to regain his composure after I told him I didn't want any of the money.

"We can leave in an hour if we get busy," he said.

Now he was all business again.

We packed everything we didn't plan to take with us into the mine along with the two bodies.

Kelly found the dynamite Andy had saved to close the mine when we finished.

"Have you used this stuff before?" I asked.

"No, but Andy showed me how to do it. He already inserted the cap and fuse, so it's ready to use. All I have to do is secure the dynamite in place, light the fuse, and run. Andy said the fuse has a thirty-second burn time like those we used to break up the big rocks. These three sticks should be enough to bring the hillside down over the entrance."

Handling dynamite scared me, so I stayed a hundred yards back behind trees to watch Kelly.

He placed the dynamite under rocks just above the mine entrance, held a match to the fuse for a moment, and turned to run. Too late! The dynamite exploded almost immediately.

Kelly had taken only a couple of steps before tons of rocks, dirt, and trees poured down the hillside toward him. When the dust settled, debris covered the entrance to the mineshaft and the scattered remnants of Kelly's body.

Getting to the boat at Stehekin was the easy part. Delivering the money to Kelly's mother, I realized, would be more difficult.

Kelly had put the money and the keys for the pickup and the boat in his backpack. I put the money and keys in my backpack and burned everything else. Then I climbed down the bluff to Cottonwood Camp, drove the pickup to Stehekin, and started down Lake Chelan in the big boat.

Ricky told us the boat belonged to his employer, but he never said where they docked it. I realized I couldn't explain having the boat or the twenty-five thousand dollars in my backpack if the police stopped me.

When I started encountering other boats on the lake, I worried someone might recognize the big boat. My fear increased the further I drove down the lake.

By the time I reached Antilon Creek, I decided the police would confiscate the money if they caught me with the boat. I coasted to a stop next to the small dock at Antilon Creek and secured the boat.

The canyon behind Antilon Creek offered an abundance of hiding places for the money. I hiked up the canyon, dug a deep hole, and buried the money, wrapped in my rain poncho and a waterproof tarp.

The next part of my plan was simple. I would tie the boat to the first suitable dock I found along the lakeshore and hitchhike to Chelan to locate Kelly's mother. Then I could hike overland to Antilon Creek to retrieve the money for her.

In hindsight, I should've realized someone would have called the sheriff's office to report a missing boat, and someone would recognize the boat tied to the Stehekin dock.

Sheriff's deputies were on their way to Stehekin in a patrol boat to retrieve the stolen boat when they spotted me a few miles south of Antilon Creek. They pulled their patrol boat alongside the big boat after they ordered me to stop.

"Found the boat at the Stehekin dock. Driving it to Chelan to return it to its owner," I said, giving them a bright smile, trying to look like an innocent Boy Scout performing his daily good deed.

They didn't believe my Good Samaritan story. One

deputy took command of the big boat. The other deputy arrested me for theft and transported me to a jail cell in Chelan.

My court appointed attorney coached me on a story to tell the judge. "Insist you were returning the boat. Throw yourself on the mercy of the court. You don't have any prior offenses, so the judge will only sentence you to time served or a couple days in jail if he finds you guilty of theft," he said.

I agreed to follow my attorney's advice if he would locate Kelly's mother for me.

Two things happened the next day that shocked me. First, the judge sentenced me to six months in the Chelan County jail in Wenatchee. Second, and even more shocking, my attorney discovered Kelly's mother was dead. In fact, she had been dead for over a year.

Obviously, I should've listened to my gut instinct about Kelly. He lied to get me to help him find the money. I have no idea what he planned to do with the money, but his plans didn't include helping his mother.

On the way to lockup in Wenatchee, I thought about the money. I was the only one who knew the money existed and the only one who knew its location. I needed to decide what to do. There was no hurry. The judge gave me six months to think about it.

Returning the money to its rightful owner wasn't an option. The mining company had gone out of business years ago. Besides, the company had reported a theft of thirty-four thousand dollars. I had twenty-five thousand dollars buried at Antilon Creek. The police might charge me with the theft of the difference if I admitted I had the money.

Like many orchard workers, I had dreamed of owning an orchard, but dismissed the idea as unrealistic. A dollar an hour worker has a hard time accumulating enough money to make a down payment on an orchard.

Along about the fourth month sitting in the county

jail in Wenatchee, it occurred to me that twenty-five thousand dollars would buy a very nice orchard. A deluxe orchard, in fact.

The next day, my draft notice arrived.

If I survive boot camp and deployment in Korea, I'm going to buy an orchard at Manson, overlooking Lake Chelan. I'll sit on my porch every evening with a big smile on my face, watching the sun drop behind Slide Ridge.

If I don't make it back to Manson, someday a patrol leader is going to send a tenderfoot scout up the canyon at Antilon Creek to dig a latrine behind their Boy Scout campsite.

Surprise, surprise!

This orphaned black bear cub visited my yard nearly every day to eat clover until berries ripened in Aug. He had brown and gold hair, which is very common around Lake Chelan.

Ring of Gold

He promised to ring her in gold,
If she would be so bold,
   As to wed a poor miner.
He could not afford a wedding ring,
Or any of those other fancy things,
   Other suitors offered for a binder,
But, they had a bond neither could define,
And she said his offer sounded divine,
   So, they wed on a northbound liner.

Far up the Yukon, he staked his claim,
And dug all winter with the clear aim,
   Of hitting pay dirt to wash when it thawed.
Thinking each foot down was closer to gold,
He dug on in the dark and the miserable cold,
   Until his back ached, and his hands were raw.
Clear to bedrock, the poor miner dug,
With no reward, save an encouraging hug,
   As miners made the strike in the next draw.

Each summer they moved to another spot,
So, he could dig all winter, and for naught,
   Just another worthless empty hole,
While she, his wife, complained not once,
As he followed each new lead and hunch,
   In pursuit of his chosen lifelong goal.
She took in wash and helped at a diner,
To grubstake the hard working miner,
   So he could keep digging like a mole.

They had four kids along the way,
Though they never found a place to stay,
   But, she made each stop a loving home.

The oldest helped their mom in town,
 As the youngest helped him up and down,
 Each hole he dug from Whitehorse to Nome.
In time, the grandchildren began to arrive,
And each one helped the poor miner survive,
 And not once, did he hear a whine or moan.

Now, fifty years have slipped away,
And the big strike still holds him at bay,
 And the family is still on the road.
Seems to him, it was only yesterday,
When they came so far north to stay,
 After he promised to ring her in gold.
He never could buy her a wedding ring,
Or any of those other fancy things;
 The poor miner had to put them on hold.

But, it is their golden anniversary today,
And he has put a few nuggets away,
 And the family is all ready to stand,
So he can thank his wife one more time,
For helping a poor miner along the line,
 While raising a family that is so grand.
He still cannot ring his loving wife in gold,
But, from nuggets he's forged a ring of gold,
 To place on a finger on her left hand.

For the first time ever, he sees a tear,
In the eye of the wife, he holds so dear,
 As she gives him a long affectionate hug.
Then, as the whole family stands and cheers,
All about him the poor miner peers,
 And realizes with a heartwarming shrug,
All the blond heads in their large fold,
Circle his wife in a cherished ring of gold,
 More prized than any he could have dug.

Remarkable Changes

The logging mill on Mill Road near Manson is gone, replaced by a park and casino. The racetrack and baseball diamond at Wapato Point are gone, replaced by condominiums. Modern homes stand where small farmhouses, rows of migrant housing, cisterns, cellars, and outhouses once stood.

The original buildings in downtown Manson remain, but with new owners, uses, and concrete sidewalks.

The Red Apple Market in Manson has a visitor's section with a coffee shop and photo albums, so tourists can see what the area looked like and old-timers can reminisce.

I recently stopped at Blueberry Hills near Manson for a delicious lunch. While reading their small brochure, I realized I remembered the owner's grandparents. They had an apple orchard near our orchard in the 1940s.

When the owner's father arrived, I introduced myself. The first thing he said was, "I remember you. We swam in the irrigation ditch by your house when we were kids." We hadn't seen each other in over sixty-five years. It seemed like yesterday as we reminisced.

Despite all the physical changes surrounding Lake Chelan, the important things remain the same. The local residents are just as friendly and accommodating as I remember them from my childhood.

Photo: Front view of Blueberry Hills near Manson where you can have a leisurely meal, pick blueberries, and view orchards and the mountains from their deck.

The War is Over

Charlie Lawrence watched three men crawl out of the pickup they used to block the road in front of him. Each man had a contemptuous smirk on his face and a hand on the revolver tucked in his jeans.

"Stop right there," the tallest man bellowed at Charlie, as the men blocked his path on the narrow dirt road.

Charlie smiled at the men. He realized they didn't know he had just returned from the front lines in Germany where he earned a bronze star killing men with a rifle—like the one he held in his right hand with the muzzle pointed at the ground.

He recognized the three men from his brother's letters. The six-footer was Bud Jr., son of rancher Bud Bowman. His two henchmen went by Jake and Luke. His brother had never mentioned their last names, just descriptions.

Bud Jr. wore thick leather gloves, Charlie noticed. The gloves would make it difficult for him to get his finger on a trigger. He would shoot him last.

Jake was big, overweight, and looked slow. He might be dangerous in a brawl. He would shoot him second.

Luke acted nervous. He would be the first to go for a revolver. He would shoot him first.

"Reckon you're talkin' to me," Charlie finally responded as he studied the three men. He continued smiling.

"Damn. Another smart-mouthed Okie or Arky," Jake said.

"It's Oklahoma for those with enough education to pronounce the word." Charlie smiled at Jake as he spoke.

The big man balled his fists as he took a step toward Charlie.

"Back off," Bud Jr. snapped, waving his hand in front of Jake as if he could stop a charging bull with a wave of his arm.

Jake hesitated before he stepped back, glaring menacingly at Charlie.

Charlie continued smiling at him. He always smiled during a confrontation. The habit was hard to break.

He was tempted to shoot the thugs to put an end to their bullying, but he remembered his promise to his attorney and Sheriff Reilly. He would shoot them only as a last resort.

The war was over for him. He had his discharge papers in his back pocket, and he hoped to start a new life here on Crab Creek.

Yet, according to his brother's letters, the killing continued along the creek. He had, it appeared, walked into the middle of the local war as he followed the primitive road toward his brother's farm on Crab Creek near Schawana.

"What're you doing here?" Bud Jr. demanded.

"I'm walkin' to Schawana, if it's any of your business."

"It's my business when you use this road. It goes through our rangeland, and we don't allow trespassers."

"I haven't seen any signs saying you own this road."

"Dumb Okie doesn't understand anything about rangeland," Jake said.

"We own all of the land along Crab Creek, so we don't need signs," Bud Jr. declared, belligerently. "This is our rangeland, so we have a right to close this road to protect our cattle from rustlers."

"Well, I ain't likely to steal many cows while I'm afoot. I probably can't pack more than four or five at a time on my back."

Charlie smiled brightly at the three men as he spoke, knowing the Bowman Cattle Company didn't own any land along Crab Creek.

Frank Jameson, his former battalion commander, worked now as an attorney in Ephrata. He was waiting at trackside to welcome Charlie when the train stopped.

He and the attorney spent several hours at the county courthouse in Ephrata, studying land titles for Crab Creek, before they talked to Sheriff Reilly. When they finished, Charlie hitchhiked to Moses Lake and started walking south along Crab Creek toward his brother's farm.

"That's the problem with you Southerners," Jake said. "You think you can joke your way out of anything."

"I can see you don't want me here, so I'll hurry along. Be off your rangeland in a few more miles," Charlie said, knowing he would waste his time debating land titles with the three thugs from the Bowman Ranch.

He knew his appearance wouldn't discourage them from trying to intimidate him. He had lived on field rations in foxholes for most of his time overseas. Three weeks of seasickness on the transport ship coming home, and a jerky train ride west to Ephrata further reduced him to skin and bones.

He still wore the tattered remnants of his army uniform. He chose to purchase the surplus M1 rifle at a second hand store at Moses Lake rather than buy new clothing. He knew he could easily be mistaken for a lost tramp.

"You'll do no such thing," Bud Jr. shouted.

"Walk back to Moses Lake. Follow the state highway to the Columbia River, and walk down along the river to Schawana like everyone else."

"That's not an option," Charlie said. "It's been a long

day, and I'm tired. I'm takin' the shortest route."

"I'm going to shoot this fool," Luke shouted angrily as he dropped his hand to his revolver. He jerked the revolver out of the front of his jeans to aim it at Charlie.

As Luke raised the revolver and thumbed the hammer back, Charlie lifted the muzzle of his rifle a few inches to point it at Luke's foot. He touched the trigger, creating an ear-piercing blast. The bullet hit where Charlie aimed, putting a hole in the toe of Luke's right boot.

Luke dropped his revolver as he yelped and started hopping around in a circle, holding his foot in both hands.

"Damn, damn, he shot my foot," he sobbed as he fell on his back.

"I'm going to kill this Okie," Jake roared as both he and Bud Jr. pulled their revolvers out of the front of their jeans.

"You're dead men," Charlie snapped as he lifted the muzzle of his rifle to aim it at them.

The sharpness of Charlie's military command voice plus the sight of a rifle muzzle aimed at them caused the two men to release the grip on their revolvers as if they were holding hot metal. Their revolvers fell in the dirt in front of them.

"You shot my man in the foot," Bud Jr. whined.

"He was lucky," Charlie said as he watched Luke remove his boot. He could see the bullet had cut a deep groove in the end of his big toe. "The next time one of you points a weapon at me, I'll shoot to kill. Now, leave your revolvers on the ground, get in the pickup, and leave."

"You can't steal our revolvers," Bud Jr. complained. "I'll have the sheriff after you."

"You'll find the revolvers in the bottom of Crab Creek—just out from the willow tree over yonder."

Jake glared threateningly at Charlie as he helped

Luke into the pickup. Tears leaked from Luke's eyes faster than blood leaked from his big toe.

Bud Jr. shouted at Charlie after he slid behind the steering wheel.

"I bet that Overstreet woman put you up to this. Is that it, she hired you to defend her place?

"Well, you're wasting your time. This is Bowman rangeland, and we're going to own every farm along Crab Creek clear to Schawana and the Columbia River."

Charlie studied his surroundings as he continued walking along the primitive road toward his brother's farm. According to his brother's letters, the original homesteaders abandoned many of the farms along the creek during the depression. Then Bud Bowman chased off most of the remaining farmers after he took over an abandoned ranch to use as the headquarters for his cattle ranch.

Looking at the desolate landscape, Charlie concluded there was no good reason for him to own land along the creek unless his brother's hunch was correct.

His brother believed the groundwater level would rise, and Crab Creek would become a valuable water source for irrigation, as soon as the government diverted water from the reservoir behind Grand Coulee Dam to the Columbia Basin Irrigation District around Moses Lake.

His brother, Clyde, bought an abandoned homestead on Crab Creek for back taxes, and encouraged him to do the same.

Settling on Crab Creek seemed like a gamble, but Charlie realized he needed to settle somewhere other than Oklahoma. His home state was part of the great dust bowl. Farmers were abandoning their farms to move west, looking for opportunity.

Shortly before sundown, Charlie spotted a farmhouse next to the road. He recalled the title search in Ephrata showed Henry Overstreet purchased the abandoned homestead next to his brother's property. He could see a woman standing on the porch with a rifle.

He remembered Bud Jr. mentioning, "That Overstreet woman," and decided this might be Overstreet's property. The woman could be Overstreet's wife, he concluded.

Charlie stopped to adjust the sling on his rifle. Then he hung the rifle over his shoulder where it would appear less threatening. He held his hands open as he walked along the road toward the farmhouse.

The attractive woman on the porch had mature features and long blond hair tied in a braid. She wore loose fitting men's clothing topped with a slouch hat. He guessed she was in her late twenties or early thirties, a bit younger than he was.

A milk bucket sat on the porch beside her. He reasoned she was returning from milking a cow in the barn, across the road from the farmhouse.

He slowed his pace as he approached the house, hoping she would offer him a cold drink from the well next to the porch.

"That's close enough," she shouted, when she noticed him looking toward the house.

"This is a public road, Madam," he shot back at her, irritated by her belligerent tone of voice.

"You can walk down the road, so long as you don't linger on my property. I've no use for drifters."

"If you'll give me directions to the Fredrickson homestead, I'll be happy to leave you far behind me."

"You walked across their old homestead for the last half mile before you reached my property."

"Didn't see any buildings."

"Bowman outfit burned everything on the property so no one would claim it for back taxes. Why are you looking for the place?"

"I own it. I paid the back taxes on the place this morning."

"You're an even bigger fool then you look," she said.

"You must be that Overstreet woman Bud Jr. mentioned," he said, remembering the title reports showed Henry Overstreet was the only person other than his brother with legal title to land along this section of Crab Creek.

"Did Bud Jr. put you up to this, so you can move next door to harass me?" she said, as she lifted the muzzle of her rifle to point it at him.

"No such thing, Madam. Do you know Clyde Lawrence?"

"I know him. He owns the next ranch down the road. You mess with Clyde, you'll be sorry damned quick."

"That's likely true now. I'm older than Clyde, so I was able to take him down and sit on him when we were kids."

"My goodness, you must be the older brother he talks about, the one that went to the war. Come here so I can get a better look at you."

"Name's Charlie," he said as he stepped toward the porch, after she dropped the rifle muzzle downward.

"Charlie Lawrence," she said, when he stopped at the bottom of the steps, "you look like hell. Didn't they ever feed you?"

"It wasn't their top priority given the circumstances."

"I can see the resemblance, if you had fifty pounds of flesh on your bones. Come on in here, so I can feed you before you up and die on me."

"I thank you, Madam."

"Don't call me madam. The word might be a sign of

respect in the south, but madam has a different connotation in the west. I'm Margaret, Margaret Overstreet."

"Is Mr. Overstreet, home?"

"You haven't heard?" she said over her shoulder.

"It's been nearly six months since one of my brother's letters caught up with me."

"You haven't heard then. Someone shot my father, Henry Overstreet, three months ago while he milked the cow. He died the next morning."

"I'm sorry," he said, feeling foolish for not knowing how to console a female.

"I'm Henry's daughter. Your sister-in-law, Marcella, and I are good friends. Sit down at the table while I pour you a cold drink. I can have food and coffee on the table in a few minutes, and then we can talk."

She must have put the stew on to simmer before she went out to milk the cow, he decided. He could smell the spices when she lifted the lid to stir the pot with a wooden spoon. The biscuits were ready to put in the oven. He could smell them baking as he drank his second glass of water.

He soon discovered the stew and biscuits tasted as good as they smelled. She dished out a second helping without asking and set a cup of coffee in front of him.

He had just started to push his chair back from the table, so she would stop pushing food at him, when he heard a vehicle. He stood up to walk to a window to look out, but she beat him there.

"It's Bud Jr. and his two goons again. They show up before dark every evening to try to intimidate me. They think they can harass me into moving."

He could see the pickup stopped in the middle of the dirt road at about a hundred yards. Bud Jr. was behind the wheel. Jake sat in the cab with him. He didn't see Luke.

"Do they just sit there?" he asked.

"Depends on what I do. If I walk out on the porch to acknowledge their presence, they turn around and leave. If I ignore them, they shoot at the house until I show myself. There are a dozen bullet holes in the siding."

"Have you shot back at them?"

"I can shoot, but I'm not very accurate. I'm afraid I might hit one of them if I try to scare them."

"Sit down and wait for them to fire a round. I'm accurate at that distance."

"You'd shoot one of them?" she said in a tone of voice reeking of disapproval.

He didn't answer, remembering he promised his attorney and the sheriff he would shoot them only as a last resort. He didn't have to wait very long. A bullet smacked the side of the house before he could finish his cup of coffee.

Margaret let out a yelp as she jumped up to look out the window.

He stepped to the door, poked his rifle out, and fired a round.

"You knocked the mirror off the driver's side door," Margaret said, surprise evident in her voice.

"I've had some practice," he said as he watched the pickup back away at a high rate of speed.

"We'll have a war now," she said.

"You're already in the middle of a war. Clyde says they tried to steal rangeland in Chelan County before the ranchers ran them out of the area. You must know they're going to keep shooting until they kill you if you don't abandon this property."

"I don't have anywhere to go. Mom and Dad are gone, and my fiancé died in the Omaha Beach landing. Besides, I believe your brother is right when he says this will become valuable farmland when they finish the irrigation project. I'm going to plant an orchard."

"I still have money from my army discharge. I could buy this farm from you. Then you'd have money to resettle someplace where it's safe."

"You didn't hear a word I said. I'll not be scared away by Bud Jr., or bought off by a scarecrow too weak to do simple chores."

Charlie smiled when she called him a scarecrow. He couldn't resist the temptation to retaliate for the insult.

"If you're going to stay, you need someone here to protect you. You might want to consider marrying me after you feed me more stew and biscuits to build up my strength."

"Why, you egotistical jerk. Why do you think I'd have anything to do with the likes of you?"

He smiled brightly as he pressed the issue, realizing she believed he was serious.

"Simple reason if you think about it. Washington State has a community property law. You'd own half of the Fredrickson homestead, and get a husband to protect you and your property."

"Sure, I'd get half a homestead with no buildings and a husband with no meat on his bones, no brains in his head, and a big mouth."

"And big dreams, you forgot the most important part. I'm goin' to build a big house with at least five bedrooms. A man should have lots of sons."

"Do I look like a broodmare?" she screamed at him.

Charlie bit his lip as he tried to control his smiling.

"You can quit your stupid smiling, and get on down the road. I can take care of myself," she howled.

"Well, you haven't done a very good job so far," he said, more seriously. "You let those goons shoot at you every evenin'. Did they shoot your father?"

She glared at him for several moments before she reluctantly answered.

"Someone shot Dad from the top of the hill just south of here. I found the bullet casing behind some brush where the shooter waited. He rode a horse."

"Did anyone backtrack?"

"I knew the tracks would lead to the Bowman ranch, so I didn't tell anyone what I found. If someone had followed the tracks, they'd have been shot."

"So you're goin' to let them keep shootin' at you until they kill you. Don't you understand no one is safe on Crab Creek until this is settled?"

"You sure don't look to be in any shape to stop them."

"It's dark out now, so I'll wait until morning to walk to my brother's place. First, though, I'm goin' to follow the tracks on the hillside to confirm what you say you already know.

"I'll sleep in your barn tonight, if you don't object, and leave at first light. The rising sun will highlight tracks, if they're still there."

Charlie realized he might've lost the tracks if Margaret hadn't given him directions to the Bowman headquarters. The wind had erased most of the horse's tracks except in a few protected areas and around a spring.

The shooter had stopped at the spring to water his horse, leaving tracks in the mud. The horse's shoes were worn smooth with no distinguishing marks. The small boot prints eliminated Jake and Bud Jr., leaving Luke as the likely suspect. The tracks from the spring pointed toward the barn and corral next to the Bowman farmhouse.

Charlie ended up sitting on a hillside watching the Bowman headquarters and four sorry looking horses standing in a corral. The horses were hanging their heads over the top rail, waiting for someone to feed them. He believed he might be able to identify the horse he had followed by checking their shoes.

A few chickens scratched the bare ground around the barn and the vehicles parked in the front yard. He decided they didn't have a dog, making it easier for him when he was ready to walk down to the corral to check the shoes on the horses.

An hour passed before Jake stepped out of a small cabin to do his morning business from the front steps. Then he walked toward the farmhouse. Luke followed him a few minutes later.

As soon as the men entered the house, presumably for breakfast, Charlie followed a brush line down the hill to the corral behind the barn. The horses walked to him to nibble the grass he held out for them. The shoes on all four horses looked the same, he discovered. They were worn smooth and in serious need of replacement.

Before he could retreat up the hill, he heard a screen door slam shut, and heard voices coming toward the barn and corral. Feeling trapped, he stepped into the barn through a back door and climbed a ladder to the hayloft.

Someone opened the front barn door, flooding the interior with light, as he hid behind hay bales. He hadn't felt this vulnerable since a German division overran his platoon.

He recalled spending the night hiding a severely wounded officer, Colonel Frank Jameson, in a muddy ditch under a brush pile. The colonel swore eternal gratitude and insisted Charlie look him up after his discharge. Now, Frank was his pro bono attorney in Ephrata.

He could hear two voices, after the barn door closed. One was a female's voice. He recognized the other voice as Bud Jr.'s voice.

With the bright light gone, he raised his head just enough to glance toward the two people. The woman was small and long past middle age.

She shook her finger at Bud Jr. as she spoke. "Next time, she'll shoot one of you fools. If you'd finished the job the first time like I told you, she wouldn't be able to shoot at you."

"Luke refused to shoot the woman."

"Then you should've gone with him."

"Mom, I don't want to shoot a woman."

"I don't care what you want or don't want. You three are going over there tonight and finish this. I want her gone and all those buildings burned."

"You know Dad wouldn't approve."

"Your father is a senile old fool. I'll make the decisions here until you prove you're man enough to run this outfit. Once that Overstreet woman is gone, we'll only have to get rid of Clyde Lawrence. Then we'll control all of the rangeland."

"You know I don't like riding horses at night. That old mare always gets spooked and dumps me in the middle of nowhere."

"You can ride over there before it gets dark, and wait until the moon comes up to attack the Overstreet ranch. You'll have moonlight for the ride back."

Charlie heard a screen door slam shut and two more voices. He assumed Jake and Luke had finished breakfast and were walking to the barn or the cabin.

"I'll fix supper early tonight, so you boys can get an early start," the female said, before she and Bud Jr. walked out of the barn and closed the door.

Charlie waited for several minutes, listening. He heard the screen door slam when Bud Jr. and his mother entered the farmhouse. He heard a door close after Jake and Luke entered the cabin.

No one fed the horses.

He walked the ten miles back to Crab Creek before

the sun reached the midday mark. He could credit the army with one thing. He could walk, seemingly forever.

Charlie approached his brother's farm from the backside. He could see Margaret's car parked beside Clyde's farmhouse, a sure sign she had spoiled his surprise homecoming.

He smiled, thinking she was probably giving Clyde hell for having such an egotistical jerk for an older brother. She might spoil his homecoming, but there was no time for a celebration anyway. They needed to get ready for the attack on Margaret's person and property.

Charlie believed he had seen the last of foxholes when his company withdrew from the battlefield in Germany. Now he was in a brush-covered foxhole at the top of the hill overlooking the Overstreet farm. It had been a busy day, and it was still daylight. He would have a long wait.

The initial joy of his family reunion that afternoon had quickly turned to a serious discussion regarding their current situation and the orders the woman had given Bud Jr. in the barn. Then Clyde drove Charlie to the small town of Mattawa, so he could use a payphone to call his attorney in Ephrata. By the time they returned to Clyde's farmhouse, Charlie had a plan.

Clyde and Marcella agreed to the plan he proposed, trusting his judgment.

Margaret didn't agree. "I'm not going to abandon my house, and I'm not going to take orders from an obnoxious newcomer," she insisted.

Marcella exploded, shouting angrily with her face about six inches from Margaret's face.

"Charlie started out as a private and ended up a lieutenant commanding a platoon due to his combat experience. He knows how to plan for an attack. You're going to do like he says, so you don't get one of us killed."

Margaret glanced sideways at Charlie during the verbal assault.

He believed he could read the look, and knew what she was thinking.

He doesn't look like a war hero.

He smiled. She was right, if that was what she was thinking. He was certainly no Audie Murphy, the little Texas boy who killed over sixty Germans to stop an attack on his platoon.

Battlefield promotions went to the survivors. Growing up on a hardscrabble Oklahoma farm in the middle of a decade long drought had taught him a lot about surviving.

Now, he was in a foxhole again. Clyde was in the hayloft in Margaret's barn. The women remained at Clyde's farmhouse with loaded shotguns.

The only part of the plan troubling Charlie was his attorney's insistence they not shoot anyone if they could avoid doing so. He had agreed, based on the attorneys promise to fulfill his role in the plan they discussed.

As expected, Charlie heard horses behind him just before nightfall. The riders stopped fifty yards below him on the backside of the hill in a patch of tall bitterbrush. Henry Overstreet's killer had tied his horse in the same spot.

"These horses better be here after you shoot the woman and burn the buildings," someone said.

Charlie believed it sounded like Jake's voice.

"I have a hundred dollar bill in my pocket if one of you will shoot the woman," Bud Jr. said.

Two men laughed. "Your mother told you to shoot her. You don't want us to tell her you wimped out, do you?" a different voice said.

"Shut up, Luke. I was just saying, giving one of you a

chance to make a quick hundred bucks."

Charlie heard arguing, but the three men seemed to have sat down to wait for the moon to appear. He closed his eyes to catnap, knowing he had a three hour wait.

"Let's do it," Bud Jr. said, snapping Charlie awake.

Charlie listened as the three men walked to the crest of the hill where they stood a few feet from him for a minute as they looked down at the Overstreet farm buildings. Then they started walking down the hill. Charlie was confident Clyde would spot the men and track their movements in the bright moonlight.

Charlie crawled out of the foxhole as soon as the three men dropped out of sight. He approached their horses and patted them on the neck to calm them. Then he removed saddles and bridles and slapped the horses on the rump to get them moving back toward the Bowman ranch.

He rushed back to the top of the hill to look down toward the barn. The three men were still a hundred yards from the buildings. He had to watch for a moment before he realized they were lighting a torch.

After the torch flared to life, the biggest man, Jake, started running toward the barn with it. Bud Jr. placed his rifle across a branch on a large bush to aim toward the front door of the farmhouse.

Before Charlie could bring his rifle up to a firing position, he heard a rifle boom from the hayloft.

Jake tumbled down the hillside, screaming in pain.

The torch flared briefly and went out.

"Help me, help," Jake hollered. "She shot my leg."

Bud Jr. fired a round at the house, breaking glass in the window beside the door.

Somebody started laughing.

"Jake, you best get to your horse, and get out of here before that woman finishes you. Just follow my dust,"

Luke yelled, as he turned and started walking back up the hill.

Charlie sat next to a large bush that shaded him from the moonlight as Luke limped up the hill toward him.

Bud Jr. fired a second round at the house, hitting the door with a dull thud.

"I'll burn the house down around you if you don't come out," he yelled.

"Help me, my leg is bleeding," Jake yelled, sounding like he was sobbing.

"Get up and torch the barn," Bud Jr. yelled.

"You torch the barn," Jake hollered back at him, as he started crawling up the hill, sobbing even louder.

Bud Jr. fired two more rounds at the house, hitting glass with the second shot.

Luke finally reached the bush where Charlie waited for him. He still had his revolver tucked down the front of his pants, and he was still laughing.

"Stop and put your hands behind your head," Charlie said, as he snapped the safety on his rifle to the off position.

Luke jerked his head up. Then he slowly raised his hands to the back of his head.

"Don't shoot my foot again. My toe is so sore I can hardly walk."

"Turn to face away from me."

"You've got nothing on me," Luke said, as he complied.

Charlie stood up, keeping his rifle pointed at the man. He reached around him to retrieve the revolver.

"Going to throw it in Crab Creek again?" Luke asked, chuckling as if it was the punch line for a joke.

"Not this time. The sheriff will want your revolver for evidence."

"I'll bet that Overstreet woman isn't even down

there."

"You might win that bet. Lie down on your belly, put your hands behind your back, and keep your mouth shut," Charlie said.

After Luke complied, he tied his hands and legs together with pigging strings.

"I'll not gag you if you keep your mouth shut."

"I'm done with these fools," Luke said.

Bud Jr. was still shooting at the house when Charlie started walking down the hill toward him.

Jake was still trying to crawl up the hill, pleading for help.

Charlie ignored him as he walked toward Bud Jr.

Bud Jr. was busy reloading his rifle. He didn't realize someone was walking up behind him until a rifle muzzle poked him in the back of the head.

When Bud Jr. tried to swing his rifle around, Charlie smacked him in the face with his rifle butt, laying him out in a prone position. As soon as he had Bud Jr. tied, he walked up the hill to get Jake.

"I didn't realize this would be so easy," Clyde said, several minutes later. He spoke as he helped load the three bound men into the back of his pickup.

"I know we weren't supposed to shoot anyone, but that big fellow didn't give me much choice. I wasn't about to let him torch the barn."

"You made a good shot, hittin' his leg," Charlie said. They had already bandaged the flesh wound to stop the bleeding. A doctor would need to clean and stitch the wound, fix Bud Jr.'s broken nose, and look at Luke's sore toe.

"Hitting his fat leg was a lot easier than dusting the squirrels we hunted growing up."

"We aren't done yet, Clyde. You know what you need

to do in the morning to finish this, so I'm goin' to use this moonlight to get in position at the Bowman ranch."

Three hours before daylight, as near as he could tell by looking at the Big Dipper, Charlie sat beside a bush on the hillside overlooking the Bowman ranch buildings.

Several lights were on in the farmhouse. He could see a woman looking out a window toward the corral where three horses paced along the outside of the pole railing. They were nickering to the horse locked inside the corral.

The woman looked out the window several times during the next hour before she finally walked out to open the gate to let the horses inside the corral. She was the small woman Bud Jr. called Mom. She wore a long white bathrobe, holding the hemline up with one hand to avoid soiling it.

After she closed the gate behind the horses, she stood beside the corral, looking all around as if she expected the three riders would walk down from the dark hillside.

After she returned to the house, he could see movement during the next hour as she frequently passed in front of a window and stopped to look out toward the barn and hillside. Then she started packing suitcases and boxes out to a vehicle parked beside the pickup Bud Jr. had driven the day before. She was fully dressed now, in a fancy dress with long sleeves.

Charlie could see the first hint of daylight in the east when the woman walked out to the car wearing a coat and hat. She stood beside the vehicle for a minute, looking around as if she still hoped the riders would return.

She seemed finally to exhale a deep breath before she climbed into the vehicle and started the motor. She looked like she could barely peer over the steering wheel to see the driveway as the vehicle lurched forward.

As the car started to move, Charlie aligned his rifle sights to squeeze off a round. His first shot hit the radiator. His second shot blew out a front tire.

The car came to an abrupt halt. The woman scrambled out of the vehicle and scampered back into the house.

Charlie waited. Full daylight finally arrived a half hour later. He could see the woman peeking out from behind a curtain.

She was looking toward the hillside where he had sat prior to moving to burrow down behind a rock outcropping.

Another half hour passed before she attempted to leave again. She yanked the front door open and ran toward the pickup. She carried a shotgun this time.

Charlie punched a hole through the pickup radiator before she was half-way to the vehicle. The bullet made a frightful racket when it ricocheted off the motor block.

She pointed the shotgun toward the hillside and fired. Then she ran back into the house.

"We're both going to wait right here," Charlie mumbled, as he watched her slam the door shut.

His only concern now was Mr. Bowman. He hadn't seen him. Despite having heard Mrs. Bowman say he was senile, he couldn't dismiss the possibility he was looking for the three missing men. The man might've gone to the Overstreet ranch or Clyde's ranch.

Charlie had a long nervous wait before he spotted vehicles approaching the farmhouse. He believed it was nine in the morning. If so, his attorney was right on schedule.

The first vehicle was a sheriff's patrol car. Clyde's pickup followed behind the patrol car. Three, hog-tied prisoners rode in the back of the pickup. Margaret's car brought up the rear of the little caravan. He didn't know why she was following them.

Charlie kept his rifle aimed at the farmhouse, knowing the woman still had the shotgun. He didn't know how she would react to having a sheriff's vehicle in her front yard.

As the sheriff's car coasted to a stop, the woman opened the front door and looked out. Then she ran toward the patrol car. Tears streamed down her cheeks.

Sheriff Reilly stepped out of the vehicle as she ran toward him. She flung herself into his arms, gesturing toward the hillside where Charlie sat watching them.

Attorney Frank Jameson stepped out of the passenger side of the patrol car. He looked up the hill, trying, apparently, to spot Charlie.

The sheriff ushered the woman onto the backseat of the car. Then he turned, with his revolver drawn, to walk into the house. He returned to the porch in a few minutes, helping a man dressed in nightclothes. Sheriff Reilly gently placed the man on a chair on the front porch.

Even at a distance, as he walked down the hill toward the vehicles, Charlie could see something was wrong with the man. He looked wasted away and seemed disoriented.

Charlie walked to the pickup to look at the three bound men. Jake was pale. He obviously needed a doctor. Luke looked at him and chuckled as if he still thought this was a joke. He concluded the man was crazy. Bud Jr. had streaks down his cheeks where tears had trailed through dust. His swollen nose still leaked blood.

Clyde said, "Sheriff Reilly and Frank arrived at my place at first light this morning, just like you said they would. The sheriff has signed statements from each of the men we caught at the Overstreet Ranch. They've implicated each other and Mrs. Bowman."

"Good. We're done here as soon as I feed the horses and turn them loose. We can get on with buildin' our farms," Charlie said.

"Not yet we can't," Margaret said as she walked up behind him.

Charlie turned to look at her, puzzled.

"How many bedrooms did you say you plan to have in the big farmhouse you're going to build?" she asked.

"I said five, but I'm still thinkin' on it."

"Five at least," she said, as she took his hand.

"A woman needs lots of sons, Charlie. The war is over. You best come home with me. I have stew simmering, and the biscuits are ready to go in the oven. You're going to need your strength."

Sunshine Farm Market is on Hwy 97 coming downhill from the tunnel. This is just one of many roadside, fresh fruit stands a visitor will see on the way to Lake Chelan and around the lake. Thanks to controlled-atmosphere storage facilities, fresh fruit is available year-round. Most stands will have a special attraction such as a petting zoo, homemade cider, pastries, or a gift shop.

A Dream Vacation

Wayne Bailey stormed out of his office at Washington State University in Pullman shortly after a ten o'clock faculty meeting, convinced he would never return. He carried everything he valued in his briefcase and a cardboard box.

He couldn't stop Professor Mintzer from flipping the switch on his electromagnetic pulse experiment. The test, Wayne was convinced, would destroy the nation's electrical grid. Modern civilization would cease to exist at midnight tonight because the professor was determined to proceed despite the risks involved.

Wayne didn't confide his intentions when he walked out of the building. He knew colleagues believed he was paranoid. They had good reason, he supposed, since no one else objected vehemently.

This was his first year at the university after teaching high school physics in Spokane for twenty years. Tenured professors didn't want to listen to a first year teacher despite having hired him because of his groundbreaking electromagnetic-pulse research. His expertise made him uniquely qualified to voice concerns about Mintzer's risky venture, he believed, but no one would listen.

Professor Mintzer stood to lose future research grants if he didn't continue after receiving millions of dollars to prepare for the big event. He had to conduct the experiment to prove he could control high frequency, sunspot radiation and prevent global warming.

The professor certainly looked the part of a genius. He took great pains to groom, dress, and act like his idol, Albert Einstein.

Wayne suspected Mintzer and Einstein had little in common beyond looks. If Professor Mintzer had any genius, it was his ability to obtain global warming research grants.

After tenured professors shouted down his objections at the faculty meeting, Wayne decide he had no choice other than to retreat to his summer home to await developments.

Wayne stopped briefly at his furnished apartment in Pullman to collect personal items on his way north toward Spokane. He owned very little other than his summer home near Hunters. A judge had recently given their home and dog to his wife in divorce proceedings. He still missed the retriever, his constant companion prior to the divorce.

He stopped at Wal-Mart in Spokane to fill the back of his pickup with nonperishable, ready-to-eat food. Customers eyed him suspiciously, as he filled carts and lined them up at a checkout counter. He realized a food bank would get a large donation if he had misjudged what was about to happen.

The sun shone brightly on spring flowers in full bloom as he drove his overloaded pickup west on Highway 2 to Davenport. He turned north on Highway 25 and crossed the Spokane River to drive toward Hunters. He filled his gas tank at Fruitland, since Hunters doesn't have a gas station.

Wayne reached the small town before closing time at the hardware store. He purchased seed potatoes, garden seeds, 100 pounds of fine-grain salt, and 200 pounds of cracked corn.

A brief stop at the grocery store netted him a quart of Jack Daniels Whiskey and a case of Budweiser. He would've maxed out his credit card at the town's only two stores if he hadn't already overloaded the pickup.

He took his time driving five miles out of town and up a steep mountainside road to his isolated cabin. He closed and locked gates behind him.

Twice, he had to stop to let grouse and turkeys move off the primitive dirt road. Deer disappeared behind the brush and trees lining the road after stopping just long enough to identify the intruder. Bear, elk, and moose tracks were visible on game trails that crossed the road.

Despite his despair, Wayne relaxed as he drove the final quarter-mile down a shady lane to his cabin. He felt at home here.

There was nothing impressive about the cabin's size or style, but it was all his. He had designed and built the cabin from the ground up to blend into the surrounding environment. His property was prime wildlife habitat, and he didn't want to do anything to upset the balance of nature.

He planned to live at the cabin when he retired. He didn't expect it would happen so soon, or that he would be all alone. He still missed his dog.

Time passed quickly as Wayne packed his supplies into the cabin. When he finished, he moved the pickup out of the way. Then he turned on the well pump to fill every available container with drinking water. He didn't believe the pickup or pump would work after midnight.

The sun dropped behind a hill as he finished his preparations. He cooked dinner and enjoyed a long, hot shower, convinced it would be his last. The hot water tank wouldn't work without electricity.

Finished, he poured a double shot of whiskey, opened a beer chaser, and sat down to consider his situation.

He had grown up on a ranch near Chelan and listened to his father and grandfather talk about weather cycles. He experienced the cycles at the ranch and witnessed the results. Rainfall and temperature, he learned, increase and decrease in a predictable pattern.

His interest in physics started in junior high school when he read an article in a magazine suggesting the sun's eleven-year sunspot cycle might affect the earth's weather.

He studied sunspots and their connection to weather and long-term global warming and cooling patterns while majoring in science in college. More recently, he completed his master's degree. His thesis documented his research on electromagnetic pulses from sunspots and how they affected weather.

Now, he was a recognized authority on the subject, but still, colleagues wouldn't heed his warning when he told them Mintzer's sunspot experiment had the potential to destroy the earth's electrical grids.

The whiskey and beer chaser soothed his nerves. He poured another double and opened another can of Budweiser. He decided he would get rip-roaring drunk while he waited to see what would happen at midnight.

The ceiling lights would be his indicator.

At midnight, the zealous professor would flip the switch on his experiment to try to influence sunspot activity. He would destroy the electrical grid. Then the lights would go out.

Modern civilization would cease to exist.

Wayne jerked awake with a start. The sun shined brightly through a bedroom window, causing him to blink his eyes. He was in bed. He had no idea how he had gotten there.

The last thing he could recall was sitting in his easy chair in front of the fireplace, drinking whiskey and beer while he waited for midnight. He must have consumed too much alcohol, forgotten what he was doing, staggered into the bedroom, turned off the lights, and crawled into bed. He rarely drank more than a single beer, so that seemed like a logical conclusion.

He glanced toward the electric clock on the nightstand. The clock's hands pointed straight up to twelve o'clock. Alarmed, he jumped out of bed to rush toward the bedroom door to flip the light switch, even though he realized the lights wouldn't work. The sun was rising from the east, so he knew it was morning, but the clock stopped working at midnight.

The fanatical professor had flipped the switch, destroying the electrical gird. He could only hope the damage involved only the northwest region of the country. Potentially, he realized, the damage could be nation or even worldwide.

If the experiment damaged just the northwest power grid, repairs would take a few weeks with massive outside help. Most rural residents could survive that long. City folks wouldn't survive unless they received water and food from out of the area. Food on grocery shelves would disappear in a couple of days. City water systems couldn't replace the water supply in their reservoirs without electricity.

If Mintzer destroyed the electrical grid nationally or worldwide, it would take years or generations to repair the damage. Rioting and looting followed by starvation and disease could decimate the earth's population—all because no one would stop an obsessed professor from performing a dangerous experiment to try to get additional research grants.

The refrigerator light didn't work when he opened the door to look for cold water to wash down a double dose of aspirin to treat his throbbing headache. He tried a water faucet, knowing the well pump wouldn't work.

He had no drinking water other than what he had stored the previous evening. He would need to remove the well cap in a few days. Then he could dip drinking water using a long rope attached to a small container. He could pack water from the small pond next to the cabin to flush the toilet.

His electric furnace wouldn't work, so he would have to depend on his wood-burning fireplace for heat. Surviving winter would necessitate cutting several cords of firewood. He would begin by cutting trees close to the cabin, using his chainsaw and the gas on hand. He would have to use an axe and handsaw when he ran out of gas.

The experiment would've fried computerized electrical

systems in vehicles, so it didn't matter that gas stations couldn't pump gasoline. He would eventually siphon gas out of his pickup to use in his chainsaw.

He would listen for airplanes. Highflying jets would indicate the damage was localized or regional. No jets would indicate something much worse. He hadn't heard any planes, but he hoped that would change.

Serviceberry, raspberry, and currant bushes would provide gallons of berries he could collect and dry for winter use. His property was a natural wintering area for wildlife, so he could obtain fresh meat as needed. He would use corn to lure animals close to the cabin. He could cook food outside over a campfire during the summer and indoors in the fireplace come winter.

Despite the seriousness of the situation, Wayne realized he had an opportunity to fulfill the living-off-the-land fantasy he had nurtured since his Boy Scout days. He was in the right place with the proper resources and experience to survive.

Days turned into weeks as Wayne methodically prepared for winter. Turkeys nested in the brush around the cabin during the summer, grouse and deer fed on the clover in his yard every day, and he noticed an occasional moose track.

Bear sightings during the rut in early July caused him to carry a shotgun loaded with slugs for protection while he picked berries. He shot a yearling bear in August when it refused to leave his garden. He rendered two quarts of lard, roasted the tenderloins, and buried the hams in salt in his woodshed.

Deer rubbed velvet off antlers in late August and elk bugled during the rut in early September. He tended his garden and added to his woodpile every day.

By the time the first frost arrived in early October, he had acquired a deep tan and lost several pounds of excess fat. His toned muscles allowed him to work endlessly without tiring. He went to bed at last light every evening and woke up refreshed at first light.

Snowflakes, freezing rainstorms, and ice on the pond announced the arrival of winter during the last week of October. The first serious snowfall fell overnight during the second week in November. The temperature dropped to the low twenties at night and daytime temperatures seldom reached forty degrees—perfect for storing meat in his woodshed.

Had there been anyone there to ask, he could've truthfully said he was having the time of his life. His summer had been a dream vacation. He had proven he could survive, and he was eagerly looking forward to winter.

His only concern was for those who didn't have his resources or experience. After five and a half months with no sign of human activity, it was apparent the professor's experiment had caused widespread damage resulting, most likely, in catastrophic human suffering.

He realized there was nothing he could do to help. His ex-wife and the irrational professor in Pullman would be among the first casualties, he believed. He tried not to think about his dog.

Then he spotted tracks in the snow. Someone was watching him.

Wayne had circled the cabin an hour after daylight looking for deer tracks in the fresh snow. He hoped to find the barren whitetail doe he had seen almost daily near the cabin. What he found instead startled him. Tracks! Human tracks!

Someone had stood on the hill overlooking his cabin. The trespasser stood there long enough to trample the fresh snow—cold or nervous. The tracks came from the other side of the hill and left in the same direction.

He decided the tracks were less than an hour old. After he followed them for several hundred yards, he realized they pointed toward a small pond at the south end of his property. Abruptly, the tracks turned at a ninety-degree angle and lengthened, suggesting the trespasser was trying to run away from him.

Rather than follow the tracks, he hiked to the top of the next ridge where he could look down at the pond. He wasn't surprised to see a wisp of smoke from a small campfire under trees next to the pond. A few minutes later, he spotted the trespasser, sneaking through the trees toward the fire.

Fresh snow made it easy for Wayne to approach the campfire without making any noise. What he discovered saddened him.

A man, woman, and two small children huddled over a small fire. Their only shelter was a primitive, brush lean-to with its open side facing the fire. They didn't have any supplies or a firearm.

Wayne chambered a round in his rifle as he stepped out from behind a tree.

The man beside the fire jumped up. He seemed to wilt when he spotted Wayne's rifle.

"I don't have a gun," he shouted. He held out his hands to show he wasn't armed.

The woman and children slowly stood up. The children started crying.

Wayne didn't like what he could see. They were wearing summer clothing. The children didn't have jackets, just a single blanket wrapped around them. They looked to be seven or eight years old. He noticed the man was wearing work boots, but the others wore street shoes.

"You followed me from your cabin," the man said. "I meant you no harm. I was exploring the area, looking for food for the children. I'm Leonard Charmin. This is my wife Alma and our children, Leon and Alexia."

"I'm Wayne Bailey. I own the cabin and all of the property surrounding it, including this pond and the area around it. How long have you been here?"

"Since yesterday. We had a good campsite down on

278

Wolf Creek until several men stormed into our camp two days ago. They stole my rifle, all of our supplies, and ran us off. They didn't leave us much."

"Where did you come from?"

"We moved to Hunters for a construction job, just before the power went out. Residents deserted the town to live with local relatives or friends on ranches and farms. We didn't know anyone we could ask for help, so we had to take to the hills to try to find food. I thought we could survive the winter until the men took our supplies and the rifle."

"Do you have any food?"

"We haven't eaten since they forced us out of our camp and took the dried berries and jerky we were storing for winter."

"I have a tarp you can use to cover your shelter and a couple of sleeping bags. You're welcome to use my spare axe and rifle. I can give you some food to hold you over until you get a deer. Would that help?"

"That's all we need. I'm a carpenter. With an axe, I can build a proper shelter to keep us from freezing. If I can kill a deer occasionally, we'll survive. Will you allow us to stay here by the pond?"

"You're welcome to stay as long as you don't disturb the animals near my cabin."

Wayne went to bed that evening feeling good about having helped the family. He was concerned, however. Would others follow?

He had his answer the next morning when he spotted new tracks in the snow. Two people had stood on the hill, looking down at his cabin.

The next morning, he found tracks all around the cabin. Someone had pried the door open on his woodshed during the night. They took a sack of potatoes and carrots he had grown in his garden.

He heard a shot later in the day. He initially assumed Leonard had shot a deer since the shot came from the direction of the pond. Abruptly, however, several rapid shots followed.

Wayne stayed in the cabin for the rest of the day and watched for trespassers. He didn't see anyone.

They were standing on the hillside the next morning. He could see four men. One of the men held the old rifle he had given Leonard.

He thought they would leave when he stepped out onto the porch with his rifle. They watched him for a moment, and then the oldest man in the group leaned his rifle against a tree and walked down the hill toward the cabin.

Wayne chambered a round in his rifle as the man approached. He noticed the man was wearing a blanket with a hole cut out of the center of it to form a Mexican style capote. The blanket looked like the one the children had wrapped around them.

The man stopped next to a large pine tree when he was within talking distance.

"We've been watching you. You're all alone in the cabin," he said belligerently. "There're four of us. We don't think it's fair that you have a nice warm cabin all to yourself while four of us are out in the cold."

"You're trespassing on private property."

"There ain't anyone here to enforce property rights, so we have as much right to this cabin as you do. You might be smarter than the people by the pond were. If so, you'll leave, and we won't have to kill you."

Disgusted by the man's comments, Wayne fired a round at the pine tree near the man. The man jumped behind the tree and ran up the hillside.

Immediate rifle fire from the hillside knocked out the window in the front of the cabin as Wayne stepped back inside and slammed the door shut. The men were still on the hillside when daylight faded away, firing an occasional shot at the cabin.

Wayne considered his situation as he watched his thermometer. These men would shoot him without a second thought and feel justified in doing so, he realized. He believed they had already killed Leonard and his family.

The temperature in the cabin dropped below freezing during the night. The men weren't going away, and he didn't dare use his fireplace. A fire would illuminate him, making him an easy target. With broken windows and no heat in the cabin, he would freeze.

He reluctantly concluded he couldn't defend his property indefinitely against determined killers. It was apparent that roving bands of desperate, destitute people wouldn't hesitate to steal from him or kill him. He swore softly as he decided he had to abandon his cabin.

When he had his pack ready, he sat in the dark in his easy chair with a quilt wrapped around him. He cradled his rifle in position for a quick shot if the heard the men approaching the cabin. He decided he would wait until midnight. Then he would escape into the depths of the surrounding forest where no one could find him.

Exhaustion overtook him as he waited. Despite his anxiety, he drifted into a deep sleep.

Wayne jerked awake with a start. He was sitting in his chair in front of the fireplace. Bright sunlight shined through the living room windows.

Alarmed, he glanced at a window and the hillside, expecting the men to shoot at him.

He didn't see any men. Then he realized the windows weren't broken. There was no snow. Spring flowers were still in full bloom. The Aspen trees had green leaves on them. He could hear an airplane.

The lights were on, he noticed. The clock said eight minutes after seven.

He had electricity.

He also had a wicked, splitting headache.

A whiskey bottle and several beer cans littered the floor beside his chair. Several moments passed as he tried to clear the fog from his skull, so he could understand what had happened. Finally, he realized he had drank too much, fallen asleep, and started dreaming.

The electrical grid hadn't collapsed at midnight. He could think of only one explanation. Professor Mintzer hadn't flipped the switch on his experiment as planned. Something had happened to cause him to delay it for a day.

His dream flashed in front of him, making him shudder. He had experienced firsthand, albeit in a dream, what would happen when the professor flipped the switch. The consequences had been devastating.

He needed only a moment to make his decision. He couldn't just wait at his cabin and do nothing. Someone had to destroy the obsessed professor's experiment to keep him from destroying modern civilization.

Within minutes, Wayne Bailey was driving down his primitive road on his way back to Pullman. He didn't expect he would ever be able to return to his cabin because there would be a severe penalty for the action he had to take.

The only thing he took with him was a large sledgehammer.

Two fawns in my yard. They are born about the first week in June and may not show any fear when a human approaches them. They are not orphans. Don't touch them. A doe may refuse to nurse a fawn with human scent on it. Take photos and enjoy their antics.

Incriminating Evidence

"My husband works long hours and I'm bored," Samantha said during our phone conversation. "He says I need a hobby, so how soon can we get together?" She laughed playfully as she suggested a time and place.

A week later, I drove to Olympia to meet her at a cheap motel. We met at ten in the morning, half way between her home in Oregon and my home on Lake Chelan's south shore.

Samantha smiled as she stepped out of a new Mercury Cougar. "A Christmas present from my husband," she explained. As we walked toward the motel office, she started giggling. "I was afraid you'd look like a homicidal maniac," she said.

That's nice. I won't mention you're much older than I expected.

"Special rate for three nights," said the woman in the office, as Samantha placed cash on the counter. The photo on the wall confirmed the elderly woman and her husband owned the motel, which had obviously fallen on hard times after the new highway bypassed them.

"Only need it for a few hours," Samantha said. Then she snickered as she handed me two, crisp, hundred-dollar bills—my usual fee.

I shoved the money in my pocket. Embarrassed.

The motel owner ignored the transaction, which didn't surprise me. *She must expect strange behavior when guests pay cash and don't show identification.*

Samantha continued laughing shamelessly as she packed an ice cooler toward our motel room.

"You need to learn not to blush if we're going to meet at a quickie-stop motel once a month," she said.

My face was still red when I followed her into the

room with my cardboard box.

Our time together passed swiftly with only a short break for lunch. Samantha was eager, joyful, and a quick learner.

"I can't believe I did this," she laughed, when we finished.

"You have amazing talent for an amateur," I said.

The same woman stood behind the office counter when we returned the key at four in the afternoon. She didn't look surprised.

As we walked to our vehicles, I said, "Bet she rents the room again."

"A couple of times before closing," Samantha joked.

Samantha's infectious humor kept me chuckling until a state patrol vehicle pulled behind me near Tacoma. The vehicle followed me past Fife.

Then a sheriff's patrol car pulled alongside my pickup. Multiple blue lights started flashing.

Uh-oh, they don't look friendly.

In seconds, it seemed, they had me standing beside the busy, four-lane highway with my hands cuffed behind my back. Passing drivers slowed down to stare at me.

"We have probable cause, so keep your mouth shut," an officer barked to stifle my feeble protest. He laid the contents of my pockets, including the two, hundred-dollar bills, on the hood of my pickup.

More police arrived. They used a dog to search my pickup.

One officer talked on a radio. I heard enough of his conversation to know the state patrol stopped Samantha on the freeway south of Tumwater. *They're giving her the same treatment they're giving me.*

The woman at the motel must've vacuumed our room. Found the white powder we spilled on the carpet. Called the police.

In a couple of minutes, as I expected, a deputy

yelled, "Bingo." He held up a large bag full of white powder. Then he plopped the plastic bag on the hood of my pickup.

Another deputy dumped the supplies from my cardboard box onto the pickup hood. A small bottle of clear liquid, a hypodermic needle, surgical grade scalpel, cotton, and the rest of my supplies spilled out of the box.

The two officers gave each other high-fives.

More police arrived with blue lights flashing.

A huge, bug-eyed, deputy sheriff with a conspicuous pug nose made sure they understood what was happening.

"Shared a room with a woman. Doing drugs," Pug Nose shouted. "Paid him two hundred dollars for you-know-what. Hope they let me flip the switch."

Shooting seems more likely. Don't give him just cause. Keep my mouth shut. Hold my hands up. Oops—handcuffs. Don't move.

As usual, my allergies picked a bad time to act up. My nose started itching. I cringed. *A runny nose combined with the bag full of white powder is going to be even more incriminating.*

"Five pounds," an officer shouted as he lifted the bag of white powder as if he could weigh it. "Worth a fortune."

He guessed wrong, but I kept my mouth shut. The bag held five pounds when I met Samantha, but we used some of it, and spilled some on the carpet.

I could still hear the state patrol officer talking on his radio. "Found drugs. Money's in her car. Hidden. Tear it apart."

I cringed again. *Samantha might end up in jail with nothing but a pile of scrap metal. Husband's going to be furious. Might not give her money for a room and my fee for our next meeting.*

A plain-clothed officer arrived, assumed command,

and issued orders. *He looks like a detective from a narcotics unit, or a Sargent Joe Friday impersonator. His skin will crack if he smiles.*

"Where'd you get *that*?" he said, as he pointed at the bag of white powder.

I smiled for the first time. *Finally, I get to explain the incriminating evidence.*

"Safeway," I said.

"What?" he shrieked. "How much did you pay?"

"Two dollars and thirty-five cents," I said. "I had a coupon."

"Boy's gonna go to Hell, sure enough," yelled Pug Nose.

My allergies were completely out of control now due to the ragweed growing by the freeway. My nose itched uncontrollably. I couldn't scratch my nose with my hands cuffed behind my back, so I sniffed and wiggled it.

Pug Nose seemed to interpret my action as an attempt to make fun of his flat snout. His eyes bugged out even more than usual. His face turned red as he started hyperventilating. He took a threatening step toward me. Then he clamped a hand to his chest, gasping for air.

This isn't good, I thought. *He's about to have a heart attack.*

"The white powder is Twenty Mule Team Borax," I yelled. "You can buy it at a grocery store. The clear liquid is formaldehyde from a drug store."

"Take us for fools?" Pug Nose stammered, as he gasped for air.

I ignored the question. *Telling him the truth might kill him.*

"Look at a business card in my billfold," I pleaded. "The card explains why I have the supplies you found."

The plain-clothed officer glared at me for a full minute before he picked up my billfold. He dumped the contents on the pickup hood to find my business card.

His lips moved slowly as he read the card. Then he glared at me again, seemingly confused.

Doesn't understand what's on the card. Need to explain it.

"The card says I give private lessons by arrangement," I said, speaking loud enough for everyone to hear.

Pug Nose interrupted me before I could finish my explanation.

"Told you what he was doing. Bound for brimstone and fire," he shouted, sounding like Burt Lancaster in his Elmer Gantry role, exciting a crowd before he passed the collection plate. Then he started sucking air again with his hand clamped to his chest. An older deputy grabbed him by the arm to help him into the back of a patrol car.

A city police officer arrived a few moments later. He inspected the items displayed on the pickup hood. Then he started laughing.

"This stuff has to belong to a taxidermist," he said in a deep Southern drawl that made his large belly bounce.

"My crazy brother-in-law has stuff like this on a workbench in his garage. He uses borax to preserve bird skins, and a hypodermic needle to inject formaldehyde into soft toe pads and wattles. He replicates bird bodies for his mounts with this other stuff. He'll stay up all night to stuff a stupid bird."

I realized this might be my last chance to explain the incriminating evidence and avoid a trip to jail.

"The woman I met at the motel is learning taxidermy as a hobby," I shouted. "She paid me two-hundred dollars to teach her how to mount her husband's trophy pheasant. She's taking it home so he can display his trophy in his law office. Her finished mount is absolutely gorgeous."

"Not anymore," said the officer who had been talking on the radio. "They tore the bird apart looking for drug money."

His statement startled me.

How is Samantha's attorney husband going to react to having his wife intimidated, his trophy ripped apart, and her car damaged?

I started to protest, but an officer interrupted me.

"You've wasted enough of our time," he said. "Get out of here so we can get back to work."

I could see a retired taxidermist would get no respect from this group, so I kept my mouth shut while they removed the handcuffs.

The officers disappeared by the time I finished tossing my taxidermy supplies back in the cardboard box and shoved the hundred-dollar bills into my pocket.

During the drive back to Lake Chelan, I decided incriminating evidence makes teaching taxidermy as a sideline too risky. I needed to find a new pastime.

Over coffee the next morning, a friend made me laugh by suggesting I should join his writers group.

"We have fun and make a few dollars selling our stories," he said.

Then I remembered friends always accuse me of telling tall tales. I decided to join the Wenatchee Senior Writers Group to learn how to put my *stories* on paper, hoping a publisher would print them. One did. I hope you have enjoyed the results.

Additional Visitor Information

LAKE CHELAN, The Official Visitors Guide of the Lake Chelan Valley. This is an annual publication of the Lake Chelan Chamber of Commerce. It is available at the Visitor Information Center, 216 E. Woodin Avenue in Chelan. You can view a page-by-page copy of this visitors guide on line at **www.lakechelan.com**.

LAKE CHELAN, Visitor Guide. This is a publication of the Lake Chelan Mirror, 315 E. Woodin Avenue in Chelan. Their website is **www.lakechelanmirror.com**.

Useful websites:
> **www.lodgeatstehekin.com**
> **www.ladyofthelake.com**
> **www.chelanseaplanes.com**
> **www.holdenvillage.org**
> **www.cascadeloop.com**

Suggested Reading

Lake Chelan Valley, by Kristen J. Gregg and the Lake Chelan Historical Society.
Glimpses of Manson History, by Wayne Stanford.

Books are available from the Lake Chelan Historical Society at the Chelan Museum, 204 East Woodin Avenue, in Chelan.
You can get a complete list and ordering information at **www.chelanmuseum.com**.

ALSO BY JIM TARBERT—*on Amazon.Com*

THE CAYUSE KID

JEREMIAH JOHNSON—*Available Nov. 2015*

BLOOD TRAIL—*Available May 2016*

WILD WEST WOMEN—*Available Nov. 2016*

Jim Tarbert lives in East Wenatchee, Washington. He has retired from teaching and business careers to devote more time to wildlife activities and writing.

Jim is a member of the Wenatchee Valley Writers Group and the Wenatchee Senior Writers Group and wishes to thank members and Sue for their suggestions and encouragement and Doug McComas for editorial assistance.